THE MANCHESTER MAID

VICTORIAN ROMANCE

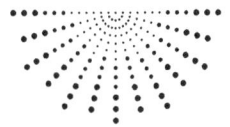

ROSIE SWAN

PUREREAD.COM

CONTENTS

PART I
Prologue — 3
1. A Cold November Wind — 17
2. A strange quirk of destiny — 32
3. An unpleasant surprise — 49
4. The Mansion — 63
5. Meeting the young Master — 79
6. Accepted — 93
7. Dear God, he can't die — 115
8. A daring plan — 133
9. Caught — 150
10. A solemn pledge — 167

PART II
11. About Letters, Lies and Changes — 185
12. A bend in the road — 200
13. A visit to Broughton — 215
14. The great debate — 232
15. About Good Plans and Wicked Plans — 252
16. The hour of darkness — 269
17. Separation — 283
18. Payback Time — 298

Epilogue — 316
If you loved The Manchester Maid — 321

Love Victorian Romance? — 333
Our Gift To You — 335

PART I

PROLOGUE

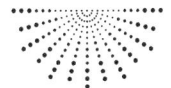

The dream
The Irish Sea
1840

It was the third night in a row that Harvey Matthews dreamed of home. Every night the dream was the same. His dear wife Hazel would come to him while holding a precious bundle wrapped up in a colourful baby blanket. "Harvey," she would say, hardly able to contain her joy, "Look what God gave us." She would then pull aside part of the blanket, so he could have a good look at the package in her slender arms.

And as Harvey looked, his eyes widened.

There, safely tucked away against Hazel's chest, was the pink scalp of a new-born babe with a tiny tuft of auburn colored hair sticking out right in the middle. It was a sight so precious, so pure and fresh.

A child? Was that baby his? He had not known Hazel was pregnant.

"Is it… mine?" Even in his dream, he knew it was an offensive question, but he had to know. When had all this happened?

Hazel however, wasn't disturbed by his attitude. Her joy was too great to be spoiled by Harvey's sceptical approach. She was just radiant and carried a beauty that Harvey had rarely seen in his life. While he dearly loved his wife, it was common knowledge she could not be classified among the prettiest of women in town, at least not by the worldly standards most men adhered to. But now, in his dream, it seemed an angel from heaven had dipped his celestial paintbrush in some sort of heavenly veneer and had not been stingy in applying the glorious elixir to his wife. She no longer resembled the somewhat slovenly woman with her tense lips and nervously darting eyes that he was so used to. The look of tension and difficulty that would tell him she worried about a thousand-and-one things, problems she should never be worried about but that made him feel like a poor fisherman from Blackpool, and a stumbling husband who could never do right.

But not in the dreams.

In the dreams she had not just been *touched* by an angel, rather she *appeared* as one. Instead of answering Harvey's rude question in a way that he would have deserved by saying something like, "Are you suggesting I've been unfaithful to you, Harvey Matthews? Shame on you," she gave him the sweetest smile and whispered, "Yes, love… this child is yours. This is God's blessing."

And every night he dreamed this part, his reaction was the same. It was a feeling of joy, unbridled joy. The baby was *his*. Truly his. Upon hearing Hazel's gentle reassurance, he allowed her happiness to spread to his own heart. "A baby… I am a father now." As he stared in awe at the tender miracle before him, he realized this was a sacred moment. This was one of those rare instances where heaven touched the dreary world of the common life. The veil between this life of toil and suffering and the unseen realm of perfection had been pulled away, and he was allowed a rare peek into eternity. That baby came from a sphere of perfection where everything made sense and where sin, poverty and evil could not molest.

And in the dream it was a girl, every time. How could dreams be so similar? Hazel would show her to him. She would pull back a bit more of the blanket so Harvey could have a better look. Wonderful… The child stared at him with large green eyes while sucking on one of her tiny fingers, and looked at him as if he were the best man in the world.

A girl… He had been given a girl. If it had been a choice, Harvey would have opted for a boy. Boys could bring in more money, but right now he was too excited to think about that. Who was he anyway, to complain about such a wonderful blessing?

But then the dream would take a turn for the worse. It happened every night. Right when he held out his hands, expecting Hazel to hand him the babe, he was pulled back by an unseen force; terrible and dark. A gale had come out of nowhere, a wind so strong that there was nothing he could do to fight it. A scream erupted from his throat and he began to wave his arms around in a futile effort to stand his ground, but he never succeeded. He was powerless and faster and faster he was being pulled into a dark pool of nothingness.

He could still see Hazel's face from a distance. It no longer carried the heavenly expression of grateful joy but had turned into a desperate grimace of helplessness and fear. "Harvey!" she cried out. "Don't leave me!" It was a despondent wail, so loud and clear that it shattered Harvey's heart. He wanted to tell her he loved her, but he could not. No words would come out of his mouth and a sickening reality dawned on him that maybe he was just about to… die. But he *could* not die. He had a wife and a baby to take care of.

At that point Harvey would wake up from the dream; three times in a row now.

It had been the exact same thing every night. He woke up, confused and bewildered, his heart pounding and the images of the dream still sharply etched on his conscious perception. Again that dream…

For just a brief moment he did not know where he was, but then, as the sound of creaking wood entered his ears and he felt the swaying and the rocking of the boat, he remembered again. He was still sailing on The Bullfrog, somewhere out in the middle of the Irish Sea, and he and the others were on their way home after a successful fishing trip. The days had been sunny, and the nights still. Perfect for fishing, but now the wind had increased in strength. He could feel it by the force with which their little vessel was being tossed up and down on the waves. Judging by the force with which the vessel shook and creaked, he realized they needed him on deck. Recently, he had become the First Mate, which meant he worked right under Master Farren and was qualified to handle the boat in rough weather.

Still, that dream… it troubled him. Why did he have this same dream, three nights in a row? It always started so wonderful, almost heavenly, but then it would end like a regular nightmare. He could not shake off the memory of the look of panic on Hazel's face and could still hear her screams, even now, as he sat up straight on the straw ticking on which he had been lying.

But then, this was only a dream. Dreams were not to be trusted. Dreams were no signs or guides for the way one was to live his own life. Most likely, as Master Farren claimed, dreams were caused by a mixture of your heart's unfulfilled desires, worries about life, and the overload of tea, fish and more fish, so annoyingly present while out at sea for five days in a row. That was probably true. Last night, he had just eaten too much treacle with his potatoes.

Nevertheless, true or not true, Harvey was shook up. He rubbed his eyes and shook his head in a futile effort to shake off his visions of the night. The others needed him. What time was it anyway? He looked up and squinted his eyes as he scanned the room. Above him, in the ceiling and right around the hatch that led to the deck, was a small trickle of light that seeped through the cracks, signifying the new day had made its appearance. Only one more day of sailing and they would be home in Blackpool.

The desire to take Hazel in his arms and pull her close to his chest became almost overwhelming. He was not a man that was easily given over to unstable emotions and fickle feelings. He was better than those foolish people who fell apart at the least bit of trouble and would whine like a baby. But after having had these disturbing dreams, he desperately wanted to see Hazel again and hold her and take care of her.

Tomorrow. Then he would ask her straight out if she was with child and after they had had a good laugh about his silly behaviour and she would have chided him for having these weird dreams, he would close the curtains of the bedroom in their small rented place in Gloucester Street and kiss her. Yes, that was what he would do… Tomorrow, after they had disembarked in the harbour and he had helped to transport the fish they had caught, he would see Hazel and everything would be all right.

He threw off the coarse blanket that had kept him warm throughout the night, got up and made his way to the wooden steps that led up to the deck.

When he opened the hatch and stuck out his head, he was welcomed by a cold, harsh wind filled with heavy raindrops that gushed down his face. Corwine Musselwhite, the third mate, was just passing by and cast him a wide grin. "Right on time, sir. I hadn't counted on rain," he exclaimed. "I was just going to get you. Farren wants you."

Harvey climbed out all the way and walked over to the railing with difficulty. Wherever he looked legions of dark clouds, like angry horsemen from an invading enemy, swept over the foamy wild sea.

Normally, Harvey loved such weather. It was always a fight to steer their boat right through the storm into the safety of the Blackpool harbour. A fight with the elements, but a fight he and his buddies would always win.

But today Harvey wasn't so sure of himself. The dark pull toward death in his dream had been so real, and Hazel's face had been so terrified…

Master Farren was standing near the back of the boat, holding the wheel, and was impatiently motioning for him to take over. No doubt the Master had been sailing for hours on end while he had been sleeping... and dreaming.

Just then the boat went down again in a valley of water, surrounded by massive walls of salty foam. As Harvey made his way forward, he held on tight. This was no ordinary storm and it was fast getting worse. Right above his head, he heard the desperate shriek of a seagull. He spotted the little fellow and stared at it in amazement. Seagulls, so far out at sea, and always hoping for a handout and an easy dinner. But there would be no handout today, and it appeared the struggle against the gale was getting too much for the little fellow. The bird simply landed on the bobbing, furious waves as if he was sitting in an easy chair. A grim smile appeared around Harvey's mouth. Smart bird. If you can't beat it, just join it. But for him and the crew, it would not be so easy.

"It's going to be quite a storm, Harvey," Master Farren cried out above the wind when Harvey had reached him. "But nothing you and I cannot handle."

"Of course, Skipper," Harvey replied. He admired the older fellow with his bushy beard and large, unkempt wild brows and deep-seated eyes. He had never seen the old tar afraid in all the years he had been working under him. First as a boy and a deckhand, then as fourth mate, third mate, and now, a few months ago, Master Farren had promoted him to First Mate. A wonderful change it was, as it meant better pay and more responsibility.

"Not afraid, are you?" Farren asked without looking at Harvey. Harvey couldn't help but grin. He wasn't afraid, but even if he was, Farren would be the last person he would show it to. "Of course not," he answered indignantly. "You want me to take over?"

The seasoned sailor nodded. "Just for a while. Nature is calling, but I'll be back. This is going to be a serious challenge. It's getting worse, you know. Have you seen it?"

"Seen what?"

"There," Farren took one of his hands off the wheel and pointed in the direction from where Harvey had come. "Look south."

Harvey turned in the direction Farren was pointing and swallowed hard.

The clouds that were rolling in from there were darker than any he had ever seen at sea, and they were spreading fast. Even though it was still morning, they would soon be plunged into total darkness.

"Take the wheel," Farren ordered in a loud voice. "I'll be back in a minute."

Harvey grabbed the wheel as Farren walked off. Afraid? Afraid of a minor storm…? Of course not. He was worth

11

his salt. But true, this was going to be a storm unlike all the others he had experienced.

Earlier, Farren had already given the orders to lower the mainsail and raise the smaller storm sail that would help them manoeuvre more speedily. Cormine Musselwhite and Tate Hample, the fourth mate, were struggling to do as they were told. The work was progressing slowly, because of the violent shaking and bobbing. Too slow to Harvey's liking. If these two sailors didn't hurry, the mainsail could rip. "Hurry up with these sails," he yelled from a distance, knowing full well his statement would not make any difference as they could not even hear his voice over the roaring wind.

But then, right at a crucial moment, Cormine slipped on the rain-soaked deck. The sail came crashing down. The unfortunate man was still holding on to one of the ropes with both of his hands, but as a monstrous, surging wave washed over the deck and pushed the boat precariously to its side, the sailor disappearing from sight. A second later, a bright flash of lightning, much closer than Harvey liked, illuminated the raging waves around, and Harvey saw Cormine struggling to stay aboard. To Harvey's relief he saw how he crawled back to safety. The lightning flash was instantly followed by the terrifying roar of a thunderclap, so close and so loud that Harvey feared the ship had been hit and had snapped in twain.

"Come on," Harvey shouted into the wind, wanting to

encourage himself. "I am not afraid of you. Is that all you got?"

But he knew this was no regular storm. It appeared the mouth of hell had opened and all its ugly demons had been unleashed and were now letting down their fury on the helpless vessel. Harvey held on to the wheel with all of his might, gritting his teeth, barely able to think. It was all he could do to keep from being swung overboard as the ship tilted down again to the side and Harvey saw how the foamy, dark green waters now almost reached his boots. Then, with a violent shake, the ship was pushed back up again. Dear God, have mercy…

Sail right into the storm... right into the storm, Harvey mumbled as he kept following the procedures he had learned from Farren, but it was so difficult to keep the ship steady.

"Let me have the wheel," a voice shouted in his ears. Farren was back. "Right into the waves, Harvey."

Right when he was about to step aside to hand the wheel back to Farren an unexpected wave threw Harvey off and the wheel slipped out of his hands. Instantly the helpless boat tipped precariously to its side.

Harvey had nothing to hold on to anymore, and lost his balance. As the ship tilted very far starboard he slipped and let out a guttural roar, swinging his arms around in hopes of finding something to hold onto. But he did not. Seconds later he plunged into the foaming sea.

Instantly the cold salty water was all around. He yelled for help but all he got was waves that smashed into his face, filling his lungs with salty water. They felt like they were about to burst... He needed air, but there was no air. There was only water, cold, dark and foul. Where was the surface? He could not be very far from the surface, but he could not find it.

He wanted air, but all he got was water. At that point, he understood he was going to die... He would never see dear Hazel again. His dream had been real. He was now being pulled away by the darkness, just like he had been in his dream. Hazel would be desperate. Without him, she could not take care of her own life anymore. The poorhouse was the only place she could go to. And a child... she was with child...

God, please...

"Fear not. I am with you always."

What? Who was talking?

It was the strangest experience, but despite being in the depths of the belly of the sea where nobody could talk, Harvey heard a distinct voice. It was as loud and clear as he had heard Master Farren say only moments earlier that he wanted to take over the wheel. But this voice was calm, almost tender, and spoken with the utmost of grace.

"Today, you will be with me in Paradise," the voice continued.

Paradise?

Where had he heard those words again? Then he knew. The Saviour had spoken these words to the thief who had been hanging on a cross next to him. The Saviour was here, right next to him in the water. He was with him even during his last desperate moments on earth.

So all would be well then. There was no reason to be afraid.

After these words Harvey no longer struggled, but somehow allowed himself to just float through the troubled waters and, strangely enough, a deep, unearthly peace settled on his heart.

"You will have a daughter upon earth and she will be called Alice, for she will be noble and kind," the voice continued.

A daughter? But he would never see her, as he was going to die. It didn't matter for somehow, all would be well. The Saviour had told him so. And that was enough for Harvey.

Then his heart stopped beating…

1
A COLD NOVEMBER WIND

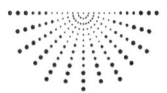

Hazel Matthews' head was spinning and a curious dizziness was making itself known. She had to steady herself in her chair as she had the impression she would otherwise fall over. It came unannounced and with no reason she could think of. Nausea welled up too and worked its way up through her stomach all the way to her throat as if a troupe of savage bandits had entered and were bent on making her life miserable. She stared at her friend Nelwyna Musselwhite whose blue eyes grew wide as she perceived something was wrong.

"A-Are you alright?" Nelwyna enquired, but Hazel could not respond. Instead, fighting her dizziness, she forced herself up from her seat and mumbled, "Sorry, love... I... must leave."

Hazel pushed her chair aside and ran off through the dingy, dark hallway to the outside door that led to the narrow plot outside. There, in the muddy area surrounding the back-to-back houses Hazel's family shared with several other families in Blackpool, was the outhouse. She threw open the creaking door and disappeared inside, closing it again with a bang.

Where did that nausea come from? At first, it had been a barely detectable sense of dizziness. Then a slight headache, like a smothering blanket had joined in the battle, but now it was all culminating in the overwhelming urge to empty the contents of her stomach.

This was so embarrassing, right when Nelwyna Musselwhite had come over for a visit. Was she getting sick? She could not afford to get sick. Today, she expected Harvey back from his fishing trip. The house needed cleaning, and she had wanted to prepare a hearty meal for him. After five days at sea, the man wanted something else besides fish.

Fish?

The thought of food did it.

Hazel fell to her knees and yielded to what her body urged her to do. Seconds later she felt better, although her headache seemed to have intensified, and so did her shame. The small outhouse, only a windy hut that four neighboring families shared, was not the most hygienic;

not the place where one was expected to kneel, but today she had no other option.

She got up and flushed the gaping hole that was carved out in the middle of the wooden seat with the murky water from a bucket that was placed right next to the lavatory for that purpose. She would have to fill it up again later, so the next person would not find himself without water to flush. But not now. She didn't have the strength just yet.

Minutes later, she stumbled back into the living room where Nelwyna was waiting with some alarm in her eyes. "What's wrong, dear? Can I help?"

Hazel shrugged her shoulders. "Not sure what it is; probably something I ate."

"What?" Nelwyna tilted her head.

"Nausea. A strange wave of nausea. I got a bit of a headache too." Hazel pressed her lips together. "I hope it's not contagious." She let out a deep sigh and plopped herself down in the chair again. "I don't feel feverish though," she added as she felt and rubbed her forehead.

Nelwyna studied Hazel for a moment and then shook her head. "I am no doctor," she began, "but if you ask me, I don't think that what you've got is contagious."

Hazel looked up. "You don't think so? How do you know?"

"*I said, I'm not a doctor,*" Nelwyna explained, "but could it be that you are pregnant? Could it be there's a little one on the way?"

A ripple coursed through Hazel's body. "Pregnant... a little one?" She repeated the word as if Nelwyna had just told her Queen Victoria herself was scheduled to visit Hazel's humble home. "B-But that's not possible."

"Why not?" Nelwyna said with a slight frown. "Have you and Harvey not been... well, you know, you two have been married for quite some time now. It's time you two fill up the nest."

For a moment, Hazel stared into space and then without making much of a sound she whispered to herself, "Pregnant.... I might be pregnant."

A wide smile had now formed on Nelwyna's face. "You know when I had my Patrick, I felt just like you. I don't think there's anything to worry about. If I am right, it is a time to rejoice."

"How can I be certain?"

Nelwyna shook her head. "You can't. Not right now, at least. But these are the symptoms: They call it morning sickness. You are suddenly overcome with nausea. Sometimes you have a headache, you may sweat, and there are women who have painful and enlarged breasts... is that the case with you?"

Hazel blushed. "I am not sure I like to talk so freely about such things."

"I am just telling you," Nelwyna answered as she narrowed her eyes. "Of course, once your tummy swells... well, then you don't need to wonder anymore. There's no more hiding the fact then."

Hazel leaned back in her seat and shook her head, but she could not suppress a smile. *Pregnant... Maybe she was pregnant.* The moment Nelwyna had hinted at this possibility, Hazel felt better. Nelwyna was right. Something told her she was going to have a baby. She was not sick at all, on the contrary, she had never been healthier. "A baby...," she whispered. "I am going to be a mother, and Harvey will be a father."

"I was just suggesting it," Nelwyna said. "Of course, I can't be sure, but it would not hurt to go see Doctor Barnaby. He may not tell you if you are pregnant, but at least he can give you a check-up. If there's nothing else wrong with you, it can only be pregnancy."

Hazel shook her head. "No need for that, Nelwyna. I am fine. I just know you are right... I am with child." A smile appeared. "Imagine, telling Harvey he's going to be a father. What a wonderful homecoming that will be. He has been talking about wanting a boy." She frowned and added, "You think I am going to have a boy? It sure feels like a boy."

Nelwyna grinned but shook her head. "You can't feel such things, Hazel. You know better than that."

"But it is a boy, Nelwyna… It's going to be a boy. Mark my words. And if it's all right with Harvey, I am going to call him Moulton. I have always liked that name."

"Moulton?" Nelwyna frowned. "What kind of name is that? Does it even have meaning?"

"It's old English. I think it has something to do with *spirit* or *courage*. I am not sure, but I like it. Doesn't it just sound adorable?"

At that moment there was an excited, loud knock on the door, followed by the high-pitched voice of Fernham, the ten-year-old neighbour boy, who cried out, "The Bullfrog is docking. Mrs. Matthews, your husband is home."

Both Hazel and Nelwyna jumped up with one accord. This was what they had been waiting for. The safe return of their husbands. After all, the ocean was unpredictable, dangerous, and even merciless at times. Most everyone in Blackpool knew of somebody who had died while out at sea, and every time the Bullfrog sailed out, the women had to swallow away a dark sense of dread in the pit of their stomachs. Of course, Master Farren, Harvey, Corwyne, and the other crew members all boasted on being highly experienced fishermen, still the women knew all too well storm waves could be as high as the old oak tree near the harbour, and such monstrous waves would be no match for any man.

Thus, all the women of Blackpool would accompany their husbands on every trip with their daily prayers and then linger in anticipation for their safe return on the appointed day.

"Thank you, Fernham," Hazel cried back. "We are coming." The boy did not answer. Instead Hazel could hear his receding footsteps on the cobblestones of the narrow alley and he was gone on his way to the wife of another crew member.

Hazel grabbed her woollen shawl and put it around her shoulders to protect herself against the biting wind. While it was not yet winter, the weather was cold this year and Hazel often wondered how these fishermen would fare out there at sea, with the harsh November winds ripping at their clothes and showering them with the salty spray of the fearsome waves. Never mind the cold… today Harvey and Corwyne were back in the safety of their homes.

Both women stepped out onto the street and hurried toward the harbour which was not too far from where Hazel and Harvey were living.

At the end of her alley, they needed to go to the left on Blundell Lane. Then, about fifty yards further down or so, to the left again on Longwall Avenue, and then straight toward the harbour.

As usual, the docks were a beehive of activity. Sailors, unloading their boats, were screaming orders at each other, carts, pulled by mules or oxen were riding on and off, barrels were carelessly rolled over the cobble stones, and gentlemen, dressed in fancy suits with large hats and walking canes, passed by with stately steps while inspecting their wares. They were the owners of some bigger boats. And, as was always the case, coursing right above the men was the army of greedy, screaming seagulls, ready to dive to the ground to conquer the mangled remains of a discarded fish, thus adding to the cacophony of screeches, noises, and confusion.

As Hazel entered the harbour she was almost bursting with excitement. Soon she would hold Harvey in her arms again and she could tell him the news, the wonderful news, that she was pregnant. The wind whipped salty air into her face, and the smell of raw fish that was permeating the atmosphere was almost overwhelming, but unlike earlier in the day, it didn't bother her. She was just too charged with happiness to allow the scent to make her nauseous.

Now where was the Bullfrog?

Usually, Master Farren moored their boat near the back, the area reserved for the smaller vessels. She squinted to see if she could already spot the mast with the familiar flag Master Farren had attached to the top. Yes… there it was, all the way near the back. Master Farren's yellow flag with the embroidered black fish his wife had sown, stood out against the cloudy, grey sky like a beacon of hope and joy.

"There," Hazel exclaimed in an eager voice as she turned to Nelwyna and pointed toward the flag "It's in the same spot it's always in. It's true. There they are."

She loved these moments of reunion. What was better than to see Harvey's weathered face as he walked up to her, with that twinkle in his eyes, his arms wide, before taking her in his firm embrace and kissing her on her lips? "Hello, Hazel... I am home again. What's for dinner tonight?"

Both women hurried on, pushing their way through the crowd. At one point, Hazel almost crashed into a barrel that a rough looking sailor was pushing over the quay. The man let out a curse and hissed, "Watch where you go, woman. This isn't the place for folks like you." Hazel didn't even react. She had better things on her mind than bad mannered sailors.

There it was, at the very end; the Bullfrog. They had securely berthed their vessel and were busy unloading. Master Farren was standing with his back to the approaching women and was talking to a man Hazel didn't know. And there, not even ten feet away, stood Corwyne, filling up a barrel with fish they had caught. He looked up and spotted both Hazel and his wife, but he wasn't smiling.

Why not? Why wasn't he smiling? This was a joyous occasion,

Hazel hesitated and scanned the area to see if there was a sign of Harvey. Corwyne had now alerted Master Farren, who turned around. His face was white, ashen white, and when he spotted Hazel, he lowered his eyes.

What was that? Why were they acting so oddly? He was usually such a jolly man… but not today. A dark cloud of doubt entered Hazel's heart. She ran over to Master Farren, crying out, "Where is Harvey? Is he still on board The Bullfrog?"

Master Farren was very close now. Hazel could see the worried expression in his eyes and could sense his anxiety.

"I-I am so sorry, Hazel." It was all he could say.

"Sorry for what? Where's my husband?"

From the corner of her eye she could see Corwyne embracing Nelwyna, but there was no joy on their faces either. There were no exclamations of joy and no happy squeals of laughter so common when husbands embrace their wives after a week at sea. That's when Hazel understood. Master Farren didn't even need to say it anymore.

Something had happened to Harvey on the trip.

Her fears had come upon her. Harvey, her dear Harvey, would not come home anymore. He had become the next victim of the cruel sea. Harvey would not even get to see his own son. He would never know Moulton; no, it was even worse… he had died without even knowing his wife was pregnant. How cruel, how unjust, and how unfair… and yet, it had happened.

"The ship almost capsized," Master Farren stammered. "Harvey did well, but I don't think I've ever seen waves so high. It's a wonder we didn't *all* die. Harvey slipped and fell overboard. There was nothing we could do."

Hazel took in the information. She heard the words, but didn't understand. It made little sense. Nothing made much sense. Her dizziness was back. Her headache had returned like a little intruder who had somehow climbed up to her brain and was now hammering on her skull from the inside. Hazel rubbed her forehead and noticed it was wet with sweat. Where was that coming from? She wasn't even feeling hot. In fact, she was cold, so very cold.

That's when darkness overtook her. Her legs and knees could no longer hold her up and while she let out a terrifying cry, she sagged to the ground. It had become too much; she had fainted.

Two days later

"What will you do?" Nelwyna asked Hazel. Her voice was soft, as she stared at her friend with gentle eyes. She *had* to be careful. At this stage, any wrong word could be like a hammer crashing and shattering the glass of Hazel's fragile emotions. Careless remarks would only add more sorrow and suffering to her dear friend's heart. She had never seen Hazel like this. Dark circles were etched around her eyes, otherwise so full of life and zest, but now they were only drooping pools of misery. What could she do to help?

Hazel did not answer. She stared ahead, not seeing anything in particular, and just when Nelwyna wondered if Hazel had even heard her question, the answer came in a flat tone, "I am going to Manchester."

Nelwyna frowned. "Manchester? But that's a big city. It's not safe there." She shook her head and added, "Corwyne said you can stay at our place, at least until you've gotten yourself back on your feet. We'll help you. That's what friends do."

Hazel cast her friend a weak smile. "Thank you, Nelwyna, but there's no future here for me. My mother lives in Manchester and there I can find work."

"You can find work here," Nelwyna objected.

"I never liked it here," Hazel answered, and a dark shadow flashed over her face. "Fishing was Harvey's life, but it was never mine. Don't you tire of always having to wonder if your husband will make it safely back to shore? I hated that sense of insecurity."

"Corwyne is a fisherman, just like Harvey was," Nelwyna argued back. "Fishing is what we do, and it's not like he is in constant danger there at sea. He's been sailing for years."

"Sure," Hazel replied, pressing her lips together and casting Nelwyna a sour glance. "You tell that to Harvey. Just in case you forgot, I just lost him to the angry sea."

Nelwyna blushed. "Sorry, Hazel. I did not mean it like that." She scolded herself. She had wanted to be so careful, but she came across as harsh and uncaring. "It's just that I hate to see you go. We are friends, aren't we?"

"Listen," Hazel said fierily. "Of course we are friends, but that's beside the point. Friendship will not pay the rent. You yourself told me I am probably pregnant. A few months from now, I will be grand with child. Who is going to hire me then? Now I can still make the needed changes."

"I told you, Corwyne has opened our door to you."

"I am going to Manchester. Your house is even smaller than mine. I don't want to be a burden to you or Corwyne. I hate Blackpool. I hate fishing villages, and I hate having to go to the poorhouse." Hazel pressed her jaws together and seemed unwilling to consider any other option. Thus, Nelwyna let out a sigh. "I see," she said. "When will you leave?"

"Tomorrow."

"Already? How will you travel?"

"I have only one option," Hazel sighed. "By foot, of course."

"But that's going to take you ten hours. Why don't you wait until we can find you someone who travels to the Manchester market?"

Hazel cast her a fiery stare. "Thank you, Nelwyna, but I have made up my mind. I'll travel tomorrow." A cynical laugh escaped her throat. "I'll be ever so glad when I have left Blackpool with its stinking fishing boats and the cruel sea who snatched my husband and my happiness away from me." She leaned back in her seat. "I appreciate what you are trying to do, Nelwyna, but I have made my decision." She forced a smile on her face, but it was clear there was no smile in her heart as she said, "Forgive me, but its best you go now. I have to make my preparations."

"Please do not harden your heart," Nelwyna still whispered, but judging by the empty stare that had returned to Hazel's face, she knew her words were meaningless. Hazel, at least for now, had locked her heart and only God could still find entrance. "I'll be praying for you," she mumbled. "Corwyne and I will always be there for you."

"Thank you," Hazel said as she got up and opened the front door, to show Nelwyna she wanted her to leave. "So at least, somebody will pray. Goodbye, Nelwyna. I wish you all the best."

As soon as Nelwyna's feet touched the cobblestones outside, the door closed behind her with a bang and deep sadness entered Nelwyna's heart. "Dear God, don't take your hands off my dear friend. Help her, dear Father."

2
A STRANGE QUIRK OF DESTINY

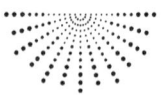

8 MONTHS LATER

Teryl Dewar was not in a good mood that dreary morning as he sat down in his dining room. He drummed his slender fingers on the perfectly crafted wooden table, while waiting for Baxter, his faithful servant, to bring in the breakfast. It should have been there already, but it was not. At least the candles of the sparkling chandelier hanging above the table were already lit. They cast a curious golden glint throughout the richly decorated room, which was just about the way it should be. Normally, being here cheered his heart as everything around him was a clear witness of his success in business. But today he mainly focused on the dark shadows lurking in the corner of the dining room, as those seemed to perfectly fit his depressed state of mind.

. . .

Not that it was all that strange for Teryl to feel that way. At least so he told himself. After all, he'd hardly slept again, and of course, as usual, that was all due to his wife's ill behaviour. Her constant nagging and murmuring was just getting too much. Somehow, she managed to always unleash her complaints on his weary mind right when he was craving rest and sleep. A rare talent, but not one to be treasured. He had a business to run. He needed his strength, but that thought did not ever seem to occur to her selfish mind. She forgot that he was the means to her happiness. The reason his wife was able to enjoy such a cushioned life, filled with parties and luxury, was entirely due to *his* fortitude and shrewd business sense. Normally, her complaints did not bother him all that much. He would simply nod, politely whisper a *"Yes Dear", "Of course Dear"*, and turn his head to his other side, but last night it had really been annoying. She had actually prodded him every single time with her outrageous little stupidities, and thus made it impossible for him to sleep.

"Dear, are you awake?"

"No."

"Good, then will you please hand me a handkerchief. My nose is blocked. So awful."

"Eh… but I am sleeping."

"Thank you, dear, and while you are at it, will you rub my back too. I have such terrible heartburn…"

"Heartburn? Arabella, rubbing your back isn't going to do a thing for your heartburn. Ask the maid to make you some ginger tea."

"I don't like ginger tea. You know that. Please, Teryl…. Will you hold my hand?"

"No, I *don't* want to hold your hand, I want to sleep. I have an important meeting with Perkins Tremble tomorrow."

On and on it went, and of course she used her pregnancy as an excuse to get his attention. As if pregnancy was an illness. The poor people in his factory never complained about *their* pregnancies, so why would she? He had seen plenty of pregnant women in his cotton mill, working with their bulging stomachs, sweat on their foreheads, and their messy hair stuck together in unsightly buns. They never uttered a complaint, but just took it as a woman should do. Maybe Arabella just had it too good.

Admittedly, he had no idea what it was like to carry a baby around all day in your belly. If he was entirely honest, something which did not happen too often, he understood that having the added weight of a baby growing within would possibly have some disadvantages. He already hated those rare moments when he had to offer a hand in the factory and carry a few sacks of cotton around. And that was only for a minute or two. Still, having a baby was only natural, so it couldn't be that bad. To make matters worse, old Doctor

Timothy had told him he needed to consider this baby a miracle.

"This is a wonderful gift from heaven, young man," the doctor had told him. While he didn't particularly like to be called *young man* by his personal physician, he had to admit Arabella's pregnancy had come as somewhat of a surprise. Arabella, having been sick during childhood, had been declared barren. She had told him she would never be able to bare him children. He would have no heir to his cotton kingdom, and he would never know the joy of fatherhood. Big deal. He had been fine with it. That meant he would have all the more time to throw himself in the industry without the distractions of whining, unruly children. And yet, here she was… pregnant.

But now he wanted his breakfast… Where was Baxter with the soft-boiled eggs he had each morning?

He switched his attention away from the dark corners of the dining room to the large window that looked out over the grassy lawn in front of their estate. While aimlessly playing with his knife he noticed it had begun to rain. A grey day it was. Just like his mood.

The door opened and Baxter appeared, carrying a silver tray stacked with buns, Teryl's customary soft boiled eggs, cold meats, cheese, and a jug of home brewed ale. "Good morning, sir," the servant said as he placed the tray on the table and arranged the dainties in an orderly row before Teryl. "Did you sleep well?"

"No Baxter, I did not sleep well." Teryl cast his servant an angry stare. Baxter had been in his employ for a good number of years, and generally served him well. The man was always obedient to his master's whims, but he was getting older and that was irritating. He claimed to have arthritis which caused him to limp a bit. His brown eyes, that used to be full of life, had lost some of their splendour and his dark hair had turned to an ugly shade of grey. As far as Teryl was concerned it wouldn't be long before he needed to place an ad for a new servant. He had mentioned it already to Arabella, which of course had paved the way for another volley of her negative and silly complaints.

"Why are you so late?" he asked the man.

Baxter remained unperturbed. "I am sorry, sir. The cook is not feeling well."

"I've been waiting here for just about forever, Baxter. I don't feel well either, but I am not making a big deal out of it. Most people in this world don't feel well, and yet they have to get their work done."

"Yes sir. I am sorry, sir." Baxter replied politely without even moving a muscle in his face. "It's just that…." His voice trailed off.

"What?" Teryl grunted while checking his egg by tapping it with his knife. "What's wrong with the cook anyway?"

"Well… eh…," Baxter began. "As you know she's pregnant. Grand with child, just like Mistress Arabella."

"Of course I know," Teryl fired back. "But that's no reason for my breakfast to be late. I have a schedule to follow, you understand?"

"Yes, sir. Of course. But she's—" Baxter tried to explain, but before he could come to the point, Teryl interrupted him.

"— I don't want to hear about it, Baxter. You deal with it. I've no time for such irrelevant and minor issues. Dismissed." He did not want to waste more time on such unimportant details and motioned for the servant to make himself scarce. He had work to do. He pulled the silver butter tray closer and took too large a scoop of butter that he smeared with short, jerky movements on the bun he had put on his plate. In an hour Perkins would appear. The workers in his cotton mill were unhappy and a shipment of raw cotton that was expected from Liverpool through the Bridgewater Canal to his factory on Miller Street was delayed. Nagging little problems that all cost money, and he hated losing money more than anything else. Decisive action was needed.

"But sir…"

"No, Baxter. I told you to go." Teryl looked up from the

breakfast table, his eyes flashing and half a bun in his hand. "Out."

Right then, the glass door opened again and as Baxter stepped out, clearly distressed, Arabella entered, dressed in her wrapper, or tea-gown, as some used to call it.

Teryl sighed. Why was she here? He needed to eat in peace and prepare for his meeting with Perkins. Arabella would never come near the table in the morning. Sick as she was with that dreadful disease called pregnancy she would prefer to have breakfast in bed. But here she was, looking rather suspicious. Teryl braced himself for more arguments.

"Good, Teryl… Here you are."

Of course he was *here*. Where else would he be?

She strode forward. As she did, her dress made it appear as if she were gracefully flying and flowing. Teryl leaned back as he studied his pregnant wife. In spite of his angry mood, he had to admit she looked rather radiant at times, almost regal. Not quite beautiful enough for him to forget about his anger, but pretty enough to admire the view. When actually had she become so big with child? It almost looked like she was about to give birth, but that couldn't be. It was not her time yet. Arabella's long brown hair was not yet made up and hung in loose, happy curls over her shoulders. He did not really want to, but he couldn't help but marvel at that bulging tummy of hers. It was indeed a true testimony of something extraordinary to come, and he almost agreed with Doctor Timothy that he was witnessing a small miracle.

Almost, but not quite. After all, he had no time for such simple-minded and sentimental gibberish. Thus, he pushed the thoughts away. Arabella's face did not carry a scowl for once. Rather her face reflected serenity. Why could she not always be like this? Maybe it was just because of her wrapper. Ever since Arabella had heard she was pregnant, now almost eight months ago, she had immediately ordered at least three such dresses from a tailor in London, but somehow, he had never really noticed any of them before. He had only noticed the bill. It had been a small fortune, but at least Arabella had been delighted and her incessant complaining had stopped… for a few days.

He expected her to pull out a chair and sit down next to him, but she glided past the table toward the large window with the elaborate curtains and looked at the rain outside.

"Is there… anything you want?" he began, squeezing the bread with his fingers. "You are not usually up so early. Are you still ill? Baxter can call for Doctor Timothy."

She turned away from the window while placing one of her hands on her bulging tummy. "It's not for me. I am here on behalf of Hazel."

Teryl stared for a moment at his wife, not quite comprehending. "You mean... Hazel, the cook?"

"Yes. She's the one. We've only one Hazel in our employ."

Teryl shook his head, fearing a new set of problems he *could* not and *did* not want to deal with. "Baxter already mentioned her," he hissed. "She was late."

"I told him to tell you. But I guess you didn't give him a chance."

Ha, there it is. He knew it. She had begun to complain again, trying to make him feel bad with that guilt projection of hers. Teryl broke another piece off his bun and dipped the whole thing in the butter without using his knife. "Tell me what?"

"That he called Doctor Timothy, of course. Hazel needs him."

Teryl choked as he swallowed a large piece of bread in one go, causing him to choke. He grabbed his ale and flushed the whole thing down. When he had somewhat recovered he glared at Arabella. "Why did Baxter call Doctor Timothy for Hazel? He is our doctor, not Hazel's, and since neither of us is ill, there's no need for the man to come down here."

Arabella furrowed her brow. "Hazel's labour started."

Teryl wrinkled his nose. Was he the only intelligent person around here? "Of course her labour started," he snapped. "It started at six this morning when she got up and had to prepare for her day's work. What is that to me?"

"No, Teryl," Arabella raised her voice. "She's *in* labour, She is having her baby and she needs help."

Teryl blinked his eyes. He was just about to stick another piece of bread in his mouth but he threw it back on his plate, glaring. "I see... but what is that to me?" He thought about it for a moment and then added, "Just send her home then. We don't want all that commotion here anyway. Give Doctor Timothy a drink and send him back home." He rubbed his forehead and sighed. Problems, problems, problems... and none of these were work related. "You think someone else could take her place cooking until she'll be back tomorrow?"

Now it was Arabella's turn to blink her eyes. "Listen, Teryl... she *can't* go home. She's *in* labour. She needs help, which is why I told Baxter to go ahead and call Doctor Timothy. He should be here soon. I just wanted you to know, that's all."

Teryl had to think for a moment but at last the truth of what Arabella had just told him sank in. He pushed his chair away and shook his finger in Arabella's face. "You do not make such decisions without consulting me, do you hear me? This is Broughton. This is not a place where every alley cat can have their baby. She can go home for the day, give birth to her baby right where she belongs, and return again to service tomorrow. Doctor Timothy is a busy man and there are plenty of others who can help to deliver that baby."

Arabella flinched but something Teryl had rarely seen welled up in her eyes. Anger, fury... perhaps even disgust. "Doctor Timothy is coming," she spat out. "That's all there is to it. I just wanted you to know."

For a moment Teryl stared at his wife. She had never, ever stood up to him. This was a first, and he had better make sure it would never happen again. Rage welled up, he forcefully pushed his chair away, and rose. All his frustrations about her whining, complaining, and him losing sleep last night, came out and he bristled with anger. No longer was there anything beautiful or regal about her; rather she had morphed into a mound of rebellion that took way too much space in his precious dining room. A bible verse flashed through his mind... Ah, that was helpful. Not that he believed in the Bible, a book that some would call *the Holy Book,* but he had heard other men say that quoting Bible verses to your wife was quite helpful in keeping a rebellious woman in line. He licked his lips and blurted out in a hoarse voice, "Wives, submit to your own husbands. I say this for your own good."

It seemed to have the desired effect. Arabella stared at him wide-eyed for a moment, but then she broke out in a wail. "I want to submit to you, Teryl, but you don't understand pregnancy. Sometimes, I think you don't even understand women."

. . .

Teryl broke out laughing. That was funny. Of course he understood women. Women just needed to keep quiet and do what they were told to do. Arabella really had no idea how much he was sacrificing for her.

"I am pregnant too," Arabella sniffed while her voice was reaching a hysterical pitch. "What if it was *me* in that kitchen, being in labour?"

"I *know* you are pregnant too," Teryl grunted, failing to see the connection. He plopped himself down on his chair again raking his hand through his hair. A headache was coming on. Great, that was just what he needed. He grabbed the mug of ale and finished the last large gulp in the hope it would calm down his nerves somewhat. Surprisingly, it did. His fury was diminishing. He licked his lips and added, "But there's a difference between you and a mere cook. Never compare yourself with her. We are the Dewars."

"I know Hazel is just the cook," Arabella cried. "I am not comparing myself with her. But I will not ever forgive myself if something goes wrong. It's why I called for Doctor Timothy and it's why I told you."

Teryl shook his head. "What's done is done. Just let the doctor in, but don't count on my support." He narrowed his eyes, scoffed and then, still riding on a small wave of anger, he added, "I sure hope you will not make such a scene when your baby is born."

"W-What did you say?" Arabella's lips quivered. "I thought it was *our* baby."

"Sure," Teryl grunted. "As long as it is a boy. I want you to bear me a boy. I do not need a girl. I cannot handle more females in my life. They all drive me crazy."

Arabella's mouth went open to answer, but no words came. Instead a terrifying yelp escaped her throat as if she was in pain and she grabbed her belly with both of her hands.

"What?" Teryl asked. "Why are you acting so strange?"

"My…. My…" But Arabella did not finish her sentence, rather she stared with large, fearful eyes at her husband.

Teryl raised his brows as he stared in horror at the rich carpet on which Arabella was standing. A large puddle of water was sinking into the fabric. "What is that?" he groaned. "Are you messing up the carpet?"

"The baby…" Arabella whispered while tears rolled out of her eyes. "My water bag broke… The baby is coming, but it's too early…"

The baby? For a moment, Teryl did not understand, but then it dawned on him what had just happened. The strain of their conversation had been too much for Arabella, and she was about to give birth.

"The doctor," he shouted as he felt his stomach turning. Arabella didn't look well... not well at all. He ran toward the door and shouted through the large hallway, "Get Doctor Timothy. Somebody call the doctor. My wife is in trouble. She's having the baby."

∽

That day two babies were born in Broughton.

By the time Doctor Timothy arrived Hazel was just about to give birth. The doctor, not having the time nor the energy to confer with Teryl, ordered Hazel to be brought to one of the guest rooms where she was placed in a luxurious canopy bed. It was a room Hazel was not normally allowed to enter, but Doctor Timothy did not care. There, surrounded by draped curtains, silk sheets, and on two soft mattresses that were stacked on top of each other, Hazel gave birth to a healthy, chubby baby.

A girl it was, with a tiny, adorable tuft of auburn hair sticking out right in the middle, and with curious green eyes that beheld the world around her with great wonder.

As soon as the baby was born, Hazel, with fearful eyes, insisted on getting up. "Doctor... this room isn't for us. The master will not like me being here."

Doctor Timothy just smiled. "You leave that to me," he reassured her. "You may stay here for as long as you need to. I'll talk to Master Teryl."

He did. Master Teryl never showed his face and she stayed in that room for more than a week.

The Master had something far more important to worry about than a poor cook that resided with her baby in one of his guest rooms. Arabella's birth was not nearly as easy as Hazel's. After her water bag had broken, to Teryl's horror, Arabella began to bleed severely. Doctor Timothy had been rather alarmed, and together with Baxter's help moved her to her bedroom. That was a moment of truth. It hit Teryl full force when Doctor Timothy ordered him out of the bedroom and the door was shut before his very eyes. He could only hear Arabella's wailing and the nervous, hushed mumbles of the doctor and his assistant filtering through the door. Her labor took until nearly midnight and Doctor Timothy, nor his assistant, would take time to explain to him what was happening. At last, Teryl almost resorted to prayer. When fear knocks on a man's heart even the hardest of characters are tempted to pray and Teryl Dewar was no exception. When Arabella at one point let out a particularly alarming scream Teryl Dewar considered calling on heaven's help and struggled with the thought for several hours. Still, it never came to that, as it was then that the door opened and the smiling face of Doctor Timothy appeared, holding a new-born baby, wrapped in swaddling clothes, in his arms.

"Congratulations, Teryl," he said. "Your wife has birthed you a son."

A son... Just what I wanted. Teryl stared at the bundle in the doctor's arms, barely able to comprehend what he saw.

"Can I hold him, Doctor?"

Doctor Timothy nodded. "You can, but I must be honest with you. The baby was born premature and does not seem as healthy as he should be. We need to keep a good eye on him. The next week or so will be crucial."

Weak? My son is weak? "Will he be fine, Doctor?" Teryl asked while he stretched out his arms so the doctor could hand him the baby.

The doctor gave him a weak smile and gently placed the baby into Teryl's arms. "Things are looking good, but I just want you to be careful. I can't say for sure, but I think baby's heart is weak, and his breathing is laboured."

"And… Arabella? How is she?"

"Tired, very tired, but she'll be all right."

At last, a smile appeared on Teryl's face. "My boy will be strong, Doctor. He may be weak today, but he'll be strong in the end. He is a Dewar. Therefore, I will call him Silas. I know a bit of Latin and I believe that means 'man of the forest.' He'll be strong like a tree."

Doctor Timothy grinned. "It means something else in the Hebrew tongue, the language of God's chosen people."

"What?" Teryl stated with a frown.

"It means 'prayed for,' Doctor Timothy replied, his face carrying a serious expression. "I think we all prayed for the safe delivery. I am sure you did too, right Teryl?"

"Of course, Doctor," Teryl replied half-heartedly, not wanting to pursue the subject any further.

"Good," the doctor said. "If you don't mind, my assistant will stay here for the night, just to keep an eye on things." After these words he turned around and walked out the door.

And so it was that Alice Matthews and Silas Dewar saw the light of life in the summer of 1841. Two babies from two very different backgrounds, but brought together by a strange quirk of destiny on the very same day and in the very same house.

3
AN UNPLEASANT SURPRISE

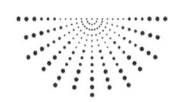

Hazel returned late that night, her feet aching. Her work at the Broughton mansion had gobbled up her time, and now she was late. Much later than she had wanted. Master Dewar had wanted her to surprise his six-year-old son Silas with what he called *Marshmallows*. Hazel had not known what they were, and neither did Master Dewar himself. "It is some sort of sugary delight," he told her. He had heard about it from eavesdropping on some of the workers at the mill. Since it was supposedly some sort of revolution in the world of sweets, he wanted his son Silas to partake of that.

Hazel had been forced to drop her other duties, go to town, and find out. One of the other servants, an unpleasant fellow by the name of Ricky Maloney would take care of the dinner cooking, at least that was what Hazel had been told. But it turned out Maloney had done nothing of the sort, and thus, by the time dinner was supposed to be ready, instead of serving the customary Wednesday roast, all Hazel could offer the family was a gooey, sugary mess of Marshmallows that Silas didn't even like. It brought down scowls from the family, and instead of Maloney, she got the blame. After having received a severe scolding from the Master, complete with several threats about being fired, she still had to prepare dinner, even though it was late.

It didn't matter. Such was life as a servant. She could do nothing about it other than saying, *Yes sir, you are right sir*, and more of such nonsense.

But now this long and horrible day was over and soon she would be able to warm her cold body by the open fire, drink a cup of hot beet soup, and if she was in luck, her little girl Alice would still be awake. She could just forget about everything, if only she could have a small moment of heavenly joy, away from the biting cold on a dreary winter's night in the slums of Manchester.

But it was not to be. She knew it as soon as she stepped through the wobbly, half rotten door of mother's ramshackle dwelling in *the alley without a name*. For there, in the gloomy living room, was only the dim light of a flickering oil lamp without the warmth of a cosy open fire. There was no steaming pan full of hot beet soup, and there were no joyful squeals of delight from a young child crying out, "Mama, you are home."

Instead of all those pleasantries there was an uncomfortable grunt from Nana who hung over the rough, wooden table in the middle of the living room while the scent of liquor pervaded the air.

Whiskey... Nana had been drinking again.

"You are l-late," Nana slurred. She stared at Hazel with large, droopy eyes and did not even attempt to hide the empty bottle that was lying on the table before her. The wretched thing had fallen over and rolled over in a puddle of its own poison. "Really late," she mumbled again. "T-That's no way to r-raise a daughter."

Hazel closed the door to the street and tossed her bonnet on a stool near the table. She shivered. "Nana, it's freezing in here. You let the fire go out."

"Di-Did I?" Nana attempted to move her sluggish body upright in a weak effort to appear strong, and explained, "We've got n-n-no more wood, Hazel. I suppose t-that's why."

Hazel frowned. "Don't do this to me Nana. Not again." Nana was the name little Alice had called Hazel's mother once. Mother had been touched, and if anything touched mother it was something to treasure. Thus, the name Nana had stuck.

"D-Do what? I've done nothing," Nana tried to answer.

. . .

"What do you mean you've done nothing? Where is the money I gave you yesterday? I gave you all of my earnings. That should have been enough to carry us through this week."

Mother shook her head and answered in a thick voice. "No, it w-wasn't enough. Not nearly en-enough."

"It *was* enough," Hazel muttered, "more than enough, but instead of food and wood you bought liquor again."

"J-Just a li-li-little," Nana defended herself, her voice thick and tired. She cleared her throat and added, "B-But you were l-late. It's y-your fault. What-what else was I supposed to do?"

"My fault?" Hazel felt rage rising. She had been giving all of her earnings to Nana who was supposed to care for Alice, keep the house clean, and prepare the meals. Was that too much to ask? But instead Nana was drinking her sorrows away, spending the precious little money Hazel had given her on liquor.

"How is Alice?" Hazel asked in a voice that sounded about as cold as the living room, hoping to change the conversation. She pulled her shawl closer around her shoulders. Her thin cotton dress was not nearly warm enough to keep the cold out.

"I-I suppose she's all r-right," Mother managed to slur back.

"Has she eaten?"

"I don't know," Mother grabbed hold of the side of the table to steady herself and shrugged her shoulders. "I told her to eat. I-It's her own fault if she didn't."

"Mother, Alice is only six years old. Are you not hearing yourself?" Hazel lifted both of her hands in desperation. When had it ever gotten to be so bad here? She knew Mother had an inordinate desire for the bottle. That had started when father ran off with that shady woman who had bewitched him years ago. Hazel still remembered that fateful morning when she had stumbled upon her father as he was saddling his horse outside. How could she forget? It had been a few years before she had met Harvey.

"Good morning, Father... where are you going?"

Father had looked up, his eyes so dark that for a moment Hazel had thought she was mistaken and she was talking to a man who just looked like father. That only lasted for a second for as soon as he opened his mouth it was clear she was indeed talking to her father. "Sorry, Hazel, but I am leaving and I will never come back."

Never come back? It was a terrible shock and instantly Hazel's eyes had filled with tears. "But father... what about me and Mama?" she remembered asking.

"You can go to the poorhouse," Father smirked. "I don't know. You figure it out. You are a big girl now and you can work too."

"The poorhouse?" As Hazel thought about that terrible moment, she could still feel the anxiety and the dread that

entered her heart. She remembered yelling, *"People in the poorhouse are living like forgotten animals, and it's rife there with disease, filth and gigantic rats."*

"It's the best I can do," Father smirked. "I should have never married your mother. Sorry."

She had not understood it then, and she still did not understand it today. How was it possible that people you'd thought you knew, people you trusted, and who were supposed to be your security, all of a sudden turned out to be like... strangers? Impersonal, uncaring, and cold strangers. That day was the last she ever heard from her father. He just took off without another word, leaving her and mother behind, complete with bills, poverty, and a deep sense of misery.

The next two years had been rough. Mother found work cleaning the streets of Manchester, and Hazel worked as a matchstick girl in the factory of Master O'Brady, a cruel man who feared neither God nor his fellow man. But then she met Harvey, and things got better. She moved to Blackpool, pleading with mother to come along. Harvey was not rich either but he had a steady income as a fisherman and was willing to care for mother too. But mother, proud as a peacock and stubborn as a donkey, refused help. "I am a Manchester girl," she insisted. "This is where I was born, and this is where I will die. I am well able to take care of myself and I do not need charity."

Hazel had left Manchester, together with Harvey. Those had been wonderful years, until that horrible day when the news had come that her Harvey had died. Oh misery of miseries. Hazel had returned to Manchester, moved in with mother, and had started to look for a job. Not just any job, but a good job. A job that would pay enough to support not only herself but would get mother off the streets too. But where would she find such a job? There was work... but not the kind Hazel was looking for. She would rather die than to become a leech collector, a job that would require her to wade through dirty pools of water and become a human trap for the leeches. She could then sell these ugly creatures to quacks and questionable physicians who would use these pests to treat certain diseases.

She was offered a job as a *pure finder* as well, but that job was no good either. As a pure finder she would have to collect dog feces from the Manchester streets and then sell it on street corners. Someone, most likely a man with a bizarre imagination, had discovered dog droppings were an excellent way to purify leather, something that was in great demand with the richer families.

No, there had to be a better way to make money.

And there was. One fortunate day, only a week after she had arrived from Blackpool, she ran into Baxter. He turned out to be the main servant at the Broughton estate, a house where a rich and well respected landowner by the name of Tyrel Dewar resided. They needed a cook as the previous cook had been fired after stealing silverware.

A cook? Hazel's heart jumped for joy. This was the chance she had been looking for. "I can cook," she told Baxter.

He studied her for some time. "We've had several cooks. One was incompetent, the other a thief. How can I be sure you are not just lying?"

"One week," Hazel pleaded. "Give me one week. I will not demand wages for that week. Let the Master decide. If he doesn't like my cooking, or if he doesn't trust me after that week, he can just throw me out. It will not cost him a penny."

Baxter had looked at her with his faithful, brown doggy eyes. He seemed like a kind-hearted older man and agreed with a warm smile. "Sounds good, Miss Hazel. Let me discuss it with the Master. Can you start tomorrow if the Master agrees?"

"I can," Hazel replied, barely able to contain her joy. "It's actually Mrs. Hazel," she added. "But my husband died at sea."

"Sorry to hear that," Baxter replied. "I will let you know tomorrow if the Master agrees."

The next morning, Baxter came by and that was it. She passed her cooking test at the Broughton estate with flying colours and after only two weeks in Manchester she was cooking for the Dewars.

She had expected Nana to be delighted. After all, she would now make enough money for the both of them, so Nana could take care of Alice while she was working, but after a while Nana wasn't happy anymore. The power of the bottle proved to be too strong. Nana, calling herself a Manchester girl, wasn't doing well at all.

Often she was found drunk when Hazel came home and there wasn't enough food for the little family. Something had to change. This could not go on much longer.

Over the years the problem continued off and on. Nana would do her best for a while, but there were days that Alice wasn't taken care of properly and Hazel was never really sure in what state she would find the house after she was done with her work at the estate.

So today Nana had outdone herself with the bottle.

"Mother, things will have to change," Hazel began, trying to sound calm and gentle, but her words came out tense. "This cannot go on. You squandered all my money on drink again... What are we going to do?"

Nana wanted to answer, but at first no words came. She cast Hazel a dumb, empty stare and then lifted her finger which she pointed in an unsteady fashion at Hazel. "We will buy wire food…eh… f-fire wood tomorrow. Y-You give us some more money, you hear."

"No, I will not," Hazel said while she stomped her foot. "I cannot trust you anymore. This is not the first time it happened, but now it's winter and we have *no* heat and *no* food. Alice can't stay here anymore, and neither can I."

With a surprised look Nana coughed while she rubbed her finger through the spilled whiskey before her on the table and mumbled, "If it makes you f-feel good, I'll drop stink...stop d-drinking. At least for a day or two."

"You have said that a thousand times," Hazel grunted. "But it never changes. In fact it's only getting worse. I love you, Mother, but I can't live like this any longer. I have to protect Alice."

"D-Don't tell me you love me," Nana fired back. Her eyes flashed and for a moment she almost appeared sober. "You know not what you are saying. You are j-just like your father, running off when things get tough." She slapped her open palm on the table causing the empty whiskey bottle to roll off the table where it shattered into pieces on the stone floor. The spilled liquor on the table splattered in all directions.

"Excuse me?" A thousand things to say flashed through Hazel's mind, but she gritted her teeth and said nothing. She was *not* just like her father and she was *not* just running off. She was giving her life for Alice, and would even give her life for mother if only the woman would be more reasonable and would show a sincere willingness to change. But lately things had gone from bad to worse and it appeared only whiskey managed to still reach Nana's heart. She needed to stop wallowing in her self-pity and fight back. She wasn't the only one who had been abandoned by father. What about the pain *she* had felt as a daughter when father told her he was taking off and would never return? At times, when it was dark outside and dark in her heart, Hazel still struggled with father's incomprehensible treachery. She had tried to help Nana. She had talked, and talked some more, but it was as if she were talking to a wall. Nana was not willing to have a meaningful conversation about such things. Not tonight, and not tomorrow either.

Nana, apparently thinking she had won the argument, let out a giggle and then, to Hazel's horror, mimicked what Hazel had just told her. She cleared her throat and said in a pompous, exaggerated voice, "Mother, I c-can't stay here a-anymore." While she spoke she lost her balance and crashed into the backrest of the chair, causing the wood to groan in creaking protest. Nana did not notice it and added, "Then g-go. Leave me too, just l-like all the others. Take Alice and f-find yourself a nice little safe haven somewhere. You were never happy here."

Hazel's lips quivered. Seeing mother like this was not what she wanted. "Mother, stop it."

"N-No, I won't stop," Nana raged, her unreasonable anger fuelled by the alcohol in her blood. "You *don't* love me. You only love yourself. Perhaps you can knock on the door of that estate of your employers. Brou-Br-Brombey, whatever the name. I am sure they will be delighted to have a spoiled, dirty little brat like Alice

59

running through their spotless marble hallways in her ragged clothes." She shook her head in drunken disgust and added in a barely comprehensible snort, "I want you out."

"Please stop it, Nana," Hazel now cried out. "You are talking nonsense." She walked over to her mother, placed both of her hands around mother's neck and gently kissed her sweaty forehead. "Come… let me put you to bed. Tomorrow will be a better day."

But Nana turned her face to Hazel and slapped both hands away. "D-Don't you patronize me. I will not have it in my own home. And don't you give me the Judas-kiss."

Hazel stared in horror at the woman before her. Was that really her mother? Oh, what horrors this world was afflicted with and what a terrifying grip alcohol could have on people. For a moment Hazel was almost certain she heard cackling, victorious laughter coming from a dark corner of the room. That would be fitting and she imagined a herd of foul demons were hiding out there. Nonsense of course. Such things weren't true. But what *was* true was the dark fury she spotted in the eyes of her mother.

And then it came to her in a flash… She *had* to move away. She could *not* stay here. For her own good, for the good of Alice, and possibly even for the good of her own mother, she would have to leave.

But that was easier said than done. Where would she go?

And then, unannounced, as if a dike broke through and flooded the land, overwhelming fears rolled in, choking her and pressing in on her chest. An ox, resting on her chest, would not have been heavier.

"O God...,"she whispered, "… this is too much. Please help." And then, just like that, the pressure was gone again. The room was as dreary, cold and miserable as before. Mother was still sitting there sneering in her drunken stupor… and yet something had changed, A curious conviction filled Hazel's heart, and the cackling of those so-called imaginary demons was no longer heard. Rather there was peace. No words were spoken but an unfamiliar confidence took over and Hazel just knew she needed not to fear. It would all work out.

Where did that come from all of a sudden? Was that God?

She had once heard a preacher talking about a peace that was greater than human understanding, a peace like a river that would carry you through this life if only you would believe. Was this the peace that man had talked about?

She stared at Nana who seemed oblivious to the change in Hazel. But in her brazen mockery, Nana had spoken a word of truth. She had unwittingly given her direction. She would indeed take Alice to the Dewars. That was the way to go… She would explain the whole thing there and ask for their help. It was a crazy idea. Master Dewar was as selfish as wicked king Ahab in the Bible, and his wife was hardly better... still, it would work out. Something deep inside whispered to her that she needed not to be afraid. She would be helped, as long as she dared to step out on the waters.

"Good night, Mother." Without waiting for a reply from mother, Hazel left and went to the bedroom she shared with Alice, her heart being a pool of conflicting emotions. On the one hand, there was a deep sadness about the state of her mother, but on the other hand there was a sense of hope and peace. Somehow she and Alice were not alone. Everything would work out. As she stepped into her bedroom she couldn't help but smile as she stared at little Alice, her head almost completely covered by a tattered blanket. The only thing that was visible was a small lock of her hair and her nose that stuck out. Alice was sleeping the sleep of the innocent, and snoring like a baby bear in hibernation. Hazel sighed as she knelt down beside her bed to say her evening prayers. Tomorrow would be the first step in a new direction.

4
THE MANSION

"Where are we going, Mama?" Alice asked, while she held on tight to Hazel's hand and looked up at her with her large, trusting green eyes; a look that always made Hazel want to do more for her precious daughter.

"We are going to Broughton, dear."

"What's Broughton, Mama?"

"Broughton is where I work, love."

"Why are we going there, Mama?"

How could she best answer that question? Alice surely would understand that life with Nana *in the alley without a name was not glorious*. But how much could she tell her, and even though Nana had gone from bad to worse, she was still Alice's grandmother. At last, she stated in simple terms, "I am going to ask if we can live there."

"In Broughton? Why, Mama? And what about Nana? Is she coming too?"

"No, love. Nana isn't coming. She wants to live her own life and now please, be quiet, love." Alice's questions made her uncomfortable. Last night, all had seemed so clear, so simple. She would simply walk out in the morning, together with Alice, leave mother and *the alley without a name* behind. Then everything, as if by magic, would work out. Somehow she and Alice would be taken care of and they would live happily ever after. But today most of her conviction had waned. Today the weather was even colder than yesterday, the sky was darker, and the wind blew harder. For all Hazel knew, it could even snow.

She was expected to be in the kitchen around eight o'clock in the morning. That way she would have enough time to prepare the breakfast. Master Dewar expected his breakfast right on time, that meant nine o'clock. The mistress stayed in bed and would notify Baxter when she wanted her food. Usually, that was around ten… *That* would be her chance. Her only chance.

Mistress Arabella, although possibly even more spoiled than Queen Victoria's children, had a bigger heart than the Master. At least, she hoped so. Master Dewar would never consider her request for help. He would glare at her with an icy stare, throw his handkerchief on the floor in anger, and then shake his head emphatically while mumbling, 'No, a thousand times, no. No poor child will ever share this house with my precious son Silas.'

But Mistress Arabella would maybe act differently. Hazel had seen her cry once, and had also seen rare moments of kindness... sometimes. Still, it was clear that her chances of success were virtually nil. Yet she had to try. That wonderful sense of assurance that had come over her last night *had* to mean something. She had not cooked up those feelings herself.

"I like Broughton, Mama." Alice's cheery voice broke through Hazel's musings. They had just reached the outskirts of Manchester. Now, they needed to follow the road through the open fields for about two miles until they came to a small forest where they would take a left to the Broughton estate. It was even colder here than in the city and Hazel shivered. She put her arm around Alice in hopes of keeping her precious child warm. Neither of them possessed a winter coat.

"You like Broughton?" Hazel replied hoping she sounded cheerful. "Why my child? You don't even remember the place."

Alice blinked her large eyes and wiped a brown curl off her face. "I like it, because you are there, Mama. I don't like to stay back in Manchester when you are gone."

"I know, love. That's why I am trying to change things... Just don't get your hopes up too high. I am only trying."

Alice seemed unaware of Hazel's misgivings, and in spite of the freezing cold, she seemed ever so happy to go with Mama to that mysterious place called Broughton.

"Have I been there before, Mama?"

"Where, my love?"

"Broughton, Mama. You said I don't remember the place."

Hazel smiled. "Yes love, you were born there."

That statement produced a squeal of delight from Alice, as it made the place all the more special and inviting, and she insisted on hearing more.

And Hazel told her the story as they walked on, until they reached Broughton at last.

The mansion rose before them; intimidating, large and impressive. A garden path led over the grassy lawn to a patio that was made of solid stone with several large marble steps that led up to the wooden front door. The walls of the main house were composed of rows of grey river stone, interrupted by equally large rows of shimmering red bricks, and held several big, white and slatted windows. The whole thing was topped off with a slanted roof, entirely covered by carefully crafted pieces of brown slate. Part of the wall was covered with dark green ivy, which seemed to be a haven for the doves who were flying in and out; their gentle cooing bringing joy and relaxation. Truly, it was a house fit for kings. Hazel peered at Alice. How would she react to this place, which surely would look to her like a palace?

. . .

"This is it?" Alice cried out in jubilation. "It's so big... and I was born here? I wish we could live here again, Mama. Can we? Oh, that would be so jolly nice."

Hazel bit her lower lip but said nothing. As she stared at the stately house, it was as if she saw it again for the first time, but now through the eyes of Alice. How fortunate she was to be working here.

"Is that part of it, Mama?" Alice asked as she looked at another building on the left. It was connected to the main house, had the same red bricks and the roof was made from the same material, but it was a lot smaller and had only one floor.

"Those are the servant quarters," Hazel answered. "That's where the kitchen is too. The entrance is at the back." She guided Alice to a set of wooden steps on the far end that led to a walkway that guided you toward the back of the building.

"I have never seen such a beautiful place," Alice stammered in sincere admiration. "And we can live here, Mama?"

. . .

Hazel squeezed Alice's hand and cleared her throat. "I said I would ask the Mistress of the house. Nothing is certain. What we need is a little help from God, so I want you to only do what I say, and not anything else, do you understand?"

Alice looked up, her eyes questioning. "Am I not always doing what you say, Mama, and isn't God always helping?"

"Yes, dear, He does and you always do what I ask you to do… But now I want you to be still and just wait."

"Wait for what, Mama?"

Hazel grunted. How could she explain to Alice what was at stake here? "Don't ask, love. Just do as I tell you to."

"Yes Mama."

She gently pulled Alice with her in the direction of the wooden porch.

"Why can't we go through the front door, Mama?" Alice pulled on Hazel's arm and pointed to the large front door that was surrounded by the ivy and the cooing doves.

. . .

"Never the front door, love," Hazel stated in a flat tone. "That is not for us. The front door is only for Master Dewar, his wife, and their guests. We have our own door."

"Yes, Mama." Alice said and to Hazel's relief she just meekly followed her onto the porch. Soon they came to a door in the back. Not nearly as impressive as the main door Alice had wanted to go to, but it was still nice as it was painted in a cheerful red colour with a nice small window right in the middle so you could look in or out. In any case it was much nicer than the mouldy, half rotten door in the *alley without a name.*

As Hazel opened the door, she saw how Alice's eyes grew large. Alice had never seen such a luxurious kitchen and Hazel took great pride in keeping it spotless, shiny and clean.

"This is where I work, Alice," Hazel said in a soft voice. It almost felt as if she were apologizing. It was such a contrast with Nana's cold, uninspiring hovel and Hazel could only hope her little plan would work. The kitchen was set up in an L-shape and Hazel allowed Alice to storm in and check it all out for herself. First, Alice ran over to the large slatted window on the opposite side that looked out over the green grass and the path over which they had just walked.

"We just walked there, Mama," Alice cried out as she looked out while pressing her nose against the glass. The next thing Alice examined was the large wood stove that was placed against one of the walls. The stove was about as big as Nana's table and a pot, much larger than any of the pots in Nana's place, was standing on the fire with boiling water.

"Baxter put it on, early this morning," Hazel explained. "That way we have hot water for coffee and tea." She expected Alice to ask who Baxter was, but the question never came. Instead, Alice admiringly let her fingers slide over the pretty ceramic white tiles that were covering most of the wall around the stove. Several frying pans, smaller pots, and a great assortment of ladles, knives, and other kitchen ware hung from a rack that was attached to the tiles, and on the right, next to a table that Hazel used for cutting and cleaning, was a water pump.

"This is where you work, Mama?" Alice asked, scarcely able to comprehend the beauty of it all.

. . .

"Yes, love… this is my domain," Hazel nodded.

"And I was really born here?" Alice went on.

A smile erupted. "Not here, silly. This is the kitchen. Nobody is born in a kitchen."

"Oh," Alice replied, not quite understanding. "Can I see where I was born, Mama?"

"Not right now, Alice, maybe later. Remember, I told you to sit still. I need to prepare the breakfast for Master Dewar." She pointed to a stool in the corner, right near the window, and ordered Alice to sit on it.

Alice did as she was told and when Hazel had reassured herself all was well, she opened a cupboard door, pulled out a large black dress, draped it over her own clothes and smoothed out any wrinkles. When she was satisfied all was as it should be she took a large white apron out of the same cupboard, and in one short move, slipped it over her neck so the straps of lace rested on her shoulders. She fastened it with two loose strings at the back. "Fastening the apron on the back is the difficult part," she grinned to Alice who stared in wonder at her mother.

"You are so very pretty, Mama," the girl blurted out. "You look like the queen."

"No, I don't," Hazel said as she shook her head. "These are my work clothes. I can't walk around in my own ragged dress in here."

"I love you Mama," Alice said while she stared at Hazel. "I am crushed on you."

Hazel started laughing. "Where did you hear that?"

"Bill Gripper, the fishmonger said it, Mama. He said he was crushed on someone and told me it meant he loved that person."

"The saying is 'having a crush on someone,'" Hazel corrected Alice. "It comes from the dance halls where the rich go. It's so crowded there that people sometimes get pushed around and are crushed into each other. But I love you too, Alice." She put her arms around her precious treasure and pulled Alice close. "I am crushed on you too."

. . .

Alice's giggled as she looked up into her mother's eyes and Hazel swallowed hard. Just the thought that she may have to disappoint Alice was unbearable.

Hazel was just getting ready with the preparations for the breakfast when the door whooshed open and an older man stepped in. He was limping slightly but his brown eyes had a friendly gaze. "Good morning, Hazel," he said in a rather formal voice. "Master Dewar wants to see you."

Master Dewar? Worry flashed through Hazel's mind. Usually, the Master only wanted to see her when something was wrong, but she had not even served him his breakfast. "Good morning, Baxter," she answered a little unsure. "I was just about to get started on his eggs."

Boiling eggs for Master Dewar had to be done with the utmost of care. His egg had to be just about perfect. Four minutes in boiling water. No more, no less. Otherwise, he would throw out the egg in disgust, complain about it, and demand to know why Hazel had messed up so badly. She had learned quickly.

"No eggs, this morning," Baxter explained. "The Master is not feeling very well, and wants to know what you can cook to make him feel better. Mrs. Dewar moved to the guest room. She'll be sleeping in, and wants breakfast there a bit later. Master Dewar demands to see you right away."

"I am so sorry to hear that the Master does not feel well. I will go there right away."

Baxter's bushy eyebrows went up. He had spotted Alice.

He folded his hands behind his back and stood in the door opening, erect and regal as was his custom as the head-servant of the house.

"And who do we have here?" he asked in a warm voice.

Hazel blushed. "This… eh… this is my daughter, Alice. I-I brought her here since there's nobody to take care of her at home."

Hazel braced herself for a scolding. Baxter was generally very courteous and kind. Still, bringing along a child to Broughton uninvited was just not done. But she had not needed to worry as a smile appeared on his kind face.

. . .

"Bless your heart," he said. "It's a hard world out there." The smile stayed on his face and with his hands still behind his back, he took a step forward. "Hello, dear... I remember you. You were the girl that was born here the same day young Master Silas saw the light."

Hazel bit her lower lip. Would he be offended by the ripped and ragged clothes her daughter was wearing?

It did not seem so. As the man stepped forward the smile on his face only became bigger. And what about Alice? How would she react? Alice was not used to seeing such well-dressed people. All she knew were the ruffians of the slums of Manchester and Baxter was anything but a ruffian. He was immaculately dressed in a black suit with a neatly starched, white shirt underneath that had its collar standing up. It made it almost appear as if the man had no neck. His jacket was lined with two rows of large, shiny silver buttons, but they did not serve any particular purpose other than decoration as the jacket itself was closed with a shiny silver pin, as bright and shiny as the buttons.

Baxter now stopped right in front of Alice and studied her.

. . .

"I-I had no alternative." Hazel spoke, but her words came out barely audible. Why was her throat so dry?

Baxter seemed to sense her discomfort, as he turned back to Hazel and shook his head. "Don't worry, Hazel. I am glad you brought her." Hazel marvelled as the head-servant seemed almost pleased to see Alice. If only the Mistress would act like that.

Baxter turned his attention back to Alice who, like Baxter, had put her hands behind her back presumably in an effort to act just like this large, impressive man.

"So," he began, "as I said, I was there when you were born, Alice…I may call you Alice, right?"

To Hazel's relief, Alice smiled back. She was not a timid child, never had been, and it was easy for her to make friends. It appeared Baxter was to become the next one.

"Yes, sir," Alice responded. Her face was beaming. "Alice is my name, so that's what you should call me. What can I call you?"

. . .

Hazel cringed. Would Baxter be offended?

He was not. Instead he placed one of his hands on Alice's head and said, "They call me Baxter, so I assume that's what you can call me too."

"Not even Mister Baxter?" Alice asked while she tilted her head.

"No dear," Baxter replied. "Baxter is perfectly fine. I do not call you Miss Alice, either do I?"

Alice laughed. "That would be silly, Baxter."

"That's what I thought." He made a small bow, his hands still behind his back. "I hope you will convince your mother to bring you as often as possible. Maybe you can be a friend to young Master Silas."

"Who is Si—" Alice wanted to know but Baxter broke off her sentence and turned his attention back to Hazel. "The Master is waiting in the dining room." After these words he nodded a polite greeting to Hazel, gave Alice one more smile, turned around and left.

The door closed and for a moment the room was steeped in silence. Hazel cleared her throat and said, "Well… you heard Baxter. Mama needs to see the Master. I'll be back shortly. You just stay here and while I am gone you can look out of the window."

"Yes, Mama."

"Don't go anywhere, you understand. Just stay on your stool. It's very important you don't go wandering off."

"Yes, Mama," Alice replied again, pressing her lips together. Then she turned to look out the window.

Hazel hurried out of the kitchen, trying to suppress a nervous feeling. If the Master would step in the kitchen, seeing Alice in these ragged clothes, he would be hopping mad. She had now seen Alice through Baxter's eyes.

O, what had she started…? She scolded herself. No use berating yourself, Hazel. You have come this far, and there's no stopping now.

5
MEETING THE YOUNG MASTER

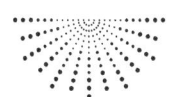

After Mama had left, Alice slid off her stool and walked around the kitchen. What a kitchen it was. She stared wide-eyed at all she saw, shaking her head in amazement. This was the place Mama worked in everyday? Alice had never been in such a clean and richly decorated place. Everything she saw; the walls, laid in with little tiles, the sturdy furniture made of solid wood, the cutlery hanging on silver hooks on the wall, and even the ceramic floor tiles, it all held her fascination. How was it even possible that Mama, being used to this standard, could be happy at the house in 'the alley without a name'?

High above, hanging from a wooden beam that ran across the ceiling was a bright and shiny chandelier. Several ornate, silver branches stretched out from the middle, all bejewelled with sparkling crystals, and each holding a large, white candle that flickered with happy, dancing flames. It cast a soft, cosy glow over the shadowy part of the kitchen. *'The house in the alley without a name'* had rafters too, but the rafters there were all covered with mould and at several places the rain water, seeping through leaks in the roof had carved out little canals through which it was continuously dripping on the floor below.

This place was vastly different. Occasionally, when Mama had been home early, she would tell Alice made-up fairy-tale stories, that usually included palaces with a prince and a princess. Now Alice understood where Mama had found the inspiration for many of such stories.

Even more staggering was the thought that she herself was born here. The desire to run out of the kitchen and explore the rest of this fairy-tale castle welled up. Dare she sneak out and see for herself what the rest of this place was like? It would be so easy to do, but then again..., Mama had specifically told her to stay in the kitchen. Her voice had been firm, almost like a warning: 'Don't leave, Alice.'

At that instant, the door opened again.

Mama already? Alice looked up, expecting to see Mama's gentle face, but it wasn't Mama at all.

There, in the door opening stood a young boy, gaping at her. He was dressed very differently from Alice, who was only wearing a simple grey dress, ripped at the seams and covered with patches that Mama had stitched on in a constant struggle to keep from having to buy a new dress. "Money is scarce, Alice," Mama always told her. "I am saving up for a new dress, but right now, your dress is just about perfect." Alice had never wondered about it, but now, seeing this boy in his fancy outfit, she realized how ragged she actually looked.

This boy had no patches on his clothes, not even a small one, and everything seemed to fit perfectly. He was wearing a white shirt with a huge bow about his neck, and funny looking velvet breeches that fitted at his knees. His lower legs were covered with cotton stockings.

"Who are you?" the boy asked, his eyes widening in surprise. He shuffled uncomfortably with his shoes over the tile floor of the kitchen. Alice couldn't help but marvel at these shoes. They were made of the finest leather and adorned with large, sparkling buckles, one on each shoe.

"I-I am Alice," Alice mumbled.

The boy gave Alice a small nod and stepped all the way into the kitchen. He closed the door behind himself.

Alice remembered what that man, called Baxter, had said. *Maybe you can become friends with young Master Silas.* Was this the young Master that Baxter had been talking about?

The boy narrowed his eyes and then asked in a gravelly voice, "Why are you wearing such silly clothes?"

Silly clothes? That wasn't a nice thing to say. Surely, her

dress was ragged and old, but Mama had made it for her and that made it the best dress in the world.

"My clothes aren't silly," Alice fired back. "My Mama made my dress. Your clothes are silly." The clothes that boy wore looked terribly uncomfortable. How would anyone be able to play in them? No, she was ever so glad for the dress Mama had made for her.

Anger flashed in the boy's eyes as he considered Alice's words. He was apparently not used to being contradicted, and wasn't sure how to react. He raked his hand through his hair, a pageboy cut that reached just to his shoulders, and then smirked. "No, yours are silly. They are dirty and ripped. What are you doing here?"

"I am helping my Mama with the cooking," Alice explained with an air as if she had been personally hired by Queen Victoria.

"Ah," the boy said. "So your mother is Hazel the cook."

"That's right," Alice said as she stepped forward. "My Mama is the big cook and I am the little cook. And who are you?"

"I am the Master," the boy answered with a smirk. "Young Master Silas."

He stepped forward, but kept his eyes glued on Alice, as if she could not be trusted and would suddenly flare up and do something bad and unexpected. "I've never seen you here before," he said. "If you are the little cook, how come I have never seen you?"

"Today is my first day," Alice replied without wavering. She confidently put both of her hands behind her back and beheld the young master. Silas stood still again, not sure what to do next. He kept staring at her with suspicion, but his eyes seemed sad. It was then that Alice noticed his pale complexion. Some of the Scavengers* Alice knew in Manchester were pale like that. Those were the boys who worked in the cotton mill and were employed to clean and recoup the area underneath a spinning mule. But they were usually ill or overworked, and always pale. Surely, this boy was not overworked. What was wrong with him? His blue eyes seemed tired and stared at her with little enthusiasm.

"Your first day?" Silas inquired.

"Yes, that's what I said. What do I need to cook for you?"

That seemed to make young Master Silas happy, as his eyes lit up. "I came for Sugarplums," he said.

Alice raised her brows. "Sugarplums? What are those?"

Now it was Silas' turn to be surprised. "You don't know what Sugarplums are? Then you are really missing something."

"Tell me."

"They are nice," Silas replied. "It's sugar in the shape of a small plum. Father says I can't have them in the morning, but he never comes into the kitchen, so you can just give me some. After all, you said you are the cook so you are in charge of the Sugarplums."

Alice scratched her head. "Where are they?"

"The big cook… eh, your mother… has them in that jar over there," Silas explained. He pointed to a stone jar with a lid that was on a shelf near where Alice was standing. "Get me some."

Alice scowled. That boy sure was cocky. Maybe that was normal. After all, he was the young Master of the house. She looked in the direction he had pointed to and spotted the jar.

Too high. She could not possibly reach it; at least not without a step. She needed a step. If she could use the stool near the window she could possibly reach it.

"That shelf is too high for us," she said. "You want to help me carry that stool over here?"

Silas grinned and nodded. "That's a good idea. If it works I can always come here in the evening too and eat as many Sugarplums as I want."

"Are they *that* nice?" Alice asked, not quite understanding. She never ate sweets and could not understand why anyone would want to climb a stool in the dark at night to get some.

"You never had any?" Silas asked, shaking his head. "I can't believe you never tasted them. What do you eat for sweets?"

"For sweets?" Alice looked up. "I never had any."

Silas halted abruptly. "You never had any sweets? That's crazy. You never had caramel or chocolate?"

"No," Alice said, feeling dumb, refusing to look at Silas.

"So you never have any foods you like?" Silas went on.

"Of course there are foods I like," Alice replied, wanting this conversation to end. This boy may be the young master of the house, but he sure was annoying. "Sometimes my mother buys me Rice Milk on the street, and for my birthday I had Plum-Duff."

"Yikes," Silas shook his head. "Those are not sweets. I never want to eat that." His face brightened and he said in a generous voice, "If you manage to get to the jar, I will let you have a Sugarplum too."

"Then you must help me," Alice answered. "I can't carry this stool by myself."

Silas nodded and walked over to the window. The prospect of getting his beloved Sugarplums had apparently softened his heart and he no longer considered Alice a stranger. She now had become an accomplice. They each grabbed a side of the stool and began to move the heavy, wooden seat toward the shelf with the Sugarplums.

"This is heavy," Silas stammered as they dragged the stool over the floor.

Alice stared at him with a tinge of disgust. His comment surprised her. That stool was heavy, but not *that* heavy. What was more, Silas was a boy, and boys were supposed to be strong. But, apparently, he wasn't strong. He was just weak… and pale. Maybe, he was ill. She had better not ask him about it.

Soon they had the stool in place. Silas pointed to the jar above them and ordered Alice to climb on the stool. "You are the cook, so you get them."

Alice sighed, but did as she was told. She hoisted herself on top of the stool and, careful not to fall off, stood straight. It was a wobbly undertaking, and she didn't particularly like standing there. But now that she had come this far, she may as well do as the young Master had asked her.

She reached out as far as she could, stretching her fingers as high as was possible, even to the point of hurting them, but it was to no avail. Still too high. The jar of Sugarplums stayed out of reach. She tried standing on her tip-toes. Very uncomfortable, but at least her index-finger could now reach the bottom of the jar. But that was not far enough.

"You try," she sighed. "I can't reach the jar."

Silas frowned. "Me, up there?"

"If you want your Sugarplums you have to climb up," Alice stated in a decisive voice.

"But you are the cook," the boy protested. "You are responsible for the food. I might fall."

"Then you will have to wait for my Mama to come back," Alice said as she jumped off the stool. "She'll be here soon."

Silas reflected on Alice's statement and then shook his head. "I will not wait," he mumbled. "She will only give me one. I'll try. Out of the way."

Alice stepped back to make room and saw how Silas climbed up on the stool with great difficulty. The boy was sighing and panting, but succeeded. At last he stood on the stool while breathing heavily, as if he had just been climbing a snow-covered mountain. He cast an eager look up and tried to reach the shelf with his outstretched hand. He too could just touch the jar. Again, that was not enough.

"Stand on your tip-toes," Alice coached him from below. "I did too."

A scowl appeared. "I may lose my balance," he objected, but apparently the prospect of the delightful Sugarplums proved to be too much for him and he did as Alice suggested. It made a significant difference as he managed to grab the bottom of the jar and in one ferocious, clumsy move, he moved it off the shelf. But that was the wrong move. He overextended himself and lost his balance. Alice looked on in horror as she saw Silas struggling on top of the wobbly stool trying to stay upright by wildly waving his arms in the air. His fingers were still clasped around the jar, but at last he let it go. It helped him to regain his balance, but the jar flew through the air. The lid came off and instantly it rained dark lumps of sugar. Then, the whole thing came crashing down on the floor. It was a small wonder the jar did not break, but the Sugarplums were scattered everywhere.

"I-I think I made a mistake," Silas whispered and appeared even more pale than he already was. He stared wide-eyed at the delicious treats all over the kitchen floor, barely understanding what had just happened.

"Quick," Alice commandeered. "We must clean up the mess."

Alice's simple statement snapped the boy back to the reality of the moment and, still panting, he climbed back down to help Alice by gathering up the hard, sugary delicacies. In the process he stuffed several lumps in the pocket of his now not so spotless pants and handed one to Alice. "Here, you can have this one."

Alice stared at the dust-covered lump in Silas' sweaty hands. It hardly looked appealing, but she realized she couldn't refuse such a generous offer from the young master of the house and decided it was best to swallow her pride.

Seconds later the sweet thing was in her mouth and softly melted away as she sucked off the hard edges.

"Well?" Silas asked. His voice was hard to hear as his mouth was full as well. "Isn't it sweet?"

"Very sweet," Alice managed to mumble while she got up and inspected the floor to see if they had overlooked a few stray Sugarplums. The floor was clean. It appeared most of the wretched things were back in the jar.

The door opened again and Mama returned. When she saw young Master Silas she blushed and her hand went up to her mouth. "M-Master Silas," she stammered. "I was just talking to your father. W-What can I do for you?"

"Noffing," Silas answered barely audible as he was still chewing on his candy. "Ih wass just lleavin. Byeh"

Hazel frowned and then spotted the jar of Sugarplums still in Alice's hands. Silas passed by her and stepped out the door without another word. Hazel sighed. "I see you met young Master Silas," she stated in flat tones. "Did he just ask you for Sugarplums?"

Alice just nodded.

Hazel shook her head. "Maybe it wasn't such a good idea bringing you here, after all."

Alice, her mouth now empty, looked up and said, "I like it here, Mama. It was a very *good* idea to come here."

"How did you manage to get the jar?" Hazel enquired.

Alice pointed at the stool.

"I see," Mama mumbled. "Let's hope Master Dewar won't hear of this." Then she added with a grunt, "Young Master Silas is always after those Sugarplums."

"I had one too," Alice confessed, "but they taste bad."

"I am sorry I had to leave the kitchen," Hazel apologized. "Master Dewar is ill and wants me to cook special things for him today. Sorry I had to leave." She took the jar with the Sugarplums away from Alice and placed them back on the shelf. "So, you got to meet young Master Silas."

Alice shrugged her shoulders. "Why is he so pale, Mama? His breathing is difficult too. He could hardly make it up the stool to grab the Sugarplums."

Hazel's face dropped and she stared in horror at Alice. "Young Master Silas climbed on that stool? *Never* let him do that again, Alice. If he falls it could be bad for him, and I may get fired if it happens in the kitchen."

"Why can't he climb a chair, Mama? All boys climb chairs." Alice asked. "Is he sick?"

Hazel nodded. "He is, Alice. Nobody know what's wrong with him. He's a bit spoiled too and can be rather rude at times. Was he nice to you?"

Alice thought about her Mama's question for a moment. Pompous young Master Silas talked with that peculiar accent all the rich people had, but as she pictured his pale face and how they had climbed the stool together in search of the Sugarplum treasure, she could not suppress a smile. Yes, she liked Silas, and he had been nice to her.

"Yes Mama, I like him. He is nice," she said at last.

Mama seemed pleased. She walked over to Alice and kissed her hair. "Good. I am glad to hear that," she said and stared at her for a moment with that warm look that is so common to loving mothers. At last, she straightened her apron and said, "Now I have to prepare a breakfast for Master Dewar. And then…" her voice faltered, "I will have to talk to the Mistress about… about us." She sighed and added, "Please do not get into more trouble while I am gone."

Alice frowned. "I did not get into trouble, Mama. Young Master Silas ordered me to get the Sugarplums. That's all."

Hazel nodded. "I know, love. It's not your fault. Now go back to your stool, and wait. Isn't the garden beautiful?"

Alice shrugged her shoulders. It was beautiful, but she had already been staring out at it for the longest time. She wanted to explore the house, but she shouldn't disobey

Mama. Later, if she ever bumped into young Master Silas again, she would ask him to show her around. After all, he was the master of the house, and he could do as he liked.

"Yes, Mama. I'll be looking out into the garden."

"Good girl," Mama answered and began her preparations for Master Dewar's breakfast.

6
ACCEPTED

Master Dewar had gotten his specially prepared breakfast. Now, the time had come to knock on the Mistress' door. As Baxter had informed Hazel earlier, the Mistress, not wanting to catch whatever cold or influenza her husband had, had moved away to one of the guest rooms. Perfect. That way it was certain the Mistress would be alone.

But would she listen? Usually, Baxter would be the one to bring her breakfast, and the Mistress did not like unexpected changes. Maybe, Mistress Dewar would be so annoyed seeing Hazel's face instead of Baxter's, that she would be thrown out before she could have even served the food, let alone talk. But she just had to try.

Hazel had asked Baxter if for once she could bring the food. "Can I, Baxter?"

He had been surprised and his bushy eyebrows shot up. "Why?"

"Because...," Hazel answered in soft tones, "... I have a request to make."

Baxter nodded and gave her a warm smile. "Fine, Hazel. Good luck."

Hazel heaved a sigh of relief and cast Baxter a grateful smile. It seemed the man could not refuse her anything and always seemed so considerate of her wishes and needs. If only the Mistress was half as accommodating as Baxter. But the Mistress had a temper. Growls and grunts were more common than smiles and a listening ear. Regardless, she just had to try and hope the Mistress would be willing to listen to her tale of woe.

Usually Mistress Dewar wanted a *simple* breakfast. That meant egg fritters, bread steak, a jar of homemade cinnamon-all-spice-peanut butter, and a pitcher of lukewarm tea. Of course, the poor never ate like that, and it was only the Mistress' personal interpretation of what a simple breakfast really meant. But today, hoping to get on her good side, Hazel added Crumpets, a couple of Cheese Turnovers, and a cup of sweet thick milk, something that was usually only served on the Mistress' birthdays. Those were the Mistress' absolute favourites.

Hazel saw Alice staring at all the goodies on the counter. Alice had never seen such delicacies, and Hazel handed her some of the leftovers. Alice's face brightened as she bit into a Cheese Turnover. "Does Nana ever have these foods, Mama?" she asked with a questioning gaze. "Can Nana come and live here too? They have enough room."

"It doesn't work that way, Alice," Hazel answered. "And remember, I'm not so sure we can live here. We need a little miracle. While I talk to the Mistress, why don't you pray for a good outcome?"

"I will, Mama," Alice replied. "But why do you say, 'it doesn't work that way?'"

"Because it doesn't," Hazel replied. The picture of her drunken mother slouched over the table welled up in her mind's eye. Nana no longer cared for Alice and wasted all the good money she had given her to buy food, on liquor and junk. No, Nana would never fit in here, and neither could they go back to *the house in the alley without a name*. "One day you will understand, Alice. But that day is not now. Now, please open the door so I can walk out with the breakfast tray. Then close the door again, sit on your stool, and say your prayers, will you?"

"Yes Mama."

"Good girl," Hazel said. She took the tray and walked out. "I'll be back soon."

∼

As Hazel stood in front of the door to the room that Mistress Dewar was sleeping in, she bit her lower lip. This

95

was it. There was no way back now. She placed the tray with the breakfast items on a small table near the door, took another deep breath, and let her knuckles fall onto the wood, hoping her knock was just about perfect. The sound was louder than she had wanted to. She listened with bated breath.

"Who is there?" came the voice of Arabella, the Mistress of the house.

"Breakfast, My Lady," Hazel replied with a cheer she didn't feel.

"Come in," came the response.

Hazel opened the door, picked up the tray, and stepped inside.

She was met by the surprised stare of Mistress Dewar, but there, sitting right on the bed was young Master Silas too. He had apparently gone to his mother's room after he had walked out of the kitchen and was now chatting with his mother. The curtains were already opened.

"Where is Baxter?" asked Arabella, her voice filled with annoyance. "Is he sick too?"

"No, My Lady, he is not," Hazel answered as she placed the breakfast tray on a bedside table. "I asked if I could bring in the breakfast this morning." She hesitated. "I have something I wanted to ask you."

"I see Crumpets and Cheese Turnovers," Silas cried out before the Mistress could answer. "Can I have some?"

Arabella frowned and inspected the tray. Her son was right. She frowned even more when her eyes rested on the cup of Sweet Thick Milk... "What's all this?" she asked. Then a flash of worry crossed her face and she gave Hazel a questioning stare. "Oh God, did I forget my own birthday?"

"No, My Lady," Hazel answered, swallowing hard. "I-I wanted to give you a special breakfast."

"Why?" Arabella's voice was sharp. "What is it you wanted to discuss with me? Is it about a raise, then the answer is no. You earn more than enough already."

"No, My Lady. It is not about money."

"Then what is it?" the Mistress grunted as she tapped with her fingers on the edge of the bed. "As you can see I am spending time with my son, and I am not in the mood for problems."

This was not going the right way. The Mistress was in her usual, grouchy mood.

"Of course, My Lady. It-It is about my daughter."

"Your daughter. Which one?"

"I-I have only one daughter, My Lady. The one who was born here."

Silas had climbed off the bed and without waiting for his mother's approval was already stuffing himself with one of the Cheese Turnovers. But upon hearing about Hazel's daughter he stopped chewing and looked up, curiosity etched on his face. "Was Alice born here?" he mumbled while wiping the crumbs of the Cheese Turnover with the sleeve of his immaculate shirt. "Where was she born?"

Arabella scowled at him. "Alice? What are you talking about?"

Silas could not reply as he had taken another bite of his mother's breakfast, and wiped his mouth with his sleeve once more.

"Not your sleeve, dear," Arabella groaned. "You have a handkerchief for that purpose." She shook her head and reached for the cup of Sweet Thick Milk. She sniffed it and gave Hazel a small, approving look. "Thank you, Hazel. It's my favourite."

Silas had his mouth empty again and blurted out, "Where was she born, Mama? Tell me."

Arabella took a sip of her drink and gave Silas a disapproving look. "It is not important, son. It was a long time ago, and it was an accident. But if you really want to know, it happened in this room."

For a moment, Silas seemed stunned, but then a smile appeared on his pale face. It was as if a ray of sunlight broke through the clouds and he turned to Hazel. "Alice was born in *this* room?"

Hazel gave Silas an insecure little nod and whispered barely audible, "Yes, Master Silas... Alice was born in this room."

"I like Alice. She is nice," Silas cheered.

Arabella choked as she had taken too big a swallow of her Sweet Thick Milk. She put the cup down, pressed her napkin against her red lips, and cast Silas a worried glance. "What do you mean, you like her? You don't even know her."

"Yes, I do," Silas replied confidently. "I met her this morning. I want her to be my friend."

Arabella's mouth dropped open. "Y-You met her this morning? Where?"

"In the kitchen. She was nice and we shared my Sugarplums."

Anger flashed over Arabella's face and she turned back to Hazel. "Is that true, Hazel. Did you bring your daughter here?"

Hazel blushed. "Yes, My Lady. She is in the kitchen right now. You see... I don't have a place to stay with her for the night."

Arabella's face could not have been more incredulous than if her husband had just told her they had lost all of their wealth. "A-Are you saying you want to stay in my… eh… our house?"

Before Hazel could answer, Silas jumped up and down for joy and began to cheer in a loud voice, "Yes, Mother. That's a great idea. Hurray. Alice is my friend."

His spontaneous outburst surprised Arabella. She stared in bewilderment at her son, and Hazel knew why. The boy was considered too ill to show his emotions like that. Any excitement was bad for him, and the doctor had ordered rest, sleep and some more rest. Apparently, he'd had breathing problems all of his life, although there was even more that was bothering him.

"Calm down," Arabella exclaimed in a loud, authoritative voice. "You know what Uncle Buddy has said. Too much excitement will make you even sicker. Stop it."

"But I like Alice, Mama," Silas protested in a small voice.

But Arabella shushed her boy and turned to Hazel. "What's going on, Hazel?"

And so Hazel told the Mistress about the cold house in *the alley without a name*. She told her about her mother's lack of care for Alice, and how she squandered all the money on drink rather than on food and firewood. As she told the story tears brimmed her eyes. When she was done she lowered her head and stared at the floor, not sure what to expect.

It was quiet for some time. Then Arabella cleared her throat and shook her head. "But you are poor, Hazel. We can't have a poor girl in our house. We have no room."

Silas, who had silently followed the conversation, grunted loud. "We have *this* room, Mama, and we have the playroom, the dusty room, the sunny room, and there is even the room with the velvet curtains. We have plenty of room."

"No Silas, we have not," Arabella fired back. "All these rooms have a distinct purpose, there's no room in the servants quarters either."

"We don't need servants, Mama," Silas stated while wrinkling his nose.

"Of course we do," Arabella snorted. "Who would be doing the cleaning, the cooking, the gardening and so forth?"

"But our cook doesn't *sleep* here," Silas muttered while scratching his head and pointing to Hazel. "And yet she cooks here every day. So why not put Alice in one of the rooms for the servants and let the servants only come in the day?"

Arabella flashed her son an angry glance. "I am *not* going to argue with you, son. Your father would have a heart attack if he finds out we have taken Alice and her mother in. We are not a guest house for poor people."

"But Baxter is poor, and he sleeps here."

"Baxter is different. Baxter is Baxter. That's not the same." Arabella turned her attention back to Hazel. "So… if there is nothing else, then—"

There was a knock on the door.

Arabella stiffened. "What now?" she grunted. "Who is it? I am busy."

"It's Baxter, my lady," came the muffled voice from behind the door. "There's a message from Sir Bud Dewar."

Arabella let out a deep sigh, finished her cup of Sweet Thick Milk, and clapped her hands. "Come in, Baxter."

The door swung open and as Baxter stepped in it seemed to Hazel a wave of freshness rolled in with him. As soon as he saw Hazel was still in the room, he mumbled an apology. "I am sorry my lady, I did not mean to interrupt, but Master Dewar's brother wants to examine young Master Silas again this afternoon. What can I tell the messenger?"

"I don't want to see Uncle Buddy," Silas jumped up once more and stamped his leather shoe on the wooden floor of the room. "He always makes me eat those horrible pills. I want to play with Alice."

"Hush," Arabella demanded and ordered her son back to his place on the bed. "You eat whatever Uncle Buddy prescribes. He is a mighty good physician. If I hear any more of this there will be consequences." She did not say what these consequences would be, but it was enough to calm Silas down, nevertheless the scowl on his face was unmistakably clear.

Arabella concentrated on her conversation with Baxter again. "He's welcome at four this afternoon," she replied. "Silas is having his nap between two and four, and then the doctor can stay for dinner."

Baxter nodded. "I will tell that to the messenger, my lady."

"Good," Arabella said and waved Baxter away with her bejewelled hand. But Baxter did not move right away. Apparently, there was something else on the butler's mind. He cleared his throat and said barely audible, "May I make a suggestion, My Lady?"

Arabella had just taken the last Cheese Turnover from the plate near her bed and was about to take a bite. "What?"

"If you will forgive me, my lady, but the conversation was so loud, I could hear your discussion about Hazel's daughter all the way in the hallway…"

"Did you?" Arabella's eyes narrowed into tiny slits, and her voice was filled with contempt. "You are a servant, Baxter. Don't you forget it." Hazel could see Baxter swallowing hard, but to his credit he dared to go on.

"I only wish to serve you, My Lady, and all I say is for the benefit of your household. May I speak…?"

103

Arabella rolled her eyes but made an impatient gesture with her hand, indicating Baxter could speak his piece.

Baxter licked his lips. "Remember what you and Master Dewar were discussing in the garden the other day, My Lady?"

Arabella frowned, she had just taken a bite of her Cheese Turnover, and couldn't answer since her mouth was full. Baxter took it as a sign he was allowed to say more. "I couldn't help but overhear as you wanted me to stay around so I could serve the cakes and the tea. You told Master Dewar, Silas needed a friend... *desperately* is the word I recall."

Arabella swallowed her Cheese Turnover, tilted her head and hissed, "So?"

Baxter smiled. It was the sweetest smile Hazel had ever seen. "Well, it seems to my rather uneducated and ignorant mind the Good Lord has answered your plea."

Arabella studied her fingers for a second, sighed and then stated with the air of a queen, "You are right about the level of your education and your ignorance, Baxter, but what does the Good Lord have to do with anything?"

"A friend for young Master Silas is just falling into your lap, My Lady. The young Master never sees anybody."

"That's because he is sick," Arabella growled. "He can't have any excitement."

"But you yourself said that being alone all the time is not good for him."

"It isn't. But there's nothing we can do about it," Arabella argued back.

"But there is. Suddenly, there *is* a friend for the young Master. I saw Hazel's daughter this morning. She's the prettiest girl I have ever seen."

Hazel stood like a frozen statue, as she listened to Baxter, who suddenly seemed to be pleading her cause. What was going on?

"You did?" Arabella asked, but her voice was not as impatient as it had been seconds earlier.

"She's a real sweetheart. Furthermore she was even born in this house. She would be an excellent friend for young Master Silas."

Silas jumped up again. "Yes, Mama… Baxter is right. Alice is really, really nice."

Arabella fell back into her carefully propped-up pillows. "This is a conspiracy," she mumbled, barely audible.

"Pardon me, My Lady?" Baxter asked, not quite understanding.

Arabella didn't feel the need to explain. Instead she asked, "Where is this child?"

"In the kitchen, My Lady," Hazel said. "I-I brought her here this morning, since she can't stay in the *alley without a name.*"

"Bring the child to me," Arabella demanded. "I want to see her for myself."

∼

Hazel rushed out to get Alice. In passing Baxter, she could feel his gaze. Warm, concerned; almost as if he wanted Alice to stay as much as she wanted it. What a wonderful and unexpected development. She considered stopping and giving him a big hug, but that would be ridiculous. No one did that. No one hugged the butler. It would ruin her chances on a good outcome. Thus, she ran out in search of Alice. Was this a miracle in the making, a fulfilment of that wonderful wave of peace that had rolled over her the night before?

She stormed into the kitchen and was met by Alice, who exclaimed joyfully, "Mama, you are back. Can I now see the room in which I was born?"

"Yes, dear," Hazel exclaimed, almost out of breath. "The Mistress wants to see you, and right now she is in the room in which you were born."

Upon hearing Mistress Dewar wanted to see her, Alice's face dropped a little. She nervously inspected her dress and tried to smooth out a few wrinkles with her fingers.

Hazel understood. After Alice had seen Baxter and young Master Silas it was painfully clear she looked rather poor.

"Will the Mistress like me, Mama? Will she let me stay here?"

Hazel pulled Alice close to her chest. "You are an angel, dear. It is the inside that counts, not the outside." Then she added, almost more to encourage herself than Alice, "If she doesn't see that, love, she has Sweet Thick Milk in her eyes."

Alice burst out in a giggle. "That's funny, Mama." She nestled herself closer into Hazel's embrace and repeated what she had told her Mama earlier. "I really have a crushing on you, Mama."

"Yes, child… now come."

It was a long walk to the guest room through the semi dark hallway over the soft and richly coloured tapestry. Hazel firmly held on to Alice's hand. She *had* to as Alice wanted to stop everywhere, and touch paintings and wall tapestries depicting knights on horses, groups of mean looking men with hounds chasing deer, and even a portrait of a staunch looking man that peered into the hallway through narrowed eyes, with a scowl that scared Alice.

"Who is that man, Mama," she asked. "I don't think he would like me very much. Is that Master Dewar?"

Hazel pulled Alice away. "No, Alice. I heard it is Grandfather Dewar. He's the one who built this mansion, but he has left this world a long time ago."

"Where did he go?" Alice wanted to know, but Hazel pulled her along. This was no time for Alice's childish chatter.

At last Hazel stopped in front of a massive oak door and knocked politely.

"Come in," came the voice of Mistress Dewar.

Hazel licked her lips, tried to flatten one of Alice's unruly curls, and opened the door.

∽

As Mama stepped into the room, there was nothing else to do for Alice but to follow. After passing the rather dark corridors of Broughton she blinked as the room was unexpectedly bright. The smell of wood mixed with a stale scent of a dust that no doubt belonged to the heavy carpeted floor entered her nostrils. At least, compared to the ghastly smells she was used to in the house in *the alley without a name*, it was like a breath of fresh air. Still, having to enter this room and meet the Mistress of the house, didn't feel half as glorious as it had seemed only a few minutes earlier. The best thing to do was to hide behind Mama's skirt, at least for now.

The light streamed in through two large windows on the side, the glass neatly divided by strips of wood. Even on a gloomy day as it was today, this room was unusually bright. It would be lovely sleeping here and waking up on the first day of spring with the large windows opened, the sun rays falling onto the bed, and hearing the songbirds outside who were raising their little throats to the heavens in a glorious concert of joy. But she would never sleep here, even though this was the room of her birth. From the corner of her eye, Alice spotted more paintings like the ones she had seen in the corridors, but she didn't dare look at them. She just quietly hid behind Mama. Standing here, in the presence of the Mistress, the woman Mama had been working for all these years and often talked about as *the rich lady of Manchester*, was intimidating, to say the least.

"Where is your daughter?" Alice heard a woman's voice asking. Surely, it was the Mistress speaking. Not altogether unfriendly, but her tone held a certain demeaning authority that had an unpleasant ring to it. At that moment Alice knew it would not be a good idea to ever cross this woman.

"Alice...?" That was Mama's voice. "What are you doing, hiding behind me? Don't be shy."

She could no longer hide. It was time to step forward.

The room was bigger than she had thought, but there was no time to take it all in. There, right before her, was an enormous four-poster bed, complete with white lace curtains hanging from the upper panel, and four intricately carved out wooden support pillars. Truly, only kings and queens would have a bed like that. The bed was covered with a stitched quilt in a colourful pattern and on the bed, propped up against two silk cushions, sat a woman. Her hair was undone and she stared at Alice with calculating brown eyes that were not smiling. Alice shrugged. She wanted to hide behind Mama again, but she knew that was out of the question. To her relief, she spotted young Master Silas as well. He was sitting on the bed, his feet dangling down, and he smiled.

"Alice," he cried out. "I want you to stay here, so we can be friends and play all day."

"Quiet, Silas," the woman barked. She wrinkled her nose and turned her gaze to someone standing near the door. Baxter was there. He too carried a smile. But when the lady spoke, the words cut right through Alice's heart.

"This is absolutely disgusting, Baxter. Why didn't you tell me this child is dressed so awful? And... I detect a smell too. It's a scent of the street." She grabbed a small jar, shook it around, and scattered a sweet-smelling liquid around.

Awful? Disgusting? Smelly? In spite of her insecurity, Alice felt a touch of anger. Didn't this lady know that Mama didn't have much money and that she worked hard in that fancy kitchen of hers to make ends meet? Did this woman not know that it was the *inside* that counted, not the outside?

Baxter spoke up.

"We can easily fix that My Lady," the butler answered in a soft voice. "What counts is the inside, and the long-lasting fruit. Friendship for the young Master will do him a world of good. It may even be more beneficial for him than the pills of Sir Bud Dewar."

Alice could see that the lady didn't like Baxter's last statement, but the butler seemed unperturbed. That man had courage. Yes, Baxter was nice. Alice had already considered calling him a friend, and this settled the matter.

The lady scowled and turned to give Alice a better look. "Let me see you up close, girl," she ordered.

"Come on, love," Mama whispered. "Show yourself to the Mistress."

Alice swallowed hard, stepped forward and stood still at the foot of the bed.

"I remember the day of your birth, girl," the Mistress said. "It was the day I gave birth to my son, Silas."

Silas beamed. "I remember," the young Master said.

"No, you don't," came the rough reply from the Mistress, and she cast him an angry glance. "I told you to be quiet."

Silas grunted, but still managed to cast Alice a smile.

"Your mother tells me you have no place to stay at night," the Mistress talked on. "Why is that, girl?"

"I *do* have a place," Alice answered. "We stay in *the alley without a name,* together with Nana."

The lady frowned. "Is that so? Then why are you here?"

Alice shrugged. She wasn't sure what to say next. One thing she *did* know was that this house was much nicer than the place she had been living at, all her life. "Mama told me to come here. You see, it's cold in our house. Here it's warm and everyone here is nice."

The Mistress tilted her head. "You don't know anybody here, girl."

"I do," Alice replied and pointed at Baxter. "I know Baxter. He's nice, and I know Silas too. We are friends, and… eh… I think I like you too."

A soft expression appeared on the Mistress' face. "You like me too, huh?"

"Yes, Miss."

There was even a hint of a smile on the Mistress' face. "I am *not* a Miss, girl. You may address me with *My Lady.* Everyone addresses me that way. You think you can do that, girl?"

Alice nodded. "Yes, My Lady, and you may address me with Alice. My name is not 'girl.'"

For a moment there was an icy silence in the room, but then Baxter cleared his throat and asked, "She sure has spunk, My Lady. The very thing that is good for Silas. The boy needs laughter and happiness, and I think Alice may be able to bring a spark of joy in Silas' life."

The Mistress gave him a curious look, but then turned her attention back to Silas. "Son... do you like this child?"

Silas nodded enthusiastically and began plucking at one of the sparkling buckles on his shoe. "Alice is nice. I want her to stay."

The Mistress shook her head and let out a deep sigh. "I suppose we could try it out for a little while. A few days, perhaps a few weeks or so."

"Nanty Narking," * Silas cried out in a joyful exclamation. "You can stay, Alice."

The Mistress' face darkened and she raised an authoritative finger she shook in Silas' face. "You don't talk like that, Son. Where did you get such language?"

Silas pressed his lips together. "Sorry, Mother. I just heard it."

Baxter blushed, and stepped in by saying, "So, it's arranged then?"

The Mistress turned to Baxter. "They can sleep in the basement, Baxter. And make sure this girl has a bath and some proper clothes."

Baxter nodded. "I shall make everything ready, My Lady. And Master Dewar?"

"I'll talk to him. I will tell him it's good for Silas, and then he won't mind." She frowned and added, "But it's a test. We will see how it all works out." She then proceeded to wave her bejewelled hand around, signifying she wanted them all to leave. Alice still heard the Mistress muttering that if it didn't work out it wouldn't be a great loss. She would show the Mistress she was a good girl and wanted to tell the Mistress so, but she was interrupted by Silas. The boy had jumped off the bed and squealed in delight. "I have a friend. We will be the best of friends, right Alice?"

Alice nodded and could not suppress an unfamiliar feeling of joy. Being the center of happiness felt very good. She looked at Mama and saw her eyes were glistening. This was definitely a good day. A very good day.

* Nanty Narking is slang for great fun and originated in the Victorian Era around 1840. It was commonly used in the tavern.

7
DEAR GOD, HE CAN'T DIE

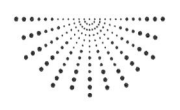

ONE YEAR LATER

Alice could hardly believe her good fortune. Living at Broughton was just wonderful. Life here could not aptly be described as a dream come true because she had never dreamed about such mansions before. She simply had not known places like this existed. Broughton was vastly different from the ramshackle dwellings of *the house in the alley without a name*. Even though the room in the basement that had been given to her and Mama was rather dark and didn't look like that beautiful room she had apparently been born in, it was still a little palace compared to the house in which Nana lived. No draft here that brought in the cold, so your nose would constantly run, no threadbare blankets that barely kept you warm at night, and no going to bed with an empty stomach because Nana had not wanted to buy food. Imagine that, here was even a toilet right in the house so you didn't have to go out in the middle of the night and struggle barefoot through the mud and the mire to the communal outhouse.

Life at Broughton was very different too. Here, Alice was required to help Mama in the morning, but what a joy that was. Cleaning, sweeping, preparing the food… it was a wonderful change, as in Nana's house she hardly ever saw Mama. There, in an effort to keep her occupied, Mama would verbally give her a list of jobs she wanted Alice to do every morning, but that list was usually so small she was done with her tasks in an hour… and then what? Most mornings, Nana would not get up until much later, and she was not much of a companion anyway. Nana was often sharp and cranky and used many words Mama told Alice to quickly erase from her memory.

"It's the curse of the bottle." Mama would explain. At such times, the expression in Mama's eyes strangely resembled the look in the sad, drooping eyes of the street dog that Gilbert Oakley, the baker, had kicked away so mercilessly one day, when the poor creature tried to steal a crust of bread. The haunted look in the brown eyes of the miserable dog had caused Alice to have a few sleepless nights. It was the look of hopelessness, frustration and fear for the future. Thus, she knew *'the curse of the bottle'* was a problem to be feared, although she wasn't altogether sure what it really meant. Sensing it was a difficult subject, she never dared to ask Mama about it, but it was best to avoid bottles altogether. So, just to be on the safe side, she would never even come near a bottle if she could help it. It caused Nana to get rather angry at times as she often demanded Alice to clean up a few of her empty ones that were strewn around on the floor or standing on the table. Sometimes, Nana would ask her to bring her a full one, filled with something Nana called *a flash of lightning*. That sure sounded scary, and that, coupled with Mama's warning about a curse being involved, was more than enough to consider disobedience the best option. Nana would be greatly angered and a slew of dark sounding mutterings that Alice had never heard before would then stream out of her mouth. It was especially at those moments Nana managed to fill Alice's limited vocabulary.

But none of that happened here.

Here, at least to Alice's narrow understanding of things, nobody needed flashes of lightning in cursed bottles. Here, everything was different, including the clothes Alice now wore. Baxter had thrown her old clothes away and had given her a dress he called *a simple dress*.

Simple? To Alice, it was anything but simple. She had never worn such beautiful clothes, and when she first saw it, a silk blue dress with pretty lace at the seams and covered in front with a white apron, her mouth fell open and she almost didn't want to wear it for fear of soiling it.

Baxter smiled at her and told her in encouraging tones it was not a big deal and that he had more of the same.

And then there was the food. While Mama had always made sure there was something to eat in Nana's place, somehow there often wasn't. But here she was allowed to eat in the kitchen and she tasted things she had never even dreamed of eating. When Mama prepared a hearty meal or a yummy desert for the Master or the Mistress, she always managed to prepare just a little bit more than was needed so Alice could partake of the blessings.

But none of that was as wonderful as not being alone anymore. Here she belonged. Here she was together with Mama and here she had a friend in Silas. Life in the *alley without a name* had been *a* lonely life. There, Mama was gone from morning till night, even on Sundays.

"Sorry, dear," Mama explained once when Alice had asked her about it, "but the Dewars have to eat on Sundays too."

Of course they did, but she missed Mama, especially on those days. Alice was a brave girl though, and refused to complain about it. Mama's work was important and it paid the bills. Often, Mama would be back in time to tell her another bedtime story and take her away to a magical world of beauty. Nevertheless, in Nana's place she pretty much had to fend for herself, filling the hours with… nothing really. As a result the streets of Manchester became her second home.

But here in Broughton, she was around Mama every morning. Working together in the kitchen was just about the best thing that had ever happened to Alice, and when Mama told her about God's house that was called heaven and suggested Alice's father was waiting there for her, she envisioned a kitchen almost twice as big as the Dewar's in which her father was the main cook and she and Mama were helping.

Here, Mama taught her a wealth of other things too. Alice learned how to sew and how to properly clean and keep house. "Life is hard, Alice," Mama would often explain. "We are very fortunate we found this job. Now you can learn things, and learning and knowing things is the key to earthly happiness. If you have no skills, you have no future."

"What is a skill, Mama?"

"Skills are the things you are good at and that people need. If you can do things for them, like I am cooking for the Dewars, people hire you. But if you have no skills you are forced to do horrible things like working all day long in the cotton mill, or being out on the streets like Nana used to do."

"Doesn't Nana have any skills, Mama?"

To Alice's surprise, the question caused Mama to blink her eyes. She didn't answer right away, but at last she said, "She does, Alice, but Nana has decided to bury them, and that's just as bad as not having them."

"Is it the curse of the bottle, Mama?"

Mama turned her eyes away and all of a sudden showed much interest in a fish that needed cleaning. She never answered Alice's question.

"And young Master Silas… is he learning skills too?" Alice asked at last.

"He is," Mama replied with a smile while wiping her eyes with her handkerchief. A piece of fish had probably gotten in her eye.

"But why then isn't he learning to cook, Mama?"

"Because he is the young Master, Alice. Young Masters do not clean and cook and that sort of a thing. They learn different skills, like reading and writing. They have to, because later on they have to run the banks, or the political parties… all kinds of things you and I don't need to ever do. Now let's get on with the work."

Alice wasn't sure she understood. She didn't want to run a bank, neither did she know what a political party was, but why couldn't she learn to read and write? That would be so lovely. Once, she had seen the bookcase of the Master in his study. In that room, truly a sacred place, there was one wall completely covered with books. There were large ones, small ones, old ones, and yet even older ones… and they all carried this particular scent of paper mixed with the leather of their bindings. Alice had never seen such a thing. That day her heart skipped a few beats and her mouth hung open as she stared at volumes and tomes full of mysterious secrets that doubtless would unlock doors to other worlds.

Looking up at Mama, she sensed the subject needed to be changed. No problem. She would ask Silas about it himself in the afternoon. Most afternoons, at least on those days that young Master Silas was not occupied with dainty responsibilities, like Mama sometimes called them, they were allowed to play together. Those too were times of great fun. Young Master Silas had a lot of toys, among them one of Alice's favourites, a large, brown rocking horse that was carefully polished. The wooden animal sparkled and shone almost as if it were a real horse. He had a skipping rope too, another toy that brought great joy to Alice. Silas didn't care for it much, and on days the young Master wanted to play with his grand collection of toy soldiers, he let Alice use the skipping rope to her heart's content. The first time Alice had tried it she had fallen. The rope had gotten tangled between her legs and she fell right on her bottom. It had caused a great outburst of laughter from young Master Silas.

Too loud, apparently, as the door swung open and Alice looked into the face of a large man who stared at her with angry eyes. Since she was still on the floor, he towered over her, his presence filling up Alice's vision. She felt like a sweaty grasshopper who was facing an angry farmer who was just about to exterminate the pest that had been nibbling on his corn.

"So, you are the new girl?" the man scoffed while rolling his eyes. Then he turned his attention to Silas who looked paler than ever and hissed, "You know what Uncle Buddy said. Excitement is bad for you. If this keeps up, that girl is out."

"Yes, Father," Silas said and lowered his eyes, the sword of one of his toy soldiers peering menacingly out of his closed hand.

Father? Then Alice knew. She was standing in the presence of the Master. It was the first time Alice saw him and knew who he was, it was just about the only time he actually spoke to her. Besides a few times in the garden, and one time in the hallway when he passed her with dark, brooding eyes of disgust, she had hardly ever seen him, let alone spoken to him. Silas just shrugged his shoulders when she asked him about it. "That's just my father. He will always consider you poor, but…," he stopped and looked Alice square in the face, "I don't care. I am happy to have you as my friend." It made Alice all fuzzy and warm inside, but she had not forgotten the warning from the Master, and from that day forth she tried to be as quiet as possible.

But that afternoon, she would ask Silas about skills. Silas had already told his mother the day before he wanted to play outside in the garden that afternoon. That was something he had to arrange ahead of time, as the Mistress usually objected to him being outside, supposedly for health reasons. (It's too cold, too wet, too dirty, or too this or too that) She was constantly worrying that Silas, having that mysterious illness, would catch a cold in the wind, or something even much worse. But even the Mistress had to admit the weather was beautiful and there was no reason for Silas to stay cooped up in the house.

That afternoon the two friends strolled out through the main door and stepped into the garden.

"I wanted to ask—" Alice began as they stepped off the porch, but Silas interrupted her.

"Look what I got," he said, while he pulled a green, silken bag out of his pocket and showed it to Alice. A mysterious grin played on his pale face. "I got it from my father last night." He dangled the bag before Alice's nose without telling her what was in it. "Nice, huh?"

"Very nice," Alice replied with a frown. "But what is it?"

Silas shook the bag around. It made a clattering sound as if stones were banging against each other. "Marbles," he explained. "Did you ever play marbles?"

"Of course I did," Alice said, not able to hide her scowl. Not everything Silas had or did was unknown to her. She remembered playing in the streets of Manchester with a couple of clay marbles she had found in a puddle. Most street kids in Manchester had marbles and it was a popular game. So when she had found them in the mud, she had carefully dried them, polished them up with the sleeve of her dress, and had for a few moments felt like a queen. But not for long, as she had to hand them over to a fat kid with buck teeth only a day later. She had not actually lost them during play, but the bully had threatened to beat her up and she would *cop a mouse* (get a black eye) if she wouldn't give them to him. The little criminal was at least two heads taller than Alice, and all of a sudden, holding on to her pride and a few dirty little balls of dark clay hardly seemed advantageous.

But the marbles Silas showed her were different. She had never seen such precious stones, made of pure marble. They all had intricate markings and shone like regular jewels.

"Do you want to play?" Silas asked and he pointed to the stone path near the front.

Alice hesitated. She wanted to, but throwing jewels around on the dirty ground, possibly losing a few, did not seem like the right thing to do. "I'd like to," she squirmed, "but what if they get dirty, or you lose one?"

Silas shrugged his wealthy shoulders. "I will just ask my father to buy me new ones. Come on…Nanty Narking, it's great fun. Although it makes me tired."

And great fun it was. Alice won almost every time, but at last she began to suspect Silas was letting her win. At all the crucial moments he would make really weird blunders, shake his head, and exclaim in surprise, "O, crickets, dear me! That was a really bad throw."

Of course, in the end, she handed all the sparkling stones she had won back to Silas who placed them back in his silken, green sack. The boy was having difficulty breathing now. But there was a smile on his face and she was touched by Silas' genuine effort to be nice to her. He really cared. Mama had warned her that Silas was a bit spoiled and would easily stamp his dandy shoes around if he didn't get his way, but somehow he never acted like that around her.

"Are you all right?" she asked him, a bit concerned about the wheeze in his throat.

He nodded. "I just want to rest. We can sit down on the grass."

"I wanted to ask you something," Alice said, hoping to get to the subject of skills again.

"You do?" Silas sat down on the grass. He noticed a green, dirty spot on his stockings and furiously began to rub it with the palm of his hand.

"Tell me about your skills," Alice began as she kneeled down next to him on the grass.

"My skills?" Silas stared at her, apparently not understanding the question.

"Yes, your skills," Alice insisted. "I am learning lots of skills, but Mama told me you are learning different ones."

He shook his head. "I don't understand."

"Aren't you learning to read and write? I heard you even know how to do calculations."

125

Silas' face brightened. "Ah, reading, writing… and stuff like that. You are talking about school." Then his face changed and he tilted his head. "But why do you ask? Doesn't everyone have those… eh skills? Don't you know how to read and write?"

Alice shook her head. "No, I don't."

"You *don't* read and write?" Silas blinked his eyes. "I mean… can't you even count to ten?"

Alice felt her ears getting red. "Mama says I don't need to know those things. Those are skills only people like you need to have. Mama says you are going to run a bank when you are older, or maybe you will be the chairman of a political party. I am learning to cook and clean. Mama says we are not made for anything else."

Silas thought about her words for a moment. Then his pale face brightened and he asked, "But that's not right. Wouldn't you like to be able to read and write? I've got a lot of books. Reading is fun."

For a moment it felt as if someone offered Alice the key to a grand treasure house. She could hardly contain the joy that bubbled up inside. "I-eh…would love to," she answered. "I saw the books in your father's study… oh, if I could read, how wonderful that would be."

Silas smiled a boyish, innocent smile. "Then let's teach you."

"But… eh…" Alice answered, scarcely believing her ears. "How?"

"I know how," Silas said in a determined voice. "I will ask Miss Greta Parsley to teach you."

"You mean, your governess?"

He nodded. "That's right."

"But I am only Alice. She will not want to."

A smile appeared. "And I am only the young Master. I can make her want to." He leaned forward and said with shiny eyes, "You are my friend, and all my friends can read and write, just like I can."

"You have more friends?"

"No," Silas stated, "only you and that's why you have to learn fast."

Alice couldn't suppress a feeling of joy. Imagine that… learning to write and read. What would Mama say? But then a dark thought crossed her mind that made her joy melt away like butter in the sun. "But I am sure Miss Parsley won't like me. Whenever I see her she looks at me with such disdain."

Silas narrowed his eyes. "I just told you, I am the young Master. She does what I tell her to do."

"You can't make people like me," Alice said with a chuckle. "Only God can do that."

"God?" Silas questioned. "Papa said there is no God. He says we come from monkeys. He has a book about that in his study. It's really big and full of truth."

Silas' statement confused Alice. That was not what Mama had told her, but before she could ask Silas about it, he said in confident tones, "That's why you need to learn to read. Then you can read that book too."

"Have you read it?" Alice asked.

"No," Silas said and a hearty laugh escaped his mouth. "I am just a beginner. But I read fun stuff. Right now I am reading 'The history of little king Pippin."

"What's that?

"It's about four naughty boys who are being devoured by wild beasts. You'd like it too."

Alice shuddered. For a moment she wasn't sure learning to read was such a good idea, but that only lasted for a fleeting second. "So, will you ask Miss Parsley?"

"I will," Silas replied. "And don't worry about her not liking you. She doesn't have to like you. All she needs to do is teach you. Tonight, I will talk to my mother about it." He leaned forward again and whispered. "Shall I tell you a secret?"

"What?" Alice whispered back.

"I don't like Miss Parsley either."

"You don't?" Alice asked. "Why not?"

"I saw her *doing the bear* * with Uncle Buddy. You know kissing and stuff like that. So gross." * (Hugging)

"Your governess was kissing Master Bud Dewar?"

"She was," Silas wrinkled his nose. "Who would want to kiss Uncle Buddy? That's just *so* weird."

Alice thought about what Silas had just told her. She had met Uncle Buddy on occasion. The man resembled his brother, the Master in many ways. He had the same build and the same prying, dark eyes, although unlike the Master, Uncle Buddy had a rather large belly. "The curse of the bottle," Mama had said. Again that curse. But that was even harder to understand as Uncle Buddy was a physician and he should know how to break curses. He was even responsible for looking after Silas' health. But she had to agree with Silas she didn't like the man much.

"Silas?"

The boy looked up. "What?"

"Why do you need Uncle Buddy? I never dared to ask you, but what's wrong with you? Are you sick?" Her voice was soft and she plucked at the lace on her apron hoping to avoid Silas' gaze. She had asked Mama about it before, but she had just shaken her head and told Alice she didn't know. But since Silas brought up the sinister Uncle Buddy himself, she took the plunge and asked him about it.

Silas sighed and then shrugged his shoulders. "They say I have asthma, among other things. Nobody knows."

"What is that?" Alice's eyes widened.

"Sometimes I can't breathe. It's really rather scary. But that's not the only thing. Uncle Buddy says I have lots of illnesses."

"And he can't cure you? He's a physician."

Silas shook his head emphatically. "As far as I can tell, he's not a very good one. Father only lets him treat me because he's my uncle. That way it all stays in the family. Father doesn't want other people to know I am sick, as it's bad for business."

Alice looked up. "What do you mean?"

Silas shrugged his shoulders. "People are scared of sickness. Uncle Buddy says I had an aunt who was sick like me." His enthusiasm seemed to drain away.

"And is she better now?"

Silas' face turned grim and he picked up a small pebble out of the grass that he tossed away. "She died."

A shock rippled through Alice's body. That was bad. No wonder Silas could look so depressed at times. And had Baxter not said that it was her job to make him a bit happier? Maybe she should change the subject, although… there was one more thing she wanted to ask.

"How do you know you have the same thing? I don't want you to be sick." *And most certainly I don't want you to die.* She was wise enough not to say her thought out loud.

"Because Uncle Buddy said so, and he is a doctor," Silas answered. "He says he knows everything."

"But you don't even like him, and clearly he doesn't know everything because you are still sick. How do you know he is not *Croak, bringing in the Crony Crowbar Brigade?*"

Silas stared at her for a few moments and then burst out laughing. "What are you saying? That's funny."

Alice wrinkled her nose. "That's what we call them on the streets of Manchester. Quacks, doctors who come up with all kinds of weird cures that never heal anybody."

"He's my uncle. He's no... *Croak that's bringing in the Pony Brigade,*" Silas chuckled and mumbled more to himself than to Alice. "That's funny. I need to remember that."

"*Crony* Crowbar Brigade," Alice corrected him. "But, isn't he giving you yucky medicines?"

Silas' face contorted in a foul expression. "Lately he is. He used to insist I drink loads of cooked carrot juice. It wasn't too bad, but recently he has taken a greater interest in me and has begun to give me this yucky stuff. It's blue and it comes in a bottle. I have to drink a spoonful every time he checks me. I used to spit it out, but father threatened to spank me if I would ever do it again. He got really mad, and believe me, it's not fun to make father angry. Lately, Uncle Buddy decided to give me more. He claims it's working, but I'm still as weak as ever. I hate it. Every Wednesday he takes me into my room and forces me to take it."

"What do you mean, he takes you into your room?"

"Just what I say. He says the stuff won't work when there are too many people around."

Alice shook her head. "That doesn't make any sense. Do you know what it is?"

"I don't know," he shrugged. "He calls it Alvexolol. I hate it."

"I am so sorry." Alice felt a genuine sadness for her friend. But there was nothing she could do about it. Then, Silas changed the subject in search of happier thoughts. "So, I'll talk to my mother and then Greta Parsley will teach you to read and write. Maybe you can even sit in on some of my classes. Wouldn't that be fun?"

"It would," Alice replied, but her original joy was gone. Her friend Silas was sick, and maybe he would even die. Right then and there she decided she would pray for Silas every night before bedtime. Maybe that would help.

A bell sounded from the inside. It was time to go back inside. They got up and walked back to the house, but it was as if a shadow had darkened both of their minds.

8
A DARING PLAN

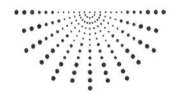

SEVERAL MONTHS LATER

Alice liked Miss Thimble. Sure the small woman, leaning heavily on a stick, was old and bent, but she carried a certain dignity that demanded respect. She had what she called arthritic joints. Alice had no idea what that meant, but it seemed to be an ailment that befell older people. Mama later explained it was the reason she shuffled with these wonky steps through the kitchen to her seat. The lines on her face were deep and saggy, and Alice couldn't help but wonder how anybody could be *that* old. But Miss Thimble's mind was still sharp and as keen as the mind of Lord Kelvin.* At least, that's what she said of herself. Alice had no idea who Lord Kelvin was, but she decided she would ask Miss Greta Parsley about that during class time tomorrow.

"Tea, Miss Thimble?" Mama offered.

"I'd love a good cup of tea," the woman answered with a smile, and while Mama turned to the stove to boil the water, the old lady turned her attention to Alice.

"So you are living here with your Mama. I bet you like it here."

"I do," Alice replied with a grand smile. "I am learning to read and write, and I can already count to a hundred."

Miss Thimble nodded, a serious, respectable nod. "Your Mama told me you are a smart girl. But you are not just smart. I can tell you are also a real giggle mug. Your smile is as pretty as the crystal dew on my herbs early in the morning." She motioned for Alice to come closer, and said, "I got something for you." She gave Alice a smile of her own which made her frail face light up. As Alice stepped forward she pulled a dry looking twig out of her pocket. "Here, child," she said, and handed it to Alice who looked at it with curious eyes.

"A twig from the garden?"

"Not everything is what it looks like," Miss Thimble replied cryptically with a twinkle in her eyes. "This is not just a bitter twig from a lonely tree in a cow patch. This is a treat, one that is much better than the candy you young girls eat on the streets out in Manchester. Unlike the foul clumps of sugar you kids swallow, and which are full of all kinds of poisonous by-products, this is healthy and completely natural."

"This is candy?"

"Stick it in your mouth and try," Miss Thimble encouraged her.

Alice wasn't sure what to think and looked to Mama for help. She had just put the water on the stove, and nodded knowingly.

"Miss Thimble knows about herbs," Mama explained. "She's our neighbour and grows all kinds of herbs. Lately, I have been having headaches and Miss Thimble came over today to bring me some herbs to fight the pain."

Herbs for healing? Alice had never heard that was possible. "I thought Master Bud Dewar the physician knows how to treat pain?"

Mama shuddered. "I don't like that man. He gives me the shivers." She stopped and giggled. "But the feeling is mutual. I don't think he even wants to come near me either, so I need Miss Thimble for my ailments. I have been friends with her almost from the day I first began working here."

The old woman chuckled. "I don't claim to be a physician," she croaked, "I just know a lot about herbs." She narrowed her eyes and said, "The Good Lord has given us everything we need for our health, and usually what we need is growing right in our own backyard. There are times we need a good physician, but at the same time people fail to understand there's a lot more we can do to keep our bodies healthy and fit. You see, our bodies are being affected in a large manner by what we put into them and how we treat or mistreat them."

Alice had never heard such things. It sounded wonderful, even logical. She kept staring and pondering the words of old Miss Thimble who sat there before her with a content smile on her wrinkled face.

"You are forgetting your treat." Miss Thimble added and pointed at the twig still in Alice's hand. "Stick it in your mouth."

"Huh?" Alice snapped back to the present and did as Miss Thimble suggested. A wonderful, sweet taste filled her mouth, and her eyes lit up. "Very nice," she exclaimed with her mouth full. "You are right. This is even better than the Sugar plums Silas eats all the time." She hesitated and then asked, "Do you have one for Silas too?"

Miss Thimble leaned back. "You mean the young Master of Broughton?"

"Yes, Mum. He likes sweets too."

Miss Thimble grinned, and reached into her pocket again. A second later she handed another twig to Alice, who stuck the precious treasure into the pocket of her apron.

Miss Thimble cleared her throat. "Actually, your Mama told me the young Master is ill. What's wrong with him?"

"He has apsma, and other sicknesses too. Nobody really knows," Alice said. "Not even Master Bud Dewar."

"You mean asthma," Miss Thimble corrected Alice. "An infection of the lungs. He needs potassium nitrate. That's in herbs too."

"Really?" Miss Thimble grew in Alice's estimation. "But he has other diseases too. He is very weak and always pale. Sometimes he seems a bit better but then he gets all worse again, but lately it's been getting much worse. Master Bud Dewar says he is going to die."

"Nonsense, child," Miss Thimble replied. "Our times are in God's hands. Nobody dies before his time. I am certain there are things that could help him."

"You think so?" Alice blurted out. "Would you want to help him?"

Miss Thimble looked down at the floor and sighed. "I don't think the Master of Broughton would want me to." She looked up again, her face a picture of sadness. "People consider me strange. Some even say I am a weird witch."

Alice frowned and cast Mama a helpless stare. A witch, like the wicked witch Mama had been telling her about a few nights ago in one of her make-believe bedtime stories? Mama had described the witch that night as a mean ugly woman whose hair was all messed up with sweaty strings sticking out in all directions. The evil creature had fingernails that were almost 5 inches long and a nose so sharp she could use it to hammer holes in the wall of her hide-out. She was a bad, wicked lady who used a giant ladle to stir a large pot of boiling stew made of frogs and snails, a brew that would be used to transform a beautiful princess into an ugly toad. But Miss Thimble was not like that. Not at all. Miss Thimble even spoke with deep respect of the Good Lord.

"You are not a witch," Alice stammered. "You are nice."

Miss Thimble gave her a weak smile. "Thank you, Alice. It's nice of you to say so. Sadly, I don't think everyone agrees."

Alice thought for some time and while she held her hands behind her back, stared at the shiny tips of the dainty shoes Baxter had given her. She had something on her mind, but did she dare ask Miss Thimble?

"What is it, child?" Miss Thimble asked, apparently sensing Alice's dilemma.

Alice looked up. "Well… eh… Silas always has to drink this medicine. Master Bud Dewar makes him drink it alone in his room, but Silas hates it, He says it tastes very, very foul. The funny thing is there are times when it goes a little better and he is not nearly as pale. I mean he's always weak and is often wheezing but he seems sort of fine. But then, as soon as Master Bud Dewar gets him to drink his medicine, he's all miserable again and much more pale. I don't understand that. He should be getting better, not worse."

Miss Thimble nodded and thought for a moment. "Of course, no medicine helps instantly," she said at last. "But I tend to agree with you. Do you know what the physician gives him?"

Alice shook her head. "Just that the stuff he has to drink is blue. It has a weird name, but I can never remember that. It's dark blue like the colour of the sky on a sunny day."

Miss Thimble pressed her lips together, and Alice could almost hear the cogwheels of her mind turning and rolling. "If you could get me a bit of that stuff," she said, I could analyse it. Maybe add a few herbs or two… Just a suggestion, of course."

"Would you?" Alice wanted to say more but Mama's voice cut her off. "Enough of this talk," Mama said. "The water is ready, and Miss Thimble is not here to discuss young Master Silas." She turned to Alice and said, "Will you serve Miss Thimble her tea?"

"Yes, Mama," Alice said, but her mind was not on the tea. If she could get some of that blue stuff in the hands of Miss Thimble, maybe it would help Silas, and that was worth taking a risk. An idea had formed. She would discuss it with Silas and see what he had to say. "Here's your tea, Miss Thimble," she said as she placed a porcelain cup with a flower design on the table next to where the old lady was sitting.

"Thank you, Alice," Miss Thimble said. "You are a real jewel."

* Lord Kelvin: British mathematical physicist and engineer (1824-1907)

~

"I don't know where Uncle Buddy keeps that yucky medicine," Silas said, his face a picture of disgust. "I wish I knew. Then I would toss it all out, secretly of course."

"Would he just give you some if you simply ask him?"

Silas shook his head with a downcast face. "I don't think so. He's always acting super-secretive about that stuff. Even claims he made it himself."

"He makes his own medicine?"

"Lots of doctors do," Silas shrugged. "I suppose they want to become famous or something. No, he will not want anybody to tinker with his precious Alvexolol."

"Can't you pretend to drink it? Alice asked with a hopeful glance. "But you just secretly keep some?"

"How do I do that?" Silas countered. "He's always pouring it out on that spoon himself and then he's checking me like a hawk guarding his eyas."

"His what?"

"Eyas," Silas explained with an air of superiority. "That's what a baby hawk is called. Learned that in one of my books. You are not there yet."

"Guess not," Alice mumbled, but decided it was not worth the argument. They should not stray from the subject at hand. It was too important. That afternoon, they were sitting in the garden again and Alice had explained her idea. She'd told Silas she had met this very dear old woman who knew everything about herbs and who had asked her what kind of medicine Uncle Buddy was giving to Silas. "She suggested she could look at it, analyse it, and possibly make it better."

"Who is the old lady you are talking about?" Silas asked. "Do I know her?"

"Miss Thimble. She lives nearby."

Silas' eyes darkened. "Don't sell me a dog.* She's a witch. That's what my father says. I've heard about her."

Alice shook her head. "She's no witch. Witches have no real fingers. They have claws, and they look at you with eyes full of fire. No, Miss Thimble is very nice."

Silas still looked at her with an unbelieving stare in his eyes.

"Now Uncle Buddy on the other hand…," Alice began a little hesitant, "… looks more like he's into witches and stuff like that. I bet his house looks like a cold, dark dungeon full of spooks that do nothing but rattle iron chains around. I don't think he even knows how to smile."

Silas broke out laughing. "You are really funny sometimes,

but in some ways you are right. He never smiles, that's true. And Miss Thimble… does she smile?"

"Oh yes, she does," Alice told him with an enthusiastic nod. "She even gave me this." She pulled out the dry looking candy stick Miss Thimble had given her. "Taste this."

Silas frowned. "Do I have to put wood in my mouth?"

"It's not wood. It's natural candy. Try it," she coaxed.

Silas' face lit up, stuck it in his mouth and soon nodded in appreciation. "I don't know if she's a witch, but this sure tastes good," he mumbled with his mouth full.

"She's *not* a witch," Alice exclaimed a little annoyed. "I told you, she is nice. Trust me. She just knows a lot about herbs and stuff that is good for your body. Maybe she can help, so you are not so sick anymore. She knows herbs to treat your apsma too."

"Asthma," Silas told her, but then thought about it for a long time while plucking blades of grass and dropping them again. At last he looked up and agreed. "Sure, I am not getting any better anyway, so why not. What do we do?"

"We give her some of that Albexocol."

"AlvexoloI," Silas corrected her.

"Right, that's what I said. We just need to find a way to get some."

Silas thought about it some more. Then his face brightened. "Maybe I *do* know where he keeps at least some of it. I think he keeps that stuff in Greta Parsley's room."

Alice looked up at him, her eyes large and round. "He does?"

"I told you he is doing the bear with her. He walks in-and-out of her room as if it were his own. Last time when he gave me the blue stuff he told me to wait in the kitchen. But I followed him and saw how he went into her room. After a few minutes he came back with the Alvexolol."

A confident smile slid over Alice's face and she mumbled, more to herself than to Silas, "That settles it. That's what we'll do,"

"Do what?"

Alice looked at him with narrowed eyes. "We wait until Miss Parsley is out and then we sneak into her room and we look for the Al… eh… blue medicine."

Silas stared at her with a blank stare, but then a grin appeared. "Nanty Narking. You sure are a bricky girl (*brave*). I am glad we are friends." Just the excitement of doing something this daring made his pale complexion almost completely disappear and a red blush washed over his cheeks. "We can do it tonight. Tonight we have the Magic Lantern."

"Tonight? And what's the Magic Lantern?"

"It's like a picture story with pretty pictures. It's really rather nice. The room is dark and a man called the lanternist projects colourful pictures on the wall while somebody tells a story."

"And you are willing to miss that?" Alice frowned.

"Of course," Silas chuckled. "What could be more exciting than breaking into Greta Parsley's room? My father said that tonight we have a story called 'The worms crawl in, the worms crawl out.' I hate worms, so I don't mind missing it. Uncle Buddy will be there and Greta Parsley is having to tell the story. Your Mama would tell it much better, but of course you and your Mama are never allowed to participate in such things. But it means everyone is busy."

"What about you? Don't you have to be there?"

"I will pretend to be too sick to attend. Nobody will miss me."

"Let's do it," Alice agreed. "Tonight we'll get some of the blue stuff."

"Nanty Narking," Silas blurted out, his eyes sparkling with excitement. "Tonight is the night. Will your Mama not be worried when you are gone?"

"She's visiting Miss Thimble tonight. Everything fits perfectly."

"Good," Silas whispered. "Tonight we do it."

* Don't sell me a dog: Victorian slang for *Don't lie to me.*

~

Master Tyrel Dewar had invited a great number of his friends for the special evening with the Magic Lantern. The living room was filled with happy chatter and a hush of excitement hung over the room. Silas counted at least twenty people. His governess, Miss Greta Parsley, a skinny woman with eyes that never seemed to focus on one single thing for even a second, was nervously prancing around while constantly looking at a sheet in her slender hand on which were the words she was supposed to read.

Silas sat with drooping shoulders on a cushioned chair looking sick. He constantly let out soft moans and forced a wheezing sound to come out of his lungs.

"What's wrong with you, boy," a harsh voice called for his attention.

He looked up and stared into the cold eyes of Uncle Buddy.

"Sick again? Maybe I need to give you more Alvexolol."

Silas shook his head. ""Please not, Uncle Buddy. I am already sick enough. I-I think I am going to throw up."

Uncle Buddy stared at Silas.

Was there a hint of satisfaction in his uncle's eyes? That couldn't be, but to Silas it almost looked as if a gleeful smile had passed the man's face. Maybe he was just imagining things. Uncle Buddy cleared his throat and said, "Don't you dare do it here. You will poke us all up (*Embarrass us*) Just go to your bed and come back when you feel better. I'll tell your mother."

"Yes sir," Silas mumbled and slid off his stool. He tried to look as pale and sick as possible as he stumbled out of the living room. Just as he closed the door behind him he heard his father ring the bell to call everyone's attention.

"Tonight dear friends, we have the honour to present to you the delightful comedy *"The worms crawl in, the worms crawl out,"* brought to you by lanternist Woody Packburn. The story will be read by our own Miss Greta Parsley." There was a loud applause and Silas's heart began to pound. The Magic Lantern show was about to start. And so was their own adventure.

∼

Greta Parsley's room, unlike Alice and her Mama's place, was not in the basement. Her room was on the second floor of the main house and Silas of course, knew exactly how to get there. He had prepared a lantern for the occasion, as he expected Greta's room to be as dark as the streets of Manchester on a winter's night. "We will have our own Magic Lantern show," he told Alice with a boyish grin and guided her up the stairs. Minutes later both she and Silas stood in front of a large oak door with what to Alice looked like a golden door handle.

"Here it is," Silas whispered.

"Let's go in," Alice whispered back. Her heart was pounding in her chest so loud she was certain Silas could hear it.

Silas nodded and turned the golden door knob. The door opened with a loud creak. That didn't matter, as everyone was busy with the Magic Lantern show downstairs. Silas stepped in and Alice followed. The room smelled musty and stale and the light of the lantern Silas was holding threw large, bizarre shadows on the wall. Alice couldn't help but shiver. The room was big, at least three times the size of the quarters Alice and Mama had in the basement, but she was glad she didn't have to live in this room. Their place was small, but happy and cosy.

"Where do we look?" she whispered to Silas.

The boy placed the lantern on a chest with drawers and shrugged his shoulders. "Everywhere."

And so the two youngsters began their quest for the Alvexolol. They looked and looked, and they looked some more. Drawers were slid open and closed again, a cupboard door was opened and Alice even climbed in, rummaging around through a colossal amount of dresses.

But they found nothing.

Silas checked Miss Parsley's private bathroom but grunted in frustration when nothing worthwhile came up. They looked up, they looked down, they looked right, and they looked left, but there was no blue medicine anywhere.

"There's nothing here," Silas said at last with a frustrated sigh. "We need to get out of here. I think the Magic Lantern show must be about over."

"Already?" Alice asked. "But we mu—"She stopped halfway through her sentence and lifted a finger in the air. "Ssh… I hear something."

"What?" Silas asked in a whisper.

Alice listened carefully, her lips getting dry. She had been right. There were footsteps coming up the stairs. "I think somebody is coming."

Silas heard it too. "You are right," he mumbled in a panicky whisper. "Somebody is coming. What do we do now?"

"Under the bed," Alice urged him, and before he had a chance to answer she dashed forward, blew out the flickering flame of the lantern and pulled Silas by the arm. "Hurry, Silas. On the floor."

"T-The carpet is dirty," Silas protested.

"Who cares," Alice hissed. "Come on. On your knees."

"I always sneeze and I get my wheeze when dust comes in my nose and lungs," he protested, but there was no more time to argue, as at that instant the door opened with the same loud creak and footsteps entered.

Just in time, Alice and Silas disappeared under the bed.

9
CAUGHT

"Listen Greta," Uncle Buddy's authoritarian voice was sharp as the fangs of a viper and cold as the hail in Siberia. It was obvious he was hopping mad as he followed Greta Parsley into her room. "You can't just walk off like that," he hissed. "People will wonder and it will jeopardize our future plans."

"I messed up," Miss Parsley sniffed in a small, broken voice. "Sorry. It won't happen again."

"I will not allow you to endanger my plans, you hear?" Alice could hear another disgusted grunt coming from Uncle Buddy.

"I said I messed up," Miss Parsley defended herself. "I am sorry."

"Sorry doesn't fix it, honey. Sometimes I wonder about you," Uncle Buddy stated as he walked to the small table near the door and lit the lantern. "You can't let your emotions run off with you."

"They all laughed at me," Miss Parsley answered with a bitter sneer. She plopped herself on the bed, her legs almost touching Alice's nose. "You laughed at me too…" she fired back. "I saw you laughing, don't deny it."

Alice could hear Uncle Buddy's chuckle. "Well… you have to admit, it was sort of funny."

"No, it was *not* funny." His remark inflamed Miss Parsley's anger, "And you didn't even stand up for me. You are just like all the rest of them."

Uncle Buddy walked over to the bed and sat down next to Miss Parsley. A second pair of legs came into view. He sighed and the youngsters heard him say in a gravelly whisper, "Sorry, love. I let my anger get the best of me. But I am *not* like all the rest of them. I am here, and they are not." It was still for a moment, then Uncle Buddy's voice came again, softer now, "Shall I maybe… rub your shoulders, love? You are so tense."

"Of course, I am tense," she snapped back. 'You don't know what it feels like when the whole world laughs at you."

"Let's leave it all behind. No serious damage got done to my… eh… our plan. And remember, it doesn't matter what people think of us. It matters what we think of them. Let me massage your shoulders…"

151

As he said it, the mattress began to move, the wood creaked, and Alice gritted her teeth as she heard the rubbing sound of Uncle Buddy's hands over Miss Parsley's shoulders. It was still for a moment, but then they heard an unfamiliar smacking sound. Miss Parsley gave a soft moan and Silas immediately poked Alice in her side while whispering, "Oh no, they are going to do the bear."

"Keep still," Alice whispered back. "Don't even move a muscle or we are in deep trouble."

Miss Parsley and Uncle Buddy seemed oblivious to their presence and continued whatever it was they were doing. Then, almost to Alice's relief, Miss Parsley spoke again, her voice hoarse and soft, "Oh Bud, I am so glad you are with me. You are my all in all. Even in my dreams I would not have ever thought my heart was capable of being filled with such streams of love and the sheer happiness you provide."

"I am glad you think so," came Uncle Buddy's response. He began to chuckle again. "I am so sorry I laughed at you tonight. I'll never do it again… but you have to admit, it was rather funny."

The mattress shook again, as apparently Miss Parsley jerked away from Uncle Buddy's arms. "It was *not* funny. Not to me." Her voice was filled with lament and once again self-pity took over. It was clear she got the morbs.* "Tell me, Bud… how long, oh how long do I have to wait and endure this miserable life teaching Silas and that ugly street kid."

Alice tensed.

"I told you," came the sharp reply from Uncle Buddy. "It takes time. Lots of time. If we act too fast, we ruin everything. But soon, we can make our final move, at least as far as young Master Silas is concerned. That street kid is just a side problem. When Silas is gone, she'll be gone too."

Alice felt a shock going through Silas' body. She was as alarmed as he was. What did Uncle Buddy mean?

Miss Parsley didn't seem to share Uncle Buddy's enthusiasm. "You are always saying the same thing, Bud," she wailed and it appeared she was on the verge of tears. "When is the kid finally going to die?"

Die? Alice froze.

"You are so impatient," Uncle Buddy spoke softly. "Just hang on. You know we hoped the asthma would do the trick, but it didn't, but now, with my Alvexolol the victory is within reach. His body is so weak by now. You should have seen him this evening, hanging over his seat. He told me he was about to throw up."

Silence again.

Alice turned in the hope of catching a glimpse of Silas' eyes, but it was too dark under the bed to see.

Nevertheless, she could literally feel his panicky stare. It was obvious these two ugly creatures were up to no good.

They heard Uncle Buddy clearing his throat. "I'll double the doses of Alvexolol. You don't have to worry, love. Once he is dead, we'll work on my brother, and then...," he paused for a moment, "Broughton is mine."

"And mine?" Miss Parsley questioned Uncle Buddy in a fearful lament.

"Of course," Uncle Buddy replied in a soothing voice. "Imagine that... You never have to teach these ugly children again, and we can sit back and relax. We can finally follow your dreams and travel to Paris and New York—"

"Oh, Bud," Miss Parsley cut him off. "I love you so."

Alice searched for Silas' hand. When she had found it she squeezed it so hard, Silas let out a stifled groan. This was truly a horrible revelation and a mixture of a thousand-and-one emotions raced through Alice's mind. This couldn't be happening. This was just a bad dream. Soon she would wake up and find herself under Mama's warm quilt in the basement of Broughton.

But it wasn't a dream. The uncomfortable floor, the dust bunnies that almost made her sneeze, her aching joints, the anger and fury... it was all too real. And so was the fear. How fragile this life really was, and how was it possible that such wicked people lived so close by, and were trying to poison the little paradise they had? Just the thought that someone was actively plotting to kill her precious friend Silas was almost too much to bear.

She *had* to do something. She could not just lie here under this bed and listen to the evil mutters of these rapscallions... The urge to climb out from under the bed and throw herself in an unbridled fury on that lousy, horrible, ungodly monster, and beat his face with her angry fists became almost overwhelming. She had never liked Uncle Buddy, but this topped everything. The depth of her rage shocked her as she had never felt such anger before. Of course, Miss Parsley was not one iota better. She was a teacher, but that was the only thing that was good about her. All the rest of what that sickening governess did was permeated with the stench of hell.

On the other hand, hearing these words was almost like a revelation. All of a sudden everything made sense. Everything fit. The reason Silas wasn't getting any better was *because* of the blue medicine. The stuff Uncle Buddy made him drink contained poison. Even Uncle Buddy said that the asthma wasn't such a serious problem and Silas was slowly growing out of it. But the drink... that wretched drink was the real cause of Silas' illness; the only cause.

She heard Silas snort. A soft moan erupted from his

throat, followed by a muffled wheeze. "I-I need to sneeze," he stammered in a weak whisper. "S-So dusty here…"

"Don't," Alice whispered back. "Please don't…"

But it was too late. Silas couldn't really help it. The dust had gotten into his nostrils and although he struggled and fought with his own nose, he just couldn't stop it.

"Achoo!"

Alice shuddered. It was over. Surely, they had been discovered. And if Uncle Buddy and Miss Parsley had not heard Silas' first sneeze they certainly would hear the second sneeze, or the third… Poor Silas kept on sneezing and sneezing.

All four legs disappeared from sight, and immediately the horrible head of Uncle Buddy appeared. The man had dropped onto his knees to see who was there. His ugly hand clawed into Alice's arm and he dragged her out from under the bed. Silas got out by himself.

"Alice Matthews?" Uncle Buddy howled as he stared with furious eyes at Alice. Then he noticed Silas. He cursed loud, an obscenity that made even Miss Parsley blush, and then he hissed, "W-What are you two doing here?"

"We got lost, Uncle," Silas cried, his lip quivering.

"Lost?" Uncle Buddy glared. "In your own home? You are lying, you miserable good for nothing scallywag." He lifted his hand in anger, ready to strike. Alice saw what was about to happen and stepped forward to protect Silas. "Don't hit him," she yelled. She jumped forward and grabbed his arm while hollering, "Stop it, you ugly man."

"I hit whoever I want to hit," Uncle Buddy hissed and struck her full force. The impact of the man's rough, hardened hand on Alice's soft cheek was unexpected and it dazed her. It was as if a hot iron had been placed against her cheek causing a hundred needles to be pushed into her face, all at the same time. She staggered for a moment, and then stumbled back to the floor. Miss Parsley shrieked in fear and ran away toward their bathroom where she slammed the door behind her.

From the floor Alice could see that Silas wasn't about to cower either. There was an angry, determined look on his face. She had never seen such strong defiance on his face, and his eyes flickered with righteous anger, although his breathing was laboured and his wheeze loud. He stepped forward and planted his brown shoe with all the force he could muster against Uncle Buddy's leg. Even though he only had the force of a child, still the wicked man groaned in pain, rocked and reeled himself for a moment, but then he found his balance again and got ready to retaliate. But Silas wasn't about to fight his uncle by himself. He began to yell. Loud, desperate, and alarming. They were veritable blood-curdling yells.

Not even a second later the door opened and Baxter's noble face appeared.

Baxter... dear Baxter. Alice's heart soared.

For a second or so, the butler stood motionless in the doorway and stared with a perplexed look into the semi-dark room. "What is going…?" His eyes rested on Alice and his mouth sagged open. Alice did not waste even a second, but crawled over to Baxter, who helped her back onto her feet. As soon as she felt the man's trusted arms she pressed herself against his chest and began to weep. Baxter folded his arms around her and whispered soothing words. Alice knew she was safe.

"O, Baxter," Alice hiccupped through her tears, "Master Bud Dewar wants to kill Silas."

Uncle Buddy roared with laughter as he heard what she just said and was quick to defend himself. "Did you hear that, Baxter…? But you didn't see what that little devil did to me, Baxter. He kicked my leg… me, his favourite uncle." He cast Silas an angry stare as he rubbed his shin. "I don't know what has gotten into these two? Turns out they are nothing but common thieves."

Baxter licked his lips, while firmly holding on to Alice. "I am not sure what to say, Master Dewar. I am certain these children are not thieves."

"Well, they sure act like it," Uncle Buddy scoffed. He slowly walked toward Baxter. Alice could hear him coming closer. With every step she grabbed onto Baxter with more force. Uncle Buddy stopped no more than a few feet away. Alice could literally feel his presence.

"It feels like these two have been stabbing me in the back. What a horrible lie… How preposterous. Why would I want to kill my own nephew?"

Alice heard him swipe the dust off his pants with that same horrible hand he had just hit her with. "He said it, Baxter. I am not lying."

"It's true, Baxter," Silas now stepped in. "We heard him say as much to Miss Parsley."

At that instant, the door to the bath chamber opened up and Miss Parsley appeared. She acted surprised, and her hand flew up to her mouth. "What is all that noise and what is going on here? What are these children doing in here?"

"Right," Uncle Buddy sneered, "that's what I'd like to know. After our presentation, Miss Parsley went to the bathroom to brush her teeth and I wanted to help her clean up a bit, but then, all of a sudden, I heard this sneeze. These horrible children were under the bed, hiding. If you ask me, I think they wanted to steal Miss Parsley's jewellery, and now they come up with this horrific lie that I want to kill them. Lies, lies, lies… nothing but blatant lies."

Baxter, still firmly holding on to Alice, cleared his throat. "I-I will have to report this incident to the Master."

"Right Baxter," Silas raged, "Call my father, and then we can tell him about the medicine that my uncle has been forcing upon me lately. It's poison. He said so himself. He wants to get rid of me so I am no longer able to inherit my father's wealth."

Uncle Buddy burst out laughing. "You hear that, Baxter? How preposterous." He turned to Silas. "What medicine are you even talking about? All these years I have been sacrificing for your health and happiness; I have given you the best treatment on the market, and this is what I get?" He shook his head in disgust.

"AlvexoloI," Silas cried out. "It's poison."

"*What?*" Uncle Buddy scoffed.

"The so-called medicine you feed me. The blue stuff. Alvexolol."

Uncle spread out his arms in hopelessness and stared dumbfounded at Baxter. "You hear that, Baxter… Have you ever heard of a medicine by that name? I don't even want to talk about it anymore." He turned and glared at Silas. "It's true that a few times I gave you a drink. So what if that stuff was blue. They were just vitamins. You are so confused, young man." He wrinkled his nose and shook his head in disgust. "I tell you, Silas, if you weren't my nephew, and I didn't respect your father as much as I do, I would ask for the liberty to give you a belting. You deserve a spanking like you never had before. Nevertheless, I do not wish to lower myself to the disgusting level of lies and fabrications on which you two seem to want to reside. Enough is enough." He turned to

Baxter and growled, "Tell your Master that I found these two little thieves under Miss Parsley's bed." He pointed to Alice and added, "Clearly, the influence this little wretch on the young Master is devastating. Young Master Silas is much more ill than we thought. I will need to look for stronger medication."

Alice shivered upon hearing Uncle Buddy's words. The man was as slick as oil and it horrified her. She looked up at Baxter and whispered, "He's is lying, Baxter. He's an awful man."

Baxter pressed his lips together, but kept firmly holding on to her. Would he believe her?

"I would advise you, Baxter," Uncle Buddy still added, "not to fraternize too much with these little liars. I believe you've been a good butler, but there are a lot more good butlers out there that would love to work at Broughton. Do I make myself clear?"

"Very clear, Master Dewar," Baxter answered politely. Then he turned to Alice and Silas. "Come children, I think it best to leave Master Dewar and Miss Parsley alone." Seconds later they were back in the hallway, but Alice's heart felt like a bag of bricks. Would anybody believe them?

* Got the morbs; Victorian slang indicating melancholy

"Unacceptable," Master Tyrel Dewar roared as he spat out the words and stomped through the room while shaking his finger in Hazel's face. "Absolutely unacceptable." He licked the spit of his lips and shouted, "I took you and your daughter in. You were given the chance to live in Broughton, away from your horrible dwelling in Manchester with that drunk mother of yours. I took your daughter off the street, but clearly the street still lives in her heart."

Arabella rose from her seat near the window and lifted her hand in the hope of calming her husband down. "Watch your heart, dear…. Remember what your brother said. You cannot get so upset."

"I am watching my heart, and I am *not* upset," Tyrel screamed. "I always knew Alice was a horrible girl."

"In the beginning she has been good for Silas too," Arabella stated lamely. "He never had a friend."

"A friend?" Master Tyrel's anger now turned to his wife. "You call that a friend? That wicked girl tempted my son to act like a common thief. She taught him to lie and cheat. I cannot even believe the depth to which these two kids descended. They called my own brother, a respectable physician, a liar? I have no words for such Tommy-rot. It's nothing but Gammon and Spinach, Bull-scutter."

Arabella's face flushed. "Don't use such words, Tyrel. We are better than that."

"These are the only words that aptly describe what just happened here." Tyrel fired back.

"Calm down, my love, please."

"I told you, I am fine," he yelled. "Nothing will happen to me, because there's nothing wrong with me. Everything is wrong with her and her daughter." While stomping his large riding boot on the floor, he pointed at Hazel who cowered in a corner. The crystal goblets in the cupboard jingled and jangled on their shelf.

Still pointing at Hazel he yelled, "You brought your daughter in here, and now you will take her out again." His voice resonated through the room. "And you will go with her, Hazel Matthews. I want you out by tomorrow morning. If I hear the pitter-patter of your feet in the kitchen tomorrow I will call the police, and trust me, you would rather not meet them."

Hazel bowed her head and just stared at the floor.

"Out of my sight," Tyrel's tirade went on. He yelled, "I never want to see you or that wicked kid of yours again."

Hazel turned and walked out the door like a beaten dog, not uttering a word.

After the door had closed behind her, Arabella desperately tried to calm her husband down. "Don't be rash, Tyrel," she urged. "Hazel has been our cook for years and years. Where are we going to find a cook as good as Hazel?

What's more, she wasn't the one who lied. It was her daughter that did."

"Of course Hazel lied too," Master Dewar stated with a scowl. "We just didn't find out. How can the mother be better than the daughter?

"But we have guests tomorrow evening? We will never find a good cook in time."

But Master Dewar was not willing to change his mind. "Sorry, Bella, but my mind is made up. I am done. I'd rather cook myself than allowing the vices of low-lifes affect and influence my son." The scowl on his face was so large he almost resembled a dragon. "In fact, why don't you get off that fanny of yours for a change and cook a meal for once. It's time you are productive."

"Tyrel…," Arabella stated while her mouth hung open. "Don't talk like that. I am the Lady of Broughton. Your anger makes you say things you will later regret."

"My mind is made up," Tyrel hissed. "They are out."

"But what are we going to do for Silas? He need friends. It's not good for him to be alone."

Tyrel nodded. "I agree. That's why I have decided to send him off to a boarding school. He's got too much time on his hands here anyway. He doesn't seem to be too fond of

Miss Greta anyway, and to be honest, neither am I. We can do without her too."

"T-The boarding school," Arabella whispered. "But then I won't see him anymore."

"You'll be seeing him during the holidays. That's good enough. Seeing you hasn't done him much good anyway. He turned into a liar."

"He's sick, Tyrel." Arabella said, now almost as pale as Silas on his worst days. "He needs care."

"He'll get care." Tyrel hissed. "There are more doctors in the land. My brother is not the only one. I tell you, he needs a different life. Work, discipline, all the stuff that made me the man I am. Idleness is the devil's workshop. He may need a firm hand more than he needs medication."

"But Tyrel…"Arabella pleaded, but it was to no avail.

"No *buts*, Arabella. This is what's going to happen. I don't care if you like it or not."

Master Dewar was done. He stomped out of the room, slamming the door behind him. Arabella stayed behind with a thousand unresolved thoughts and problems. She shivered. It was cold here, even though Baxter had just lit the fire in the hearth. Losing Alice was not a great loss. She had never liked the girl. But losing their cook was altogether a different story. A terrible headache was working its way to the front of her skull.

This was a bad day. A very bad day.

10

A SOLEMN PLEDGE

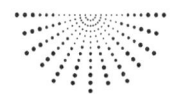

"Do we have to leave Broughton?" Alice's lip quivered and she stared with large unbelieving eyes at Mama. "Master Dewar fired you? But we didn't do anything. It's not fair and where are we going to go, Mama?"

"You *did* do something, Alice," Hazel said. "You convinced young Master Silas to sneak into Miss Parsley's room. How could you have done such a foolish thing?"

"The medicine, Mama," Alice cried. "Miss Thimble wanted a sample of the blue medicine as it doesn't make Silas any better."

Hazel shook her head. "Child, haven't you heard what Master Bud Dewar said. There *isn't* any blue medicine. The blue stuff young Master Silas took at times were just vitamins. His real medicine is different. It is… eh…" Hazel shrugged her shoulders. "Red, green, yellow… what do I know. All I know is that we are fired, Alice. You should have never done what you did." Hazel sighed and struggled to fight back her tears. "The word is you wanted to steal jewellery. Is that true?"

"No, Mama… a thousand times no. We wanted to get the medicine, but we heard Uncle Buddy say it is really poi—"

"He is *Master* Bud Dewar to you, Alice," Hazel's voice was sharp as she rebuked Alice. "That's the problem. You have become way too familiar with young Master Silas. And this is the result."

A flash of anger welled up in Alice's heart. *Master Bud Dewar… I will never call that man Master again. Never, never, never.* "But Mama, you *must* believe me. Silas has been—"

"I told you to stop this nonsense," Hazel cut her off. "You have done enough damage to last us for ten years to come."

A deep loneliness engulfed Alice as she looked into Mama's droopy, glistening eyes, which told of deep hurt and doubt and anger. Why would Mama not believe the poison story? The cold, misty streets of Manchester in the heart of winter, even without a coat, were a hundred times better than seeing Mama like this. But she and Silas were *not* lying. They were not making up stories, and they were certainly not interested in Greta Parsley's stupid jewels. The witch claimed she had found her expensive pearl necklace under the bed… how dare she? She had put it there herself as there had not been a necklace there.

At least, Alice now knew how to read and write and she was able to read some of the books from Master Dewar's study. Regardless, thinking back on her lessons, she knew her reading and writing skills were not due to Miss Parsley's teachings, but were only due to her own enthusiasm. Never once had Alice been able to spot even a speck of joy on Miss Parsley's lifeless, deadpan face when the woman explained the basics of the multiplication tables or the workings of the alphabet. The only time there had been a hint of satisfaction was when she found a spelling mistake in Alice's writing exercises and she could use her ink pen to mark the mistake.

At the time it had puzzled Alice. She was always nice to Miss Parsley herself. She treated her with the proper respect, so why was the woman so indifferent and cold? But now she knew. That woman loved nobody but herself. "Are we going back to *the alley without a name*, Mama?" Alice asked, forcing her own bitter tears away.

"I-I don't know … yet," Mama said, and Alice saw the actual tears rolling out of Mama's eyes. Oh, how Alice hated to see her cry. Mama couldn't really help it. In truth, she couldn't even be blamed for believing the lies Uncle Buddy had spread. Plotting and planning to murder Silas was such an outrageous accusation… who wouldn't be shocked?

A guilty feeling worked its way to the front of Alice's conscience. Mama's life had never been easy. After Daddy had died, her life had been one long struggle, and finally, when God was smiling upon her and they had found shelter in Broughton, misfortune struck once again. Now Mama was facing a life on the streets of Manchester again. And it wasn't even her fault. It was that horrible Uncle Buddy's fault. He was to blame for it all. He and that horrible serpent who was dreaming of taking over the estate.

She wanted to say more, but they were interrupted by a soft knock on the door. "Can I come in?"

Alice instantly recognized the voice as Baxter's.

"Just a second," Mama cried out. She grabbed a handkerchief and dried her tears. When she felt in control of her emotions, she cleared her throat and called out, "Come in."

The door opened with a loud creak, and Baxter appeared. He looked pale. Not as pale as Silas on his bad days, but Alice could see he was not his usual, happy self either. His eyes were puffy and his shoulders sagged.

"Baxter?" Mama said, with a flat voice. "What can I do for you?"

He looked like he had been fired himself. "T-There is something I wish to discuss with you, Hazel."

"All right. Speak," Hazel said while rearranging her hair.

He gave her a short nod but then turned his attention to Alice. "Young Master Silas is out in the garden near the rosebushes. I told him you'd be coming by, so you can say goodbye. In the meantime I can talk to your mother."

Silas is waiting near the rosebushes, and he wants to say goodbye? A horrible cloud of depression settled on Alice's heart. Having to say goodbye made it all so… so very final. She did not want to say goodbye. She wanted to stay here forever, together with Mama and Baxter, with Silas and without Uncle Buddy and Miss Parsley, but that wasn't going to happen.

"Thank you Baxter," Alice managed to mumble and headed for the door.

"Oh, Alice?" Baxter called after her, just before she disappeared into the hallway.

Alice stopped and turned. "What?"

"I know it doesn't do any good," he said, his voice barely above a whisper, "but I just want you to know that… I believe you. I don't think you went to Miss Parsley's room to steal her jewellery… and the other thing…," he hesitated, "…I believe that too."

His words were like a warm, balmy ray of sunshine that broke through an inky black sky on a cold winter's day. *Somebody* believed in her and Silas. Somebody knew they were not making up stories, and although Baxter's statement wouldn't make any difference as far as their stay in Broughton, it sure made a difference to Alice's heart. His words spelled hope. Hope that things would somehow work out in the end.

Her face brightened and she walked back into the room, holding out her arms, wanting Baxter to give her a hug. The butler understood and took Alice in a warm embrace. It felt safe and secure. For a moment her doubts and fears melted away and Alice knew that somewhere there was an everlasting place of rest and safety. A place where she would always feel the security she experienced right that moment. Oh, why couldn't the other people on the estate be like Baxter?

Seconds later, she was back in the hallway on her way to Silas, but there was a smile on her face and her heart was filled with a bit of hope. Fragile hope perhaps, but hope nevertheless. Someday, it would all work out.

∽

Alice found Silas near the rosebushes, just like Baxter had said. It had been raining, but he was just sitting in the wet grass soiling his best clothes, something his mother had specifically warned him against. "Don't ever sit in the wet grass, Silas." Alice could still hear Arabella's nervous voice as if she had spoken it out loud, right there. "Your clothes will get soiled and you will catch a cold. You are sick enough as it is."

When Silas saw her coming he clambered back up on his feet and gave her a sad smile.

Alice smiled back and pointed to the muddy streaks on his stockings and knees. "Your mother is not going to be pleased," she said as light hearted as she could.

"I don't care," he answered in a gruff voice. Alice could hear the rebellion in his voice. "I am mad at mother and I am mad at father. I am especially mad at Uncle Buddy, and I don't care if my clothes are black and ripped like those of the boys on the streets of Manchester you were talking about."

"But you shouldn't catch a cold," Alice stated.

"And why not?" Silas fired back. "I am apparently not any sicker than you are. Sure I have asthma, but even Uncle Buddy knows it's not going to kill me. But his poison is. As long as I don't drink that stuff, I have nothing to fear."

He pointed to a stone bench near the roses. "Let's sit down and talk about this."

The stone bench was wet too, but Alice agreed with Silas and sat down. What did it matter if they were soiling their clothes?

When Silas had lowered himself onto the bench he huffed,

"You have no idea how angry I am at my father and mother."

"I understand," Alice said. "My Mama doesn't believe me either."

"It's not just that," Silas replied. "I heard father fired you and your Mama, but there's even more."

"More?" Alice squinted her eyes. What more could there be?

Silas fumbled with his fingers and Alice could see he had been biting his nails. He only did that when he was really nervous. "Do you know what they are going to do?" he mumbled at last, barely audible.

Alice thought. "No, I don't," she said at last.

"They are going to send me to a boarding school, somewhere far away. I even heard them talk about London."

Alice gasped. "You? They are firing you too?"

In spite of the grim outlook, Silas broke out laughing. "Not firing me, silly," he chided Alice. "They don't want me to stay here anymore. They say I don't do enough, I don't learn enough, and I need discipline, like my father apparently got when he was my age. But I also think it is because they no longer want me to see you. If I stay here, we could still meet in secret."

Alice felt the blood rising to her face. "I-I am so sorry, Silas. It's all my fault," she mumbled. "If I had not suggested we break into Miss Parsley's room none of this would have happened."

"It's not your fault," Silas looked at Alice, a soft expression lingering in his eyes. "I am glad we went into her room."

"Why?" Alice did not understand.

"We went in to see if we could find out why the AlvexoloI did not work… Well, we found out, didn't we?" Silas smacked his lips. "As it turns out, I haven't even been all that sick after all. Uncle Buddy has just been slowly poisoning me, but now I can get better. I no longer have to worry about Uncle Buddy and his foul medicine, and I no longer have to sit in Greta Parsley's classes. That's all good."

"That's true," Alice said, and she gave Silas an enthusiastic nod. Silas was right. If he took good care of his body he would no longer look so pale and wouldn't huff and puff after the slightest physical exercise. Even his wheezing would possibly stop. But the thought of not seeing Silas anymore was a mountain that seemed too high. "I will miss you terribly," she muttered in a weak voice.

"I will miss you too," Silas said. "Maybe even more terrible than you will miss me."

"Not true." Alice half smiled. "I never had a friend like you."

175

Silas nodded. "That's why I am so mad," Silas replied and his face dropped. "If I could stay here, we could meet on the streets of Manchester, but now we cannot."

Alice leaned her head against Silas' shoulder, swallowing back her tears again. "I will miss you three times terrible, Silas."

He grunted. "This is not Nanty Narking."

"Not at all," Alice agreed. "Not Nanty Narking at all."

For a time neither Silas nor Alice spoke. Alice just stared out over the grass, the dark clouds above a perfect picture of the state of her heart. It began to drizzle again, but neither Silas nor Alice wanted to go back inside. Then, an idea came to her.

"Silas," she said. "Let's make a pact."

"A what?" Silas looked up.

"We make a solemn pledge. A promise to each other. A promise to God that we will always be there for each other. That we will be friends until for ever and ever, and even a bit longer."

Silas' face lit up. "I'd like that," he said. "I am just not sure if I believe in God. I'd like to, but I told you my father said that there is no God."

Alice shrugged her shoulders. "That doesn't matter. God hears you anyway. What's more, you can't believe everything your father is saying. He claims Uncle Buddy is a good man and that we are the liars. So, how can you be sure he is right when he says there is no God?"

"That's true," Silas said with a grin. "Let's make a pact. A solemn promise that we will always be together, even if we are miles apart." He got all excited and began to jump around. "And we include God. It somehow makes it more official… but… how do we do that?"

Alice thought for a moment. She had never done something so serious and it had to be done right. "Put out your hand," she said. Silas did as Alice told him. Then Alice placed her hand on Silas'. "Now you place your other hand on top of mine again, and then I put mine over yours. That way we will seal our friendship."

Silas nodded respectfully and did as Alice told him.

"Now we close our eyes," Alice said, "and I will say something."

"What will you say?" Silas asked before he closed his eyes. "It can't be just any old thing."

"That's right," Alice stated with the confidence of a regular preacher. "This is very serious."

Silas licked his lips and closed his eyes. When Alice saw he was ready, she closed her eyes too, waited for a moment, and then spoke in a firm voice: "Father God, hereby we solemnly declare Silas and I will be friends forever and ever, and even longer. Even though we will be miles apart, we will be close anyway. Let nothing come between our friendship." She paused for a moment, thinking about what she would say next. "We declare this in the name of Jesus. Amen."

"Amen," Silas mumbled his agreement, and they both looked up.

"That was… awesome," Silas spoke at last. "It felt so real." He tilted his head. "What did that mean when you said, 'In the name of Jesus?'"

Alice shrugged. "I don't know. I heard that once in church. I think you are supposed to say that after you make an important statement."

"Right," Silas said. He smiled and said, "I feel lots better now."

"Me too," Alice stated. "Now we will be friends for ever and ever." The rain had now soaked Silas' fancy suit and Alice burst out laughing. "You look terrible, like a wet cat."

"So do you," Silas fired back, his face wearing a glorious smile. "But we don't care. We are friends for ever. And we can write each other. Will you write me?"

"Of course," Alice spoke. "I will. I'd love to. That's what friends do, and we are friends for ever."

~

When Alice returned to the basement she expected Mama to severely scold her for having messed up her clothes. She had already rehearsed what she would say and she would accept everything Mama would say. Poor Mama. This was just too much for her to bear and she did not even have a friend like Silas.

But she was wrong.

When she stepped into the basement room, ready to spend her last night in Broughton, she found Mama with a serene smile, sitting on the bed.

"I-I am sorry, Mama," Alice began.

"Sorry for what?" Mama asked.

"Messing up my clothes, staying out in the rain… I just wanted to say goodbye to Silas." Alice blinked her eyes. The cloud of depression and desperation that had hung over Mama earlier was somehow gone. What had happened? "Are you all right, Mama?"

"I am," Mama said. "I talked to Baxter."

"And?"

"He is so sorry that we will have to leave, but he has a solution."

"He does?" Alice forgot that her clothes were dripping and sat down on the bed next to Mama.

"Baxter's mother is old and in need of help. She has a small house on the outskirts of Manchester but she can't take care of it anymore. Baxter asked me if we would be willing to move in with her, do the cooking and cleaning, and just be a good friend to her."

"At Baxter's mother's?" Alice wasn't sure she had heard right. "How will we pay for our stay?"

"We don't. If we take care of his mother and the house he will pay for everything. Remember, he's not fired and he makes good money here."

Mama looked up and Alice could see tears brimming her eyes again. But these were not tears of pain and sadness. These were tears of gratefulness. "We will not have to go back to the streets, Alice," she sniffed, "and we can be together. It will never be the way it was with Nana. It will be good."

"I like Baxter," Alice said while nodding her head.

"I do too," Mama replied. "He has been very nice…," she paused and thought about something. "You know what, Alice…?

"What?"

"He told me that you and Silas were probably right. Master Bud Dewar cannot be trusted and neither can Miss Parsley."

"I call her the witch," Alice stated with firm determination, "and… Uncle Buddy… I don't have a name for him yet, but that will come."

Mama laughed. How good it was to see Mama laughing again. "God is good, isn't He, Mama?"

"He is very good, Alice," Mama replied. "Very good."

PART II

11
ABOUT LETTERS, LIES AND CHANGES

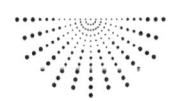

1853 Broughton

"A letter for my boy Silas?" Arabella frowned. "Who is it from?" She reached for the letter that her butler Baxter was holding and studied it with eager eyes. It stated in carefully printed out letters: *"To my friend Silas."* She recognized the handwriting and a ripple of anger flashed through her mind. That letter was from Alice Matthews and had been given to Baxter in the hopes that it would be passed on to her boy at boarding school. She looked up, and hoping to hide her anger from Baxter, she forced a smile on her face. "That girl still keeps on writing? I thought she would have forgotten Silas by now."

Baxter pressed his lips together. "Real friendship does not die easily, My Lady and as far as I can tell, Alice and Silas are very good friends."

Arabella knew Baxter was right. They were, and it greatly bothered her. That was *not* how it was supposed to be. Her Silas was too good for that horrible girl. An alley cat that was what she was. Tyrel had said so from the beginning and he had been right. They should never have given shelter to Hazel and that lying little brat of hers. She herself had been too soft again on that dreadful day when their cook Hazel had been pleading with her to take her and Alice in. It had felt charitable but even so, most of their friends had shaken their heads in dismay and they had been clear in their opinion. "You took in a street kid? That is one foolish mistake if I ever heard of one. You are going to pay the price, Arabella, mark my words."

Her friends had been right and she and Tyrel *had* paid a price. Silas had been led astray by the girl's depraved imagination. She and Silas had been caught red-handed in a wicked attempt to steal jewellery. Imagine that, her Silas a thief... They had tried to keep it a secret, but news spread fast and it had most certainly stained their good name. When they questioned Silas about it the boy had told only lies. He had claimed he and that wretched girl were only trying to find a bottle of medicine but then overheard Uncle Buddy talking about his attempts to murder Silas in an effort to become the first in line for the inheritance.

Uncle Bud... Tyrel's own brother, a murderer? That was preposterous. Not that Arabella was all that fond of

Buddy's character. The man was proud, cocky and disrespectful, but a murderer…? No, Buddy would *never* do such a thing. He was a physician and sacrificed for the good of humanity. His mission was health and hope for the sick and dying. Of course, as was to be expected, the whole episode had put even more of a strain on their relationship with Buddy and his fiancée Greta Parsley, since Tyrel had fired Greta Parsley. Since Silas was now in boarding school, there was no more need for a governess.

But worst of all, she hardly ever saw Silas anymore. Tyrel did not even allow the boy home for the holidays. Whenever she complained about it to him and told him in a tearful voice she needed to see her own son, he sneered and told her in a firm voice, "No, Silas can stay where he is. I am going to make a man out of him. You'll see him in due season."

There was no discussion possible. "You can travel to London when it's the boy's birthday, and you are free to see him when he's having holiday. But he stays in London. As long as I know that Hazel's daughter is still on the prowl and is living in Manchester, he stays right where he is." Invariably he would end the conversation by shaking his finger in her face while hissing, "One day you will thank me."

Arabella looked up from her musings and gave her servant a hard stare. "They shouldn't still be good friends, Baxter. They never see each other anymore."

Baxter shrugged his shoulders. "I would not know, My Lady, but every time when I see her at my mother's place, she talks about him."

"She still does?" Arabella grunted. She shook her head. "As your employer I insist you discourage her in that way and you tell her we do not approve of their friendship. I wish you would not allow yourself to be used as her personal mail man either."

Baxter blushed. "As you wish, My Lady."

"You see," Arabella went on, "there is no future in their friendship. Silas is my son and you know the terrible influence that girl has been on my boy. Silas is destined for greatness. But Alice will only end up in the gutter; poor and destitute, and with nothing to give to the world."

Arabella could see in Baxter's face, he did not agree with her. He swallowed hard but said nothing. "Are you not in agreement, Baxter?"

"May I speak frankly, My Lady?" Baxter said with some difficulty and waited respectfully to see what Arabella would say.

What now? Arabella wasn't in the least interested to hear what her servant would have to say, but she felt put on the spot and nodded her agreement. "Speak, Baxter."

"Your son Silas has been weak, ill perhaps, but he is a bright child and I hardly think he would ever want to cause you or the Master any pain or discomfort. You know as well as I know he is no thief and—"

"Enough, Baxter," Arabella stopped him from saying more. "I almost fear you believe their story that Uncle Buddy would want to harm him or us in an evil plot to take over our wealth. Don't you say another word. That girl is bad news, but I fear having her living in your mother's house is not working out so well. It appears her bad attitude is rubbing off on you."

Baxter raised his bushy brows. "Forgive me, My Lady, but she and Hazel are a tremendous blessing in the house. Alice is amongst the most honest and hard-working girls I've known."

A blessing... honest and hard working? How could that be? Arabella forced the smirk she felt coming off her face. "Well, I am glad to hear that, Baxter," she managed to say in polite tones. Of course, Baxter coming from a poor background failed to realize that the One-eyed man would always be the king in the land of the blind. Baxter could not be expected to understand. He himself was part of the lower classes and had it not been for Tyrel's and her generosity, the man would possibly sleep in the poorhouse himself. As long as he was doing his job properly he was valuable, but he should not push his luck too far.

She looked up at him, raising one eyebrow and said, "Anyway, I will take care of this letter. I will write my son's address on the envelope and mail it off, just like all the other letters. You may go now, Baxter, or is there anything else?"

"No My Lady," he said. He made a small bow and walked off, apparently satisfied that his little mission was accomplished. But as soon as he had left the room Arabella tore the envelope open and began to read.

Dear Silas

How I miss you. I am getting worried since you never write back to me. Why don't you answer my letters? I tell myself it is because you are so busy with your studies and all your new friends. Please, please, write to me. Life in Baxter's home is wonderful. His mother is really nice and I play Snakes & Ladders with her every afternoon. For the rest of the time I help Mama in the house. Do you know what? I subscribed to a library and that way I can read nice books. It's a little expensive (one-and-a-half guineas) but Baxter paid for it. He told me I need to read as much as I can, so I learn lots too. I've always liked Baxter... Shall I tell you a secret? I think my Mama likes him too. I saw them doing the bear the other day in the kitchen, but I don't mind. Mama needs someone who is nice and dependable.

Please write, Silas. Remember our pledge. We are friends for ever and ever, and even a little more.

Yours truly,

Alice

. . .

After she was done reading, a dark scowl appeared on Arabella's face. She crumpled up the letter and threw it on the floor. How dare this alley-cat start her letter with *Dear Silas*. Silas wasn't dear to her at all, and what was that nonsense about a pledge? The part about Baxter being fond of Hazel was almost laughable, but then again, *birds of a feather flock together*, so that was to be expected.

No, this letter would not go anywhere outside of this house. Like all the other letters Alice had written to her precious Silas and Baxter had so faithfully delivered into her hands, this letter too would go into the open fire where it would happily disappear from this world without harming anyone. Nevertheless, it was still a problem and Baxter had been right when he stated their friendship was still very much alive. Just that morning a letter from Silas had arrived too. And it wasn't even for her, his own mother. Sure, there had been a small note attached.

As usual? What did Silas think? She wasn't his little mail-servant. Of course, she had read that letter too. It was more of the same gooey stuff along the lines of what Alice had written. Silly sentences about friendship, memories, and all kinds of other nonsense. There had been one part in the letter that had been somewhat encouraging as Silas wrote he was getting stronger every day and his asthma was not nearly as bad as it had been in Manchester. But his next sentence, about being so much better since Uncle

Buddy was no longer around was disheartening. It almost appeared he believed his own lies. Sickening it was ... just sickening.

Arabella picked up the crumpled letter from Alice to Silas and stared at it one last time. A despicable piece of dirt it was and seconds later she threw it in the open fire, her face carrying a look of disgust. It ended up in the same spot where Silas' letter had landed earlier that morning. The fire flamed up and soon all these supposed words of love and faithfulness were forever gone. If Silas knew what his mother did to these letters, he would be furious. But it was all for the better. Later, when he had grown to full maturity, he would understand. Then he would be ever so grateful that she had looked after him and kept him from falling into a deep, dark abyss of despair and poverty. But no one would ever know what happened to these letters. Only... the angels knew, and perhaps God too, and that was somewhat disconcerting. Still, God seemed rather distant anyway, so there really wasn't much to worry about. She walked over to a small table against the wall and picked up a small bottle of perfume. She sprayed some on her hands as if Alice's letter had contaminated her slender fingers and nodded to herself encouragingly. Everything was under her control and that felt very good.

∼

Tyrel wasn't happy at all when Arabella told him during dinner that another letter from Alice had come for Silas. He choked, as in his anger he swallowed almost a whole potato. If it had not been for Arabella forcefully smacking his wealthy back, Broughton might well have lost its Master that very evening. But he survived, and after he had taken several large gulps of wine to wash away the last remainders of the potato, he slammed his fist on the table and barked, "This has got to stop. Now this girl almost killed me."

"Please, calm down," Arabella urged her husband. "Don't get so excited, as no harm was done. Silas never gets any of her letters."

"Are you throwing them away?" Tyrel asked as he forced himself to calm down, although he was still a little pale after the potato incident. It had given him a good scare.

"Of course I throw them away," Arabella smirked. "I wasn't born yesterday. Every time Baxter hands me a letter from her I smile at him, promise I will take care of it and then, as soon as he is out of my sight, the letter ends up in the hearth. Luckily, Baxter is a bit simple and doesn't suspect a thing. He is fully convinced Silas gets all those letters."

"What did she write this time?" Tyrel wanted to know. "I hope you read her stuff before you burn it."

"What do you think?" Arabella fired back. "I just told you I wasn't born yesterday. Of course I read it. Her letters are always filled with silly, immature nonsense about friendship and so forth. But their friendship will dry up soon, since they never hear from each other."

Tyrel carefully cut another potato into small bites and played around with his fork while he stared at his plate and then spoke in wistful tones, "I wish Silas would be as faithful with his communications to us. We don't hear much from him. When was the last time you actually heard from him?"

"This morning."

Tyrel pushed his plate away and looked up as if a bee had just stung him. "We got a letter from Silas, and you didn't tell me? What did he say?"

Arabella hesitated. "Not much. Not much at all. I pretty much memorized his letter. It said: *'Mother, as usual, please give this letter to Baxter so he can pass it on to Alice. I am doing well. Thank you.'* That was it… the whole letter."

"That was all?" A curse escaped his lips. It caused Arabella to cringe, but Tyrel didn't seem to notice. "Silas wrote to Alice, but not to us?" he fumed, "That's unforgivable, especially after all we have done for the boy. I suppose he writes Alice more often?"

Arabella rubbed her nose. "At least once a month, but sometimes even more. However we are very fortunate their communication goes through us. I am so glad Alice doesn't know where Silas is right now, and neither does he know her address. Now it's all in our hands."

"He writes her once a month?" Tyrel pushed his seat away and got up. His dinner was effectively ruined and he marched with angry steps around the dining room. "And I suppose you read his letters to her too?"

Arabella nodded. "I do. It's more of the same childish babbling," Her face lit up and she added, "Although today he wrote he has hardly any asthma and his weakness seems gone."

"That's good," Tyrel replied.

"He wrote it's because he is so far away from Uncle Buddy. I am afraid he still believes Uncle Buddy wanted to kill him."

Tyrel stood still in front of the window and looked out over his garden for some time, his hands folded behind his back. At last he turned and said. "It would be best if we never have to hear about this anymore. We need to stop this nonsense, once and for all."

"Sure," Arabella agreed. "But how can we do that?"

"You mentioned the other day that Baxter is getting disrespectful?"

"He is," Arabella admitted. "But what does that have to do with it?"

"Everything," Tyrel said as he walked back to the table and sat down again. "Hazel and that girl are living with Baxter's mother. He visits her every weekend. I can almost hear all the lies Hazel and her daughter are feeding him about us."

"Sure. And...?"

"All that communication goes through Baxter. He gives her letters to us, and Silas thinks we give his mail to him. Baxter is in the way. If we get rid of him we get rid of most of the problem. Their friendship dies and we no longer hear about it. What's more, I think it is time for a fresh start. Don't you think Baxter has had his time here? We need a young pair of hands. He is getting older... Have you seen how grey he's getting? If we don't watch out we will be held responsible for his medical bills. If we fire him, a whole lot of problems will be solved, all at once."

Arabella's eyes widened. She had not expected this course of action. It was true Baxter was getting familiar with her. Today, he had even spoken up and defied her. That had been a first. Still, he was a good servant, and had been for many years. "I-Isn't that a bit harsh? It will be hard for him to find other employment."

"He's a servant," Tyrel barked. "That's all. Nothing but a servant, and according to your own admission he's getting disrespectful. He carries the spirit of that wretched girl with him every time he comes back from visiting his mother's home." Tyrel paused for a moment and then added, "If you had not been so soft and allowed Alice in our house those years back, we would have never even had this problem. Now don't get soft again. We are the Dewars, and Dewars are smart, strong and unwavering."

It was true. Tyrel was right again. If she had not been such a softy and allowed Hazel's daughter in their home, Silas would still be living here and life would still be wonderful. She should *not* make the same mistake twice. "All right," she said. "We will fire Baxter. It's his own fault, and I'll place and advertisement for a new butler."

"Good woman," Tyrel nodded in appreciation. "And don't feel bad. We are not talking family. Baxter is only a servant. England is filled with servants and I think that most of them will beg us on their knees for such an opportunity as we have to offer them."

"I agree," Arabella mumbled. "It just feels a little bad, but as long as *I* don't have to fire him, I guess, I'll be fine with it."

"No problem," Tyrel replied. He seemed much more at peace again and there was even a small smile around his lips. "I will fire him. But don't feel bad, Arabella." He continued in the voice of a schoolmaster teaching a class of three-year-olds. "That feeling of guilt is useless. I've a friend, a scientist, who knows about this stuff. He says life is nothing but a struggle where only the strong are to survive. Nature abhors the weak. He calls it the survival of the fittest, and Baxter, Hazel, and Alice… well, they don't quite fit that picture of the fittest. Those feelings of guilt are only forced upon you by our religious upbringing and need to be avoided."

"You think so?" Arabella asked in a small voice.

"I *know* so. Science is finally overcoming superstition, so be brave and courageous, and put a smile on your face. All will be well. I will write Silas personally and tell him we had to fire Baxter and explain to him about his insolence. But I will do more…"

"What do you mean?"

"I will write that Alice has gone back to the streets of Manchester and no longer cares for his friendship. She has new friends now, friends that are better suited for her. It's the reason he never heard from her. She simply doesn't want anything to do with him anymore. It stops right here."

"Isn't that a lie?" Arabella mumbled barely audible.

"Since when are you so concerned with the truth?" Tyrel replied in a mocking voice. "But in reality this is the truth. Silas and Alice just don't know it yet, but we do. Remember what I told you… It's the survival of the fittest. Tyrel grunted and yanked the bell cord with so much force that the cord almost snapped in two. Somewhere in the hallway a loud clang was heard. Seconds later the door opened and the concerned face of Baxter appeared.

"Yes, Master?"

"Two things, Baxter," Tyrel said. "Bring in a bottle of wine. The lady and I have something to celebrate. Furthermore, I wish to see you tonight right after dinner. There is something I wish to discuss with you."

"Of course, Master," Baxter said. He made a small bow and left again in order to get one of the finest bottles from the Master's wine cellar.

12
A BEND IN THE ROAD

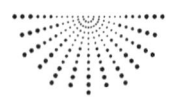

When Baxter returned home from Broughton that evening his heart was heavy. He had bad news and wasn't sure how Hazel and his mother would react. He wasn't expected home until Sunday, so his unexpected arrival would be a surprise, but since he was no longer the head-servant in Broughton and was not allowed to stay there even another night, there was nowhere else to go. He had been asked to leave at once. *Immediately.* Just like that he was fired. All those years of service apparently meant little to Tyrel and Arabella Dewar, and while he was tempted to think bitter thoughts, he had always considered himself to be a man not easily given to bitterness and anger, and he wasn't planning on allowing those ugly weeds to start growing up now. Right after the Master had broken the news to him that his service was no longer needed, and he was packing his few belongings, he had made a firm decision he would not let the bad attitude of the Dewars get the best of him. Rather than to complain about how unjust, unfair and unloving they were treating him, he wanted to treasure the memories of all the good things he had experienced in all those years of service.

Still, the rough and unexpected treatment he received from the Master would have been a blow to any man, and Baxter would be lying if he said it did not affect him. But he just had to deal with it, that was all. Obviously, he was not going to be the herald of good tidings tonight and he wasn't sure how the others would react. The front door opened with a loud creak when he entered and the comfortable warmth of the open log fire welcomed him. Hazel was sitting at the table, mending socks, and as expected, she looked up in surprise. "Baxter... I did not expect you until Sunday?"

Baxter stared at her for a moment and treasured the warm look in her eyes. Then he sniffed the air and a large grin appeared. "Couldn't miss your delicious porridge, Hazel. The cook they have now in Broughton should take lessons from you. *You* can even make porridge smell like a meal fit for kings. Is there any left?"

"There is. It's still warm," Hazel said, and called out to the kitchen where Alice was just preparing a cup of tea. "Alice, Baxter is here. Would you mind serving him some of the left over porridge?"

Alice stuck her head around the corner and cheered. "You did not eat in Broughton? Is the food getting that bad?"

"It is bad, Alice, but not so bad that I have to eat my meals here," he answered with a chuckle. A more serious look washed over him as he added in solemn tones, "No, the food is not the reason I am home tonight."

"Oh?" was all Hazel said. From the look on her face Baxter could see she knew something was wrong. Luckily, mother was already sleeping. He would tell her tomorrow.

"I was fired," he stated bluntly. It seemed his statement caused the world to stop for a moment. Nobody dared to even move a muscle and unexpectedly he felt something sting his eyes. He blinked and forced any unwanted emotions away. Hazel's hand flew to her mouth and she stared with panicky eyes at Baxter. "The Master fired you? Why? What happened?"

"Nothing," Baxter replied. "Absolutely nothing."

That was the truth. If he had broken the Mistress' collection of precious China, if he had been caught with his hand in the money jar, or if he had yielded to his temptation to sneakily sample some of the Master's fine wines, he could have understood it better. But he had done nothing wrong, at least not as far as he knew. It was the strangest thing.

He sank down on a chair, gave Hazel a sad look, and shook his head. "I don't really understand it, Hazel."

"But what did he say?" Alice piped up. She placed a bowl of steaming porridge in front of him. "He must have given you a reason."

Baxter shrugged his shoulders. "He told me it was all Arabella's idea. She apparently feels I am getting too old. *Clumsy* was the word he used."

"Clumsy? You are anything but clumsy, neither are you old. Your mother is old," Alice spoke up. "You are just grey. That's all."

A weak smile appeared on Baxter's face. "Well, on days like this I sure feel old. And I am close to fifty. That's ancient to you."

"Rubbish," Alice scoffed. "Pastor Chopple was talking in church the other day about people like Noah and Mebouzoulah, I think he said. Noah was something like a 1000 years old, and the other fellow was so old he didn't even know anymore how to die. Now *these* folks were old."

"Methuselah," Baxter corrected Alice, "and thank you for your kindness. Your youthful zeal is like medicine on my wounded heart. But whether I am old, clumsy, or athletic… it doesn't really matter. The point is that I no longer work in Broughton."

"But… what are we going to do?" Hazel asked with fearful eyes. "How are we going to pay the bills…?"

"And how will I be able to write to Silas if you cannot pass on my letters, Baxter?" Alice interrupted Hazel in a small voice.

"I don't know, Alice," Baxter said with a sigh and began eating his porridge.

Even though the fire was just as warm as before, and the light of the flickering oil lamps was still dancing in the same, happy manner, the atmosphere had changed. It seemed as if someone had opened the front door and allowed a cold winter wind to sweep through the little home.

Nobody spoke; nobody dared to speak. The only sound that was heard was the sound of Baxter's spoon in the porridge and the smacking of his lips. When he was finished he pushed the bowl away, cleared his throat and forced a smile on his face. "We are going to do what we are supposed to do."

Hazel frowned. "What is that?"

Baxter cast Hazel a loving look. "You, Hazel, were the first one that showed it to me."

"I don't understand."

Baxter answered with a weak smile. "Did you not come to Broughton, asking for help while you knew full well that your chances of being accepted by the Master and Mistress were virtually nil? You acted upon the conviction that somehow things would work out. In other words, you stepped out by faith, not knowing what the future would bring."

"But Broughton is a closed door," Hazel objected. "We were all fired. Are you suggesting we go back there, offer our apologies for being alive, and plead with the Dewars for another chance?"

"No Hazel," Baxter said with a twinkle in his eyes. "I don't think that would be very helpful. I am talking about your attitude that made you go to Broughton. You showed courage and faith. You stepped out, trusting in God and look where it brought you." He reached over the table and took Hazel's hands in his for a moment. "If you had not done that, I would have never met you and Alice, and I tell you, meeting the two of you has been worth it all."

Hazel blushed and said nothing back, but squeezed his hands in an effort to show her appreciation. It filled him with an unusual warmth. What he had said was true. He meant every word of it. He had grown so fond of Hazel over the years, a feeling he could not properly put into words, but that seemed to grow stronger by the day.

"I-I don't feel very courageous right now," Hazel stammered at last and cast him an apologetic stare, "but I think you are right. We will step out by faith. I'll look for work… Who knows; maybe there's another family that needs a cook…"

"I can work too," Alice spoke up. "I am no longer a small

child. I can read and write. I am certain I can find a job that brings in money."

Baxter let out a sigh. "I am not sure who would hire me, but I will look around too."

Hazel gave him a warm look. "It will work out, Baxter. You took care of us, maybe now it's time we take care of you. If we work you can stay home and be with your mother. Whatever we do, it will work out. God will not let us down."

"I heard the Dickens are in need of a washerwoman," Alice spoke up and looked at her mother. "I could work there, Mama. The Dickens are nice and I heard the milkman say they pay well."

Hazel smiled. "Yes Alice, that may be a good start. In any case, it *will* work out." She got up from her seat, walked over to Alice, put both of her arms around her neck and kissed her hair. "And it will work out with Silas too."

Alice shuddered. "Silas? Oh, Mama, I haven't heard from him since the day we last saw each other. That's so long ago. Why does he not write me?" She cast Baxter a hopeless glance. "You passed all my letters to him on to his mother, right Baxter?"

"Every one of them, Alice," he spoke in a soft voice. "Just pray for it, and in the meantime trust. If your friendship is meant to be, it will survive anything."

"And if it is not meant to be?" Alice asked in a small voice.

"Then you don't want it," Baxter said. "Then it will not help you, and it will be better to not have that friendship."

Alice sighed and Baxter felt his heart yearning for her. To his relief he saw the smile return on her face and she nodded. "Yes, Baxter. You are totally right. I'll just pray for it and leave it in God's hands."

And then, all of a sudden, the icy winter wind that had somehow managed to work its way into their home and had chilled them all to the bone, stopped blowing. The cold atmosphere was gone, the lights in the oil lamps were still dancing, and the happy, warm atmosphere of home where all was safe and secure, had returned. This was not the end, this was just a bend in the road. Soon they would see new vistas with new horizons and new challenges, but always with the same promise of God that He would be with them every step of the way.

∽

Ridgeview Institute for boys

London

"Come on, Silas, it's our free day. We need you." Billy Blewitt leaned over the writing desk, invading Silas' space with his chubby body, effectively making it impossible for Silas to continue his writing. "Who are you writing anyway?"

"His girlfriend," Paddy Parfitt sang in a whiney, mocking voice before Silas could answer. "He's always writing her, but she never writes back."

"Is that so?" Billy Blewitt asked. "Why waste your time on girls that don't care for you, my friend."

Silas looked up, his eyes flickering. "She does care for me. And she's *not* my girlfriend. She is much more. She is a real friend and we made a vow to always be friends."

Paddy Parfitt raised his brows. "Even more than a girlfriend? Sounds like your mother. Why do you write someone who never writes back?" He did not wait for Silas to answer but began a silly song he made up on the spot.

Silas has a little girlfriend,
Somewhere in the distant land
She never, never writes him back
Which makes his heart so droopy black
Oh, Yackety Yackety Yack

Silas is now feeling small
So he needs to party with us all
It's the only way to forget his lack
For we want our Silas back
Oh, Yackety Yackety Yack

. . .

Silas put down his pen and shook his head. "You boys don't know what you are talking about. You are talking nonsense and are just as empty as Father Tulip's whiskey bottle."

"That may be true," Paddy Parfitt replied, "but at least Father Tulip has lots of fun emptying his bottle, just like we have lots of fun in town on our free day. Come on, Silas… forget your unfaithful sweetheart and come with us to town. Near the lake we can play football with the other guys and there's lots of girls there too. Much nicer girls than silly friends who never write back. In fact, I even know of a garden party where we are welcome. We shall have lots of food, fun and fire."

"That's right," Billy Blewitt spoke up while shaking his finger in the air, delivering his opinion with the confidence of a preacher. "Leave your world of gloom behind. I heard it said the best way to heal a broken heart is to stuff it full with other loves."

Silas grunted. "I told you already that my heart is not broken at all. I am just hoping to hear from Alice. There must be a reason why she is not answering."

"Ah… the mysterious friend has a name," Paddy cried out, and right away he came up with another song.

Oh Alice is her name,

Shame on that unfaithful dame
To her is all the blame
For making Silas oh so lame

"Stop it," Silas felt anger rising. Life at Ridgeview Institute was hard enough as it was. He did not need the added scorn of the few friends he had made here. Although … friends? That was a big word. Paddy Parfitt and Billy Blewitt were not friends in the real sense of the word. They were not friends like Alice had been to him. She was a true friend… He sighed. *Was she?* However much he hated those stupid little rhymes Paddy came up with, he could not deny there was some truth in them. Why wasn't she writing?

The door to the dormitory opened and Father Tulip entered.

"Dewar?" Father Tulip croaked, standing in the door opening. "Got a letter for you."

A letter? Oh joy. Finally, there was a response from Alice. Silas jumped up from the desk and rushed forward to receive the good news Father Tulip was holding in his bony hand. Even Paddy seemed truly surprised and mumbled something about news from distant lands in Silas' merry hands. Silas had no time for his childish balderdash.

"Enjoy," Father Tulip said as he handed the envelope to Silas. "Hope it's good news."

Silas scanned the envelope, eager to see Alice's handwriting...

It was not. His heart sank. Just a letter from his father. Nothing more.

Father Tulip noticed Silas' dismay and offered helpful advice. "Not good news then? If you need to talk about it, I am in my office until six."

"Thank you, Father Tulip," Silas managed to say politely. "But that won't be necessary. It's from my father, and it's likely just business." He tore open the envelope and began to read.

Dear Silas

I hope you are well, but I am sure you are. After all, Ridgeview Institute for Boys is one of the finest in the country and I am certain you are happy there. Father Tulip assured me he would do all he could to make a man out of you, so I am trusting in his wisdom and capabilities to teach and train you in ways I could not.

I will not make this letter long, but I wanted to share some important news with you. I talked with Alice Matthews the other day. You remember her, I am sure. Well, I actually didn't talk, as she was doing all the talking, or rather, all the screaming. I was just passing by Miss Thimble's place. (You remember that witch who lives next door?) and Alice Matthews was visiting her. She just stood there on the road, blocking my passage, and refusing to move. You should have seen her... Her clothes were all ripped, her hair was grimy and unwashed, and she yelled at me... can you imagine... yelling at me? She told me she hated our whole family, and, (believe me, I write this with great pain in my heart) said she never ever wanted to see you again, and has refused to answer any of your letters we passed on to her. She said she threw them all away, unopened. The ungrateful wretch, and that after we so lovingly took her in to be your friend. Don't worry, son. There are better girls for you.

More importantly, we are fine. Your mother's parties are getting more lavish by the day and she seems happy. Oh, by the way, we fired Baxter. He had become increasingly insolent. Don't know what got into him, but all he did was rebel and argue. I am afraid he also stole money. In regards to his many years of service we will not call the police but consider the money he took our farewell gift to him. Well, that's all from Mother and me. Again, we trust you are well, and please stay out of trouble.

Lovingly

Your father.

That was it?

Silas stared at the letter and his hands trembled. What a horrible letter. Was it true that Alice did not want to see him anymore? And what about her looking so dishevelled... Father's description was so detailed, it was almost uncanny. But that was not how he knew Alice. It just didn't sound like her... not at all. But father wouldn't be lying so blatantly. Or would he? That was hard to imagine. He had always known his father to be a hard man, but even he had his good side and wouldn't just cook up a story like that. After all, he had not heard from Alice, not even once. No, there had to be some truth in that letter. But what to think about Baxter stealing money. That had to be a misunderstanding. As far as Silas knew, Baxter was as honest as Michael the Archangel, that mighty spirit-being he had heard about last Christmas.

"Bad news?" Billy Blewitt asked with a smirk.

Silas just shrugged his shoulders, but the look on his face told the whole story.

Paddy Parfitt cleared his throat and Silas feared another mocking rhyme to tumble out of the boy's mouth, but to Paddy's credit, no rhyme came. Instead Paddy placed his hand on Silas' shoulders. "Come on, friend," he said at last. "I know just the place for you to go."

Silas nodded. He may as well listen to his friends. What else was there to do for him anyway? Writing Alice was just a waste of time. He grabbed the letter to Alice he had been working on, crumpled it up and tossed it away. "All right. You win. Where do we go?"

"Good boy," Paddy said. "I told you there's a garden party. It promises to be a real hit. It's at the estate of the Davenports."

Silas frowned. "Who are the Davenports?"

Now it was Billy Blewitt's time to frown. "You don't know the Davenports? Where have you been, brother? They have one of the largest cotton mills in London. Davenport's mill is a lot bigger than your father's. Bigger, better, and broader."

"Yes," Paddy confirmed. "And you should see his daughter. I've never seen a girl so pretty."

"How do you know all that?" Silas asked.

"Told you, my friend. Unlike you, we use our free days to the full. Come on, it's time you forget about your Alice and whatever news was in that letter. Let us introduce you to Cora Davenport. She will help you to forget about your Alice in a hurry."

"All right," Silas agreed. "But can we just walk in?"

"Of course we can," Billy sneered. "There are not many advantages to being at the Ridgeview Institute for Boys, but this, at least, is one of them. We are the cream of the crop. Nobody refuses a student from the highly acclaimed school of Father Tulip. For us, any door will open." He nudged Silas with his elbow and said, "Come on, get your coat. We shouldn't keep Cora Davenport waiting."

Silas smiled, but his heart wasn't smiling. This was not a good day. No, not at all.

13
A VISIT TO BROUGHTON

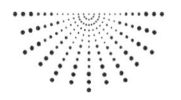

1857 MANCHESTER

Miss Thimble's house

Saturday had become one of Alice's special days. It was the day she looked forward to, as on Saturday she was not required to work in the house of the Dickens. Not that she minded working there. The Dickens were good to her, paid her well, and had come to fully trust her. She had started there as the washerwoman, but Mrs. Abigail Dickens quickly saw that Alice was a capable worker and could handle pretty much any load. Thus, Mrs. Dickens began to pile up more and more work onto her and, without it ever becoming official, Alice became the main servant in their house, and was fully employed. But on the weekends she was off, and while Sundays were filled with church and family fellowship, Saturdays were her own and she could do with them as she liked. And one of the things she liked was to visit Miss

Thimble, the dear old herb lady who had wanted to get a sample of Uncle Buddy's infamous Alvexolol.

Obviously, Alice did not go there to discuss the woes of Alvexolol, but the old woman, who now appeared to not just be old, but ancient, was like a second mother to Alice. What was more, besides her lovely garden that stretched out all the way to the walls of Broughton and was filled with the most captivating scents of herbs and flowers pretty much all the time, Miss Thimble had books. Her library was filled with many books on a great variety of subjects, and there was hardly anything Alice liked better than taking a book outside, to the porch in the balmy spring weather to leaf through it. She was learning new things and was captivated by the illustrations. Sometimes, when there was a need, Alice would pick up a few tools and help out in the garden. Miss Thimble would explain everything she knew about this herb and that flower and those were usually blessed times. And so it was this particular Saturday, as Miss Thimble had asked for Alice's help in doing the weeding in a particularly difficult part of her garden and Alice was happily digging away in the soil.

"I am so glad you are helping me with this, Alice," Miss Thimble said. "I can take care of most of the garden by myself, but this is an obstinate patch that gives my old joints a lot of trouble."

"It's a joy, Miss Thimble. I am happy to help." As she looked up, she wiped a loose string of hair off her face, effectively smearing her forehead with her muddy hand.

Miss Thimble had to laugh. "You look like a regular gardener."

"I *am* a regular gardener," Alice said with a grin, and continued her struggle with the obnoxious root of a plant that shouldn't be where it was. "At least I am on Saturdays."

Miss Thimble nodded but instructed her to be careful with the roots of a plant nearby as it appeared Alice was getting a little too enthusiastic in her efforts to show how good a gardener she really was.

"What are you trying to protect here, Miss Thimble?"

"That's Marigold, dear. It helps with skin problems and reduces pain and swelling from an insect bite."

"Really? Herbs can do that?"

"Herbs can do almost anything, Alice. Not many people think so, but there really are no worthless herbs. It's just the lack of knowledge that makes people so they carelessly pass by these plants, without realizing all the good they can do."

Alice stopped working for a moment and considered what Miss Thimble had said. "That is amazing." Her eyes fell on low-growing shrub with tiny greyish-green leaves nearby, and she pointed at it. "And that, Miss Thimble? That bush doesn't look like much."

"That's thyme, Alice. Looks can be deceiving. Thyme can be used to fight bronchitis, whooping cough and a whole string of other things. I use it to battle my arthritis. There's even a good lesson to be learned from thyme. It is one of the strongest and driest of herbs, but the bees still love it and manage to make honey out of it. So we too can take the most difficult and driest of experiences and profit from them."

Alice stared at the thyme and seemed lost in her thoughts for a moment. At last she asked, "Miss Thimble?"

"Yes, Alice?"

"Do you think I can profit from my dry and difficult experiences and can make honey out of them like the bees do?"

Miss Thimble broke out into a grand smile. "Of course you can, dear. That is what life is all about." Then her expression turned more serious. She frowned and asked, "But you are still so young. I hardly think you'd have some of these difficult experiences…" she paused for a moment and studied Alice's face, "… or do you?"

Alice felt her ears getting red. Sure she was young, but what did age have to do with it? At last she nodded and said in a small voice, "I do, Miss Thimble. I talked about it with my Mama, even with Baxter, but they say I just need to trust. Sometimes though, it's so hard to just trust."

"You've done enough for the day," Miss Thimble said. "Let's sit on the porch and while I serve you a good cup of dandelion tea you must tell me what's bothering you."

And so Alice told Miss Thimble about the solemn pledge she and Silas had made, but that he never once had written back to her. "It's so strange," she said when she had told her story. "I know it's years ago and we were just kids, but still the whole thing keeps tugging at my heart. Silas, or the young Master as you may remember him, was so sincere and we were so close… he can't just have forgotten about me. I have learned that true friendship doesn't die, and this was a very true and real friendship."

"I had no idea," Miss Thimble said at last. "I never talked much to the young Master. You know Master Dewar doesn't particular like me."

"No," Alice laughed out loud. "He thinks you are a witch. But Silas doesn't think so. Why he doesn't answer any of my letters is a mystery to me. Sometimes, it even affects my sleep and I dream about it. Really scary dreams."

"You dream about the young Master?"

Alice shook her head. "No, I wish I would. I hardly ever dream about Silas. But when I have such scary dreams I dream I am sitting at a desk and I write letters to Silas, hundreds of them. There's a whole stack of them already, but then, all of a sudden this enormous, black bird flies in. He is like a raven, only much bigger with wicked, yellow eyes. That foul bird flies in through the window and lands on my desk while I am writing letters. But then that bird begins to eat the letters... all of them. He gobbles up all the letters I wrote, but he's still hungry and then tries to eat the letter I am working on too. I shoo him away and I yell at him full force, but he just cackles back so loud and in such an eerie way that I wake up all fearful and sweaty."

"That is a bad dream indeed," Miss Thimble concluded and closed her eyes for a moment. "I could give you a tea that will help you to have better sleep."

Alice shook her head. "I don't dream it so often. Just once a month or so, but it makes me wonder about Silas. Do you think that dream means something is blocking my communication with him?"

Miss Thimble shrugged her old shoulders. "It sure sounds like it, Alice, but I am not the one to ask that. Perhaps, you should ask Silas yourself."

Alice frowned. "I wish I could. But that is out of the question. I don't even know where he is."

"He is in Broughton at the moment."

Alice looked at Miss Thimble as if her house had caved in right on top of her. "Silas Dewar is in Broughton? Why didn't you tell me?"

"I had no idea you were still thinking about him," Miss Thimble answered. She let out a groan and all of a sudden she appeared even older than she already was. While heavily leaning on her cane she told Alice what she knew. "Maralyn told me he was coming this week."

"Who is Maralyn?" Alice asked.

"She's the cook that replaced your Mama. She often comes to me secretly to ask advice about what herbs to use in the cooking. She told me last week the young Master was coming for a visit and she needed ideas for the meals." Miss Thimble chuckled. "Maralyn is a sweetheart, but as a cook she is no good."

Alice felt her heart pounding. "So, Silas is there right now?"

"I am not in charge of the schedule, but I would think so."

Alice got up. "I need to go see him, Miss Thimble. There's no time to lose."

Miss Thimble narrowed her eyes. "Be careful now dear… Master Dewar will not be particularly happy to see you again. Are you sure you have the strength for such a daring move?"

Alice pointed at a book she had been reading earlier and that was still lying on the garden table on Miss Thimble's porch. "You know Napoleon Bonaparte, Miss Thimble?"

She looked up, surprise in her eyes. "Of course, I do. Can't say I much admire the man. Why do you ask?"

Alice grinned. "I don't like him either, but he said at least *one* thing in his miserable life that I can agree with. I have just been reading it in that book I found in your library."

"What did he say?"

"He said: 'Courage isn't the strength to go on, it's going on when you *don't* have the strength.' You see, Miss Thimble, I just *have* to find out what is happening with Silas." Alice smacked her lips in a determined fashion. "I'll be back later to help you finish in the garden."

Miss Thimble shook her head. "God bless you dear. I'll be praying for you."

∼

Alice's heart was pounding as she pushed open the gate to the Broughton estate and stepped onto the familiar path that led to the main house. Nothing had changed much. The same trees that she and Silas had sat under were still there, and when she spotted the bench they had sat on while they made their solemn vow to be friends forever and ever and even a bit longer, she swallowed hard. There were a few new bushes that had not been there before and the grass was longer than it should be, but overall the place was just as she remembered. The house too looked the same. Still, just as impressive as before with its rows of grey river stone, the shimmering red bricks, and the cooing doves that were seeking shelter in the ivy. And yet, everything was different now. Alice realized that what had mostly changed, was her own outlook.

The excitement she had felt years earlier when she and mother walked up the same path was no longer there. She knew what the inside looked like, and more importantly, she knew who was living there. While she had been afraid of the Master and the Mistress at first, she now knew that character had nothing to do with status or wealth, but was a matter of the heart.

While money seemed to be a necessary evil in this present world, it appeared poor people like Baxter and Mama were living much better lives than Arabella and Tyrel Dewar. But the Dewars had a son... A son who was different, she was certain of it, and who was worth taking a risk for. For it was risky, stepping onto the grounds of the man who had fired Baxter and Mama, who called Miss Thimble a witch, and who had caused her personally so much pain by calling her a rebellious, unruly thief. Tyrel Dewar was the roaring lion of the lair with the power to call the police on her. But maybe it wouldn't get to that. God would work it all out and maybe she wouldn't even have to face the Master and she would just bump into Silas. She just had to try and find out what had happened to Silas.

Napoleon Bonaparte was right about his ideas on courage. The man was a devil, there was no doubt about it, but it sure must have taken courage to guide his beaten army back over the Alps while temperatures had dropped far below any level of endurance, they were all hungry and tired, and had not even an inch of strength left. In that light, his quote made perfect sense, and she did well to think about it. And thus, hoping Silas would just be in the garden and she would not have to face Master Dewar, she stepped courageously onward.

But that was not to be. As she passed by several berry bushes that were new, she heard laughter and voices from somewhere on the lawn. Alice craned her neck to see where the sound came from, and then she froze. There, not even ten or fifteen yards away was a garden table, complete with a red parasol, a flask of wine, and a tray of cookies and cakes. Two people were present, and Alice instantly knew who they were. Master Dewar and his wife Arabella were having tea, or rather wine, in the garden. Silas however, was nowhere to be seen. Should she turn?

But it was too late. They had seen her too. Instantly, their laughter stopped and Master Dewar rose from his seat. Even from the distance, Alice could feel the dark, hateful vibes that were coming her way. She had awakened the lion and the king of the beasts was getting ready to strike. He uttered a curse which was followed by Arabella's pitiful yelp, begging him not to use such foul language. But Master Dewar did not seem to care. He wiped his mouth with his napkin, threw it back on the table, and strode with large steps toward Alice.

"You miserable piece of vermin," Master Dewar shouted at her when he wasn't even near her yet. "Who gave you permission to come? I will call the police and tell them a thief has been spotted on my property."

The righteous are bold as a lion.* A thought welled up in her mind. It was a verse of scripture, she had just heard about last Sunday in church. She should not cower. She should not be afraid. She had done nothing wrong. She bit her lower lip and stood her ground. She made a small customary bow and looked the man in the eyes. He had aged. His hair was much greyer, there were large bags under his eyes, his shoulders were sagging, and he had gained much weight. A lion? No, he looked more like an overweight boar that was being made ready for the slaughter. For a moment, Alice felt compassion for him. How hard it was for the ungodly to live happy lives. "Good afternoon, Master Dewar," Alice said. "How are you?"

"I was fine," he hissed, "until I saw you. What are you doing here?"

Alice licked her lips. One wrong word would unleash more of his fury. "I have written many letters to your family," she said in a clear voice, "but I never got an answer." He now stood right in front of her and Alice could smell his breath. That was no wine, but whiskey. His breath resembled the breath of Nana on her bad days. Alice spotted a silver flask in his coat pocket. His eyes narrowed and he hissed, "I never got a letter from you."

"I am sorry," Alice said in a low voice. "I meant I wrote to Silas. I used to give the letters to Baxter when he was still living here, but since he can't pass them on to you, I mailed them to you. You must have gotten them. I was wondering how Silas was doing, and I heard he was here this weekend."

"Who told you that?" Master Dewar barked.

"Just heard it through the grapevine, sir." She wasn't about to involve Miss Thimble or that poor new cook.

"Silas just left," Master Dewar said, his face carrying a large scowl. "He was here, but he returned to his school earlier this morning."

"He did?" For a moment, Alice forgot she needed to be careful and couldn't hide her disappointment.

"Yes, he did," Master Dewar smirked. He paused for a moment as if he were thinking of something. Whatever it was he was thinking, it seemed to give him some peace and he added. "He told me he is done with your friendship, Miss Matthews. The reason he has not answered any of your letters is a very simple one… He doesn't want anything to do with you anymore. He throws your letters in the fire. Stop writing him, you hear me? I will no longer pass on any of your trash."

Alice was floored. Her lip began to tremble. "All my letters are burned… all of them?"

"Yes, Miss Matthews…" Master Dewar said in a mocking voice. "I tell you no lie. The fire ate all of them. He told me again this morning, just before he left, that he does not want any of your letters anymore. Don't you get it? He is too good for you. He is a Dewar, while you… well, you are really nothing."

The man actually let out a laugh and Alice cringed. She wanted to say something, ask the Master a thousand questions… How was Silas doing? How was his health and what did he look like now? But it was useless. If Silas himself had said these things, it was truly over, and the Master would not tell her anything more.

"What is it you do now for a living, little girl?" Master Dewar went on. "Sweeping the streets of Manchester? Hauling trash around?" He made a gesture as if he were throwing garbage away. "Your clothes are all soiled and your face is full of dirt, so I take it you found the right kind of work."

Alice realized she forgot to wash up after having worked in Miss Thimble's herb garden. But what difference did it make?

It was all lost anyway. Her legs turned limp. They almost could not carry her any longer and her strength was fast seeping out. She had to keep it together. She should not waver in the face of this man. But thinking straight became increasingly difficult. Her mind resembled one of Master Dewar's broken machines in the cotton mill that had been forced to work too long without proper oil and lubrication.

"I will tell you one last thing, Alice Matthews," Master Dewar spat out the words, and his voice appeared to come from far away. "If you ever set foot on my property again, I will ask the police to throw you in the deepest dungeon they can find. And just so you know, my son Silas has a new girl he loves. In time he will marry Cora Davenport and your friendship with him is over. Silas came here this week to tell me about her. In his future, there is no room for a girl like you."

Master Dewar's words kept raining down on her like blows in a fight. He was hitting her with them while her defences were totally gone. "M-Marry Cora Davenport? Who-who is she?" she mumbled barely audible.

"A respectable girl who was brought up in a respectable environment in a respectable family," Master Dewar howled. "She will bear my son lots of children so my cotton mill empire will live on forever, and you, my little thief will now have to leave my property immediately."

Leave… Of course. She had to get away from this horrible place. Tears stung her eyes as she turned around and stumbled away, out of the gate, while a thousand voices were clamouring for attention in her head. What had happened to Silas? She had cared so much for him… and had he not cared for her? Was the pledge they had made together worth nothing and had it really been only childish gibberish?

Minutes later Alice lumbered into Miss Thimble's living room again and fell down on the couch weeping. Miss Thimble shook her head and mumbled something about having feared this would happen. She prepared a hot drink for Alice, sat down next to her and hugged her long and affectionately. "It's all right, Alice. It may not feel that way right now, but everything always works out. Always."

∼

Alice had barely left Broughton when two riders on horseback entered the gate and rode their horses over the lawn toward the garden table where Tyrel and Arabella were still sitting with long, worried faces. Tyrel was tightly holding on to his empty whiskey glass and from his clenched jaws one could only conclude he was entertaining dark, miserable thoughts. The first rider was a young man with eyes that should sparkle with the joy of youth, but instead were downcast and sad. His pageboy haircut just reached his shoulders and was blowing in the wind. He was followed by a young woman. The wind was freely playing with her long, golden brown hair which would have given the casual onlooker the impression of wild abandonment and freedom, but the dissatisfied smirk on her face and her angry green eyes told a different story.

The young man stopped his horse right near where Tyrel was sitting and jumped off his horse. "Hello, Father."

"Already back?" Tyrel grunted as he looked up. "Thought you'd be gone for the afternoon, Silas. Why are you back so soon?"

"Cora doesn't like riding, Father," Silas answered. "She says it hurts. She much prefers to sit here in the garden with the two of you."

The young woman rode up to the table too, but stayed defiantly on her horse and cleared her throat. When Silas did not react right away, she cleared her throat once more and stated in a loud voice, "Will you not help me off this awful beast, my Silas? I want to join your father and mother at the table."

"Duty is calling, son," Tyrel stated while he placed his glass on the table and reached for the bottle. He looked up at the woman still on the horse. "Would you want a glass too, Cora, or would you rather have something else?"

"I'd rather have something a bit more refined," she answered while Silas helped her down and led her to a chair. "A glass of Sloe Gin would be very welcome after this horrid experience on the horse."

Tyrel nodded. "Horse riding is not everyone's cup of tea," he said as he forced a smile on his face. Then he turned to Silas and said, "Go, call our servant, Silas, and bring the horses to the stable. They do not belong on the lawn."

"Yes, Father." Silas said as he studied his father and mother's faces and asked, "Everything all right here? You two seem upset."

Tyrel cast him an angry glance. "We are not upset. I am never upset," he lied. "And why would we?" He turned to

Arabella seeking confirmation. "Right, dear? We are very happy. Things couldn't be better."

"Glad to hear," Silas mumbled, but from the look on his face it seemed he wasn't convinced. He raised his brows and walked off with the horses.

* Proverbs 28:1

14
THE GREAT DEBATE

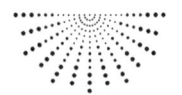

1 *860*

Alice frowned. "Do you really want to go all the way to Oxford to hear some people argue about the Bible?"

"It's not just that," Baxter replied thoughtfully. "To me, this is almost liked a turning point in history. This man Darwin wrote a book that tells us we are not made in the image of God, but that we are descendants of monkeys. There have always been unbelievers but this man even claims to be a scientist. He uses science to argue against God, and that is wrong. Science should be the greatest proponent of God, and as far as I believe, they go hand in hand."

"I am not sure what to think of it," Alice thought out loud. "It sounds rather weird. It's obvious that God made us."

She took the cup of steaming hot tea that Mama had made for her and blew on it so she could take a small sip.

"Exactly," Baxter replied, "It is weird, and that's why I have to go down there. I must stand up for what I believe."

"How do you get in? If that debate is so important it must be full with important people."

Baxter's face lit up. He shook his index finger. "I've got a friend who works in the Oxford museum where they will have the debate. He told me he'll let me in through the back."

Alice had to chuckle. "Sounds exciting."

"It is," Baxter replied. "It's very exciting." There were sparkling little lights in his eyes, lights that Alice did not see often, as Baxter was not a man to show his emotions too quickly. The first time she had seen those lights was on a very different occasion. That was the day Mama had agreed to marry him. That had been a few years ago already, but on that particular occasion, Baxter had been as happy and excited as if he were a young teen again. He had even been singing out loud in the house for three days straight, which had been a little annoying. Baxter, for obvious reasons, was not a member of the church choir, so when his singing had finally stopped, both Alice and Mama had been delighted. But today, those lights were back again, and one could only hope he would not start singing again. Of course, chances were small, as a debate between believers and unbelievers hardly seemed reason enough to break forth into song. So why was he so excited?

"I don't get it, Baxter," she said at last. "Let Darwin talk. Let the church answer. Let them fight it out. What's the big deal?"

Baxter gave Alice an incredulous stare. "The big deal? I tell you what the big deal is. There is this Irish philosopher who said: 'The only thing necessary for the triumph of evil is that good men do nothing.' * As I said, this is a turning point in history. This is a direct attack on the Holy Scriptures. I want to be in the front lines to defend the Bible."

Alice nodded. That sounded right, even noble, but it wasn't for her. Yet, if it meant so much to Baxter she was happy to hear more about it. "So… this debate… what is it all about? Who is this Darwin-fellow talking to?"

"Not Charles Darwin. He won't be talking. Apparently he doesn't like to talk to people who don't believe him and he prefers to remain silent. He said, 'To give a believer in God something to debate only means to reinforce his delusions.'"

"He said that? That doesn't seem like a very nice thing to say." Alice frowned some more. "But if he is going to stay quiet, then who is debating?"

"Among others, there is a man called Thomas Huxley."

"So… who is he?"

Baxter shrugged his shoulders. "Some claim he is a brilliant young scientist who has extensively studied fossils, apes and humans. He's apparently a spokesman for Darwin."

"And they really believe we come from monkeys?"

"They do," Baxter grunted. "They claim we all descended from apes, rather than that we were formed in the image of God. I mean, if you look at this wondrous world and the amazing way it all works… Darwin's book totally leaves God out of the picture, and that is something I cannot and will not agree with."

"It's hard to believe there is even an honest scientist who believes that," Alice agreed while squeezing her chin.

"Exactly. That's why I want to go down there. The Bishop of Oxford, a man by the name of Samuel Wilberforce will take up the challenge and will be speaking and arguing for the biblical view."

"I have heard of that man," Alice said. "He is famous as a renowned and eloquent speaker. Isn't he even a Fellow of the Royal Society?"

"I think so," Baxter replied. "I'd love to hear what he has to say against all this. Say…" he studied Alice for a moment.

"What?"

"Why don't you come with me, Alice? I sort of hate going down there all the way by myself. My walking is getting more difficult by the day and your Mama can't get free from her work."

"Me?" Alice blushed. "Going to a debate about faith and monkeys…?" She shook her head. "I don't like arguments. Let them fight it out."

"Please, Alice…" Baxter coaxed. "I am sure you'll love a break from Manchester. Oxford is quite a town and we will have a great time. But really, if I didn't believe it would be important, I would not ask you to come."

Alice sighed. She looked at the man before her. Faithful Baxter, who had now married Mama, and had been kind to her from the very first day she had met him in the kitchen of Broughton. How could she refuse? "When is it, Baxter?"

"June 30th," Baxter said instantly and stared at her with expectant eyes.

Alice smiled. "All right, Baxter, if the Dickens allow me an extra day off I will be your helper for that day. But it can only be one day. Will we be back at night then?"

"We will." Baxter's face beamed, and for a moment Alice feared he would break forth in song again. If he did, it would be her own fault. But no song came. Instead he said, "This will be an unforgettable day. We will travel by train, and as far as I know, you have never even been on a train before. That alone is worth the trip."

A train? Baxter was right. Alice had never travelled by train, and a small sense of excitement gurgled up. She had to admit, it sure sounded like an adventure. She just had to ask the Dickens and then she would be ready to go. All the way to Oxford… Baxter was right. This was going to be unforgettable.

*By Edmund Burke (1729- 1797) who was an Anglo-Irish statesman and philosopher. Born in Dublin, Burke served as a member of parliament between 1766 and 1794 in the House of Commons of Great Britain

~

To Alice's chagrin, when she woke on the morning of June 30th it was raining. Not that it was anything out of the ordinary, as it had been raining all week, but Alice had been hoping for soft, balmy weather on their journey to Oxford. It was not to be.

"That's just typical," she grunted and she envisioned having to walk around Oxford like a wet cat the whole day, tired, hungry and miserable. But her mood changed considerably when she met Baxter at the breakfast table.

"Good morning on this glorious day," he sang as Alice stumbled into the kitchen in search of a cup of coffee.

Apparently, even the rain could not dampen Baxter's enthusiasm. When Alice pulled out a chair so she could join him and she saw the eagerness with which he buttered his sandwiches, she scolded herself for looking at the dark side of things. She smiled a smile she did not feel and answered,

"Yes, Baxter, this is going to be great. Rain or shine, this day will be fine."

Baxter looked up, a twinkle in his eyes. "You are quite the poet. I was afraid you'd be having second thoughts, but I already arranged for a horse-drawn hansom cab*, so I can keep you dry and warm while we are going to the station.

"A cab? But that is expensive."

"It is not," Baxter argued back. "What's more, nothing is too expensive when it comes to taking good care of the daughter of the most wonderful woman I know."

Now the smile Alice gave him was genuine and warm. She was won over. This was indeed going to be a great day. Rain or shine, it would be fine

* The hansom cab is a kind of horse-drawn carriage designed and patented in 1834 by Joseph Hansom, an architect from York.

∼

The train journey was a marvel. It was the first time Alice left Manchester and as she looked out the window her heart soared at the sight of England's lovely country side. In her imagination the hills, valleys and dales told tales of heroic knights on horseback fighting for lovely ladies in distress and she now understood where famous painters like Turner and William Blake got their inspiration.

At last, they arrived in Oxford. Still too early for the debate, but not too early for a little sightseeing, in spite of the slight drizzle that came down from the darkened skies. But Oxford in the rain was still Oxford, and here too Alice marvelled at the sights. This had been the home of scholars and royalty for hundreds of years. Of course, Manchester too was an old city, but it could not compare to Oxford. This place was breathing with history and culture and Alice was ever so glad she had decided to accompany Baxter on his journey to the debate between believers in evolution and believers in creation.

Eventually, the time came for the debate and especially for Wilberforce to speak.

True to the word of Baxter's friend, who turned out to be one of the caretakers of the Oxford museum where the debate was held, they were both led in through the back and found a place among the hundreds of onlookers. There were mostly well-dressed men, a few women and a lot of representatives of the clergy. Thus, she felt a little out of place in her common dress. It was clear that she held no position, was not the wife of a rich banker, and could easily be mistaken for a servant girl who was supposed to make everyone feel comfortable. Her insecurity only heightened when she felt several prying eyes that were questioning her presence. Never mind. She wanted to enjoy this day to the full and wasn't about to let it get spoiled by the self-righteous eyes of the rich and powerful.

What was not helpful either was the noise level. The acoustic of the place was terrible and there was noise everywhere. It appeared everyone was already debating. The atmosphere was electric, but it was painful to the ear.

"Who will be speaking first?" Alice asked Baxter in a whisper.

"Wilberforce," Baxter informed her. "Thomas Huxley has already spoken on man's position in nature two days ago, so today the main slot of time is given to Wilberforce."

He proceeded to explain Huxley's stance in more detail to Alice, but Alice only heard half of what he said because of the noise. Nevertheless, what Darwin and Huxley claimed, appeared stranger by the minute and thus she was eager to hear what Samuel Wilberforce had to say about all this.

At last, when Alice was already getting weary, a heavy set man stepped onto the speaker's platform. He was wearing the traditional garb of the clergy that covered a white shirt with large, puffy sleeves. To Alice, he looked a bit stuffy. Not altogether unfriendly, but she had the impression the man had just learned a tad bit more than was good for him. Maybe he just looked that way because of his peering eyes that scanned the room as if he were a schoolteacher that had to explain the principles of the alphabet to a noisy group of illiterate school children. He rubbed a curl off his large forehead and cleared his throat. When he stepped up to the podium and people became aware of his presence many shouts and yells of encouragement were heard.

"There he is," someone who was pressed against Alice on the right cried out, "There is Soapy Sam himself."

Soapy Sam? Alice turned to Baxter. "Who is Soapy Sam? I thought we would hear Samuel Wilberforce."

"Soapy Sam *is* Samuel Wilberforce," Baxter whispered back with a grin. "He got that name for his slipperiness in religious arguments. He is one of England's finest orators."

So, there was the man himself, the defender of the faith. Now Alice spotted another figure too, standing on the side of the podium, somewhat in the shadows. He had been there all along, but nobody had noticed him. That was Huxley. He had a neck-beard and like Wilberforce, he carried the air of being in the possession of great and wonderful knowledge. His eyes however, unlike those of Wilberforce, were not warm. Rather, they resembled those of a nervous tiger searching for a weak sheep he could prey on.

And then it began. At last.

It was hard for Alice to follow. It was hot and stuffy in there, and Wilberforce talked for the longest time. Alice could hear some of what he was saying, but frankly, most of it eluded her. The crowd was so noisy and constantly cheered him on, which made it even more difficult to hear or understand his logic. Somehow Baxter seemed to understand it though. He seemed excited and cheered along with the others at all the right moments. That was good as now he could explain it all to her later on the way back. But right now, all Alice could think about were her hurting feet and that she was getting hot and sweaty, and much in need of a cool drink. Thus, she began to long for this debate to be over.

At last, the end came. Alice heard him say the word she had been hoping for. "Gentlemen, thus I come to the end of my reasoning. I would just like to ask the honourable Mister Huxley one thing."

Oh no… Now Huxley is going to talk even longer.

But the crowd loved it and cheered Wilberforce on.

"Mister Huxley," Wilberforce began. The crowd was now so quiet that it was easy to hear what Wilberforce was saying. "I would like to ask you one thing."

The man with the neck-beard stepped forward. "Speak."

"I was just wondering," asked Wilberforce, "if it was your grandfather or your grandmother who has descended from an ape?"

Many in the crowd laughed and began to chant for Huxley to answer. The man asked for silence by raising his hand and when everyone had calmed down, he spoke, loud and clear: "Mister Wilberforce...I tell you, I'd rather be descended from a monkey than from someone who would prostitute the truth."

For a moment it was still, but then pandemonium broke out. People yelled, some waved their angry fists in the air, and a woman, she sounded a bit hysterical, cried out that no man should be allowed to talk like that to Wilberforce. Alice heard later she had actually fainted. Alice could see that Baxter wasn't too happy with this new outburst of noise. He leaned forward to Alice and whispered, "Time to leave, Alice. It's getting too confusing here for me."

"I agree," Alice said. "Let's go." She took Baxter's hand and began to push her way through the cheering crowd to the back. Minutes later, to her great relief, they had stepped out of the stuffy, sweaty room and entered one of the corridors of the museum. "Thank God for fresh air," she sighed. "Well, Baxter, back to the trai—"

"Alice?" a familiar voice behind her interrupted her speech. "Is that really you?"

She turned and blinked her eyes.

As she stared in the direction where the voice had come from, she froze. Her heart skipped a beat as well. She blinked her eyes and as she saw who had been talking, all her strength seemed to stream out of her body. This was a mirage. This could not be happening...

But it wasn't a mirage, and it was happening. There, not even three feet away stood Silas Dewar. Next to him, holding his hand, stood a woman. A pretty woman she was, with luscious golden brown hair, that was carefully fixed in the fashion of London's high-society. She wore a gorgeous dress with a neckline that dropped low into a V-shape, and a sparkling necklace of pearls adorned her slender neck. A picture of perfection. Well, it was almost perfect, but not quite, as her green eyes were hard, jealous and mocking.

But Silas just looked like... Silas. He had aged all right, and his face now carried a few worry lines that had not been there before, but he was still Silas. Just as she remembered him, completely, totally Silas. His eyes still had the same boyish light and his pageboy haircut was still just as Alice knew it to be.

"I-I," Alice began, but she did not know what to say. She felt the burning eyes of the pretty woman in her lustrous dress stinging on her person and she knew what that woman was thinking. She did not look like a woman from the upper class.

Baxter came to the rescue, for he too had recognized Silas. "Young Master Silas," he said as he stepped forward and grabbed both of Silas' hands. "Are we glad to see you. It's been so long. How are you?"

Now it was Silas' turn to stutter. He managed to say the exact same words Alice had just mumbled. "I-I…"

Then the beautiful woman had had enough. "Silas," she smirked in a voice as if she were the queen herself, "who are these… eh… people? Remember, we are late already and have to go. We have no time for silly distractions." Her harsh voice seemed to catapult Silas back to reality, and he stammered an apology.

"Sorry, Cora. May I introduce you to Alice Matthews and Baxter." He cast Baxter a nervous smile and said, "Baxter was my favourite butler when I was young, and Alice… she was my best friend." He turned to Alice and said in a gravelly voice, as if he had just heard that his favourite dog had gone to dog heaven, "Alice… Baxter… may I introduce you to Cora Davenport, my fiancée."

"Pl-Pleased to meet you," Alice said so softly, she could not even hear her own words. Cora Davenport did not want to respond. She wrinkled her nose and sneered, "I don't care about butlers and silly little friends from your youth, Silas. We left the debate early so we can be on time to see my Daddy. We are late as it is."

Silly, little friends from his youth? Cora Davenport sure was pretty, but that didn't give her the right to speak like that. Who did she think she was?

"I am not a silly, little friend from Silas' youth, Miss Davenport," she spoke up, surprised by her own boldness. "We were best of friends. In fact we even made a solemn pledge to be friends forever and ever, and even a bit longer. Are you such a friend too?"

Cora Davenport stared in utter dismay at Alice. She was flabbergasted, and so were Baxter and Silas, although Alice, from the corner of her eye, could see an amused stare from Silas.

"Please, Alice," Baxter whispered in her ear, "she's a wealthy woman. You can't talk like that."

Alice bit her lip. Baxter, of course, was right. But what was she expected to do? How long ago had it been that she last saw Silas? How many letters had she written, and all of them had been unanswered and he had thrown all of them into the fire? Silas had made his choices, but it still hurt so bad, and now that she stood here, face to face with Silas and his ugly fiancée, it all became too much. Tears stung her eyes and she could not hold them back any longer. The dam broke. Bitter tears rolled out and dripped on the carpet in the corridor of the museum. While her shoulders shook she turned to Silas and cried, "I wrote you maybe a hundred letters, but you betrayed our pledge. You just walked off. You never wrote back. Not even once."

"What?" she heard Silas say, but she could not see his face through her tears. But then he said something strange. "You were the one who betrayed me. I was the one who wrote you a hundred letters, and not even one was answered..."

What is he saying? He wrote me a hundred letters? Where are they then?

Before she could answer, Cora spoke up again. "This so embarrassing. Silas, you come with me, and *you* little girl, you stop crying. People may think I hit you or something awful. Haven't you learned anything from the debate? Silas and I are simply higher situated on the evolutionary ladder than you are, so I have nothing to do with you."

"What?" Alice stopped crying and rage welled up. She looked with flaming eyes at Cora Davenport.

"You heard me." Cora replied and turned to Silas who seemed hopelessly confused. "Don't you agree, Silas that your former friend still looks half ape?"

Enough. Enough was enough. That woman was capable of driving anyone around the bend. Alice gritted her teeth, clenched her fists and… felt Baxter's hands grabbing hers. Just in time too. Baxter knew Alice's temperament and expected her to retaliate. And he was right. After all, Alice was still a Manchester girl, and was raised and brought up in the slums where you often had to simply fight your way out of an undesirable situation.

"Don't cop a mouse on her pretty face, Alice," she heard Baxter say. "It will make matters so much worse. You just give the devil enough rope and he hangs himself. You should not be the one to do so."

Baxter's calming words helped and Alice's rage melted away by the sun of his kind logic and concern. Alice relaxed, although her tears were still very near.

"What are you waiting for, Silie?" Cora Davenport cooed as she turned her attention back to Silas, her voice now as sugary as those despicable Sugarplums Alice had to suck on in the kitchen that day when she had first met Silas. "We are done here."

Silie? She calls Silas 'Silie'? In spite of the seriousness of the situation and the pain in her heart, hearing the nickname Cora Davenport had given to her honey pie, Alice broke out laughing. It sounded so silly, or rather it sounded Silie, and in a way Cora Davenport was right. This whole affair was dreadfully silly. Strangely enough her laughter somehow forced the last of Alice's anger and confusion away, and she felt in control again of her emotions. "Sorry, Miss Davenport," she mumbled, "I should not have gotten so angry, but your words weren't particularly filled with grace either."

"Are you lecturing me, child?" Cora's face was a mass of darkness.

"No. Miss, I am not lecturing anybody. I am just speaking the truth." Then she turned her attention to Silas, looked at him sternly and while the words did not come easy, she forced herself to say them anyhow. "Silas, I believed in our friendship with all my heart, but I guess I was wrong and naive. I never thought our friendship would end like this, but at least now I know where you stand. All the best to you, Silas Dewar. Maybe this is for the best as clearly you are walking the same road as your father has."

"No," Silas cried out. "I am not walking the same road as my father." His face had a desperate expression and he held out both of his hands. "Alice, I have been thinking of you… every day. I have written you… every month. I still think of you every day. Why do— "

Cora Davenport stepped in and interrupted Silas. "You *think* of this street woman every day, Silas Dewar?" Her voice was sharp as a razor blade and she narrowed her eyes who had turned a darker shade of green. No longer did she call him Silie. Now it was her turn to feel rage. "Explain yourself."

Alice leaned back and was ever so grateful when she felt Baxter's fatherly arms tightening around her. And then Silas said something that brought tears to her eyes once again, only these were not tears of anger or sadness, but tears of joy.

"There is nothing to explain, Cora. I have always loved this so-called street woman. I made a solemn pledge to this woman and I intend to keep it. I am already sick and tired of your whining and your complaining, but now that I have seen Alice, I know the path that I am supposed to take."

"But…But… she really is just a street girl. We've just heard the great Huxley share the truth of evolution, and how only the strong survive. The survival of the fittest. The Davenports and the Dewars are supposed to bundle their forces... We are scheduled to marry."

"Not anymore," Silas fired back. "Huxley can go fly a kite. I don't believe a word of what he is saying. I rather follow my heart and now that I have run into the love of my life once again I am not about to lose her again..." He turned to Alice and added, "... as long as you still agree to keep our pledge?"

"Stop it." Cora Davenport cried out, her voice resembling the hysterical woman in the meeting, who had fainted. "We need to see Daddy. He's waiting for us outside with the carriage."

"No I don't have to see Daddy," Silas said without even looking at Cora as his eyes were glued on Alice. "You go, Cora. I'll stay and talk to Baxter and Alice. I think we have lots to catch up on."

"You can't just shove me off like that," Cora cried, now on the verge of tears herself. "This is so... humiliating. Are you really doing this... staying with these... these... people?"

Alice could see the struggle in Silas' eyes, and she understood. He didn't want to hurt anybody, not even Cora Davenport, although, as far as Alice was concerned, she deserved a cold shoulder. *Would he really take a stand?*

He did. He shook his head. "I'll talk to you later, Cora. Bye now."

At that moment the doors to the lecture hall opened and the crowds began to stream out. The great debate was over and so was the conversation with Cora Davenport. In a desperate effort to stay ahead of the exiting crowd, she turned and rushed off. As she disappeared around the corner Alice could still hear a mixture of cries and curses coming out of her pretty mouth, utterances that did not quite befit a woman of her standing.

15
ABOUT GOOD PLANS AND WICKED PLANS

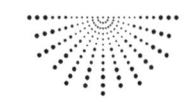

"Your fiancée," Alice cried out when Cora Davenport had disappeared from sight, "she just walked off...!"

"I know." Silas shrugged his shoulders. "But there's nothing I can do about it." His face brightened. "But meeting you... here at the debate about evolution and creation..." He shook his head and added, "How is that possible?"

The crowd that streamed out of the lecture hall was now all around, pushing into them. Further conversation was impossible. "We need to talk," Silas mumbled while trying to avoid bumping into a large, chubby man who smelled like sweat and liquor. "But not here." He pointed to the window. "I know an oyster-bar nearby. The meal is on me, of course."

Alice wanted to say something about having to go back to Manchester but she could not get the word over her lips. How could she think of Manchester now that she met Silas again? She had to find out, everything there was to find out. She glanced at Baxter, wondering what he would say. He smiled and cast her a reassuring smile. "That would be wonderful, young Master Silas. We are delighted."

And so it happened, only minutes later, that they sat in *The Solstice*, one of Oxford's finest restaurants. "This is a fish-restaurant," Silas explained, "but you can get anything you want. I come here often."

"You do?" Alice asked, while she glanced around. For a moment she had the same feeling she'd had so long ago on her first day in Broughton when she was holding Mama's hand and they entered the kitchen. Everything looked so rich and pleasant.

"Of course," Silas said with his boyish grin. "A man must eat somewhere. Whenever I'm in Oxford this is where I go."

Alice smiled back. How could she forget? Silas was, as Cora Davenport had so aptly pointed out, part of a different class altogether. She would always *just* be Alice, the daughter of cook Hazel, a Manchester girl. She let Silas order, and soon their table was transformed into a table fit for kings and queens. A great variety of fish and meats were spread out before them and the silverware, at least it seemed so to Alice, was made of pure silver. However, Alice was not in the least interested in food, and it turned out, neither was Silas. They just wanted to talk. Only Baxter seemed more than pleased with the food and he kept on filling his plate. It seemed like his smile grew proportionally with his belly.

"You said you wrote to me at least a hundred letters?" Silas began, his voice a little hesitant.

"I did," Alice replied. "And I heard you say you wrote to me a hundred letters as well?"

For a moment they looked at each other in stunned silence, and asked as in chorus, "Then why did I not receive any?"

Silas leaned back in his chair and shook his head. "My father told me he had talked to you. He said you hated my memory and that you burned all my letters. He told me you had said you never wanted to hear from me again."

"That was a lie," Alice flared up. "Of course I did not burn any of your letters. I never got any. Of course I wanted to hear from you…" She paused and then nodded. "Your father told me the same thing. He said you despised my poverty and thus you burned all my letters. And…" she paused. Should she ask him?

"What?" Silas asked.

"He said you found Cora Davenport and that in time you were going to marry her." She pressed her lips together and said barely audible, "I am happy for you, Silas."

Silas blushed and Alice could see pain flashing through his eyes. "Oh, Alice," he said, "I don't really love Cora. It's my father's doing. He insists we marry because her father has a bigger cotton mill than he does. And since you weren't around anymore, and hated me, I just gave up trying… but Cora Davenport…" He shook his head. "… she's not my treasure."

"We have been lied to," Alice said, "and we were so dumb to believe the lies of your father and mother. We never hated each other, but we just didn't know."

"Oh, horror of horrors," Silas moaned. "How could I hate the only friend I ever had? You were helping me to get my Sugarplums, you beat me at marbles, and were by my side when we discovered the story about the AlvexoloI, which was another lie." He paused and for a moment Alice feared he would break out in tears. "It seems," he continued in droopy tones, "my whole family is just full of liars. I have been so desperate, so unhappy, and so lost because I thought you had given up on me." His face took on a hard expression. "But now I understand. From the very beginning father did not like you. He has always been afraid I would fall in love with you, a woman whom he considers too low for me."

"Yes," Baxter added with his mouth full of oysters. He had been following the conversation with great interest. He emptied his mouth, took a sip of water, and said, "It must be what happened, Master Silas. Alice has been writing countless letters to you. I passed them on to your mother, thinking she would send them to you. But then, when I got fired, I could not pass them on anymore. It wouldn't have made a difference, since they just burned them all anyway."

"You got fired?" Silas' face darkened. "Why? What did you do?"

"Nothing, Master Silas," Baxter explained. "It happened already quite some time ago, but I think the Master and the Mistress were upset that I was still taking care of Alice and Hazel. But you know what?"

"What?"

Baxter's face shone. "We are married now. I married Hazel."

"You married Alice's mother?" Silas' eyes grew wide and a large smile appeared. "Congratulations, Baxter… I am so happy for you." Then he narrowed his eyes and said, "And please do not ever call me Master Silas anymore. I am no Master, I am just Silas."

"As you wish, Mast… eh Silas."

It did not take long for Silas and Alice to put all the puzzle pieces together. Their solemn pledge had not been broken. Not at all. Their friendship was still very much alive. Master Dewar and the Mistress had been plotting and planning to break their happiness. They had almost succeeded with their terrible lies and wickedness, but not quite.

"Thanks to Wilberforce and Huxley we are together again," Alice concluded.

Silas nodded. "How did you two get here in the first place?"

"It was I who asked Alice to come, Silas," Baxter explained. "I don't like what Huxley believes and wanted to hear for myself what Wilberforce had to say about it all. I was not disappointed."

"What about you," Alice asked. "Why did you and Cora come?"

Silas blew out a puff of air. "Cora and her Dad are fervent followers of Charles Darwin. They wanted me to come." A smirk appeared on his face. "As you may remember, Alice, I am not sure what to believe, but Cora wanted to convince me once and for all. She said, 'Silas, if you are going to be my husband, I want you to embrace science and leave the superstition of religion behind.' So, I came."

Alice chuckled, "And? Did you see the light?"

He shrugged his shoulders. "I didn't like Huxley much, and I don't care much for what Darwin has said. I think these fellows are a bit strange. Anyway, I haven't made up my mind yet what to believe."

"It's not a decision between science and religion," Baxter brought up. "I think they are both compatible."

"Surely, you are right, Baxter," Alice said, but seeing the confused stare on Silas' face she did not want to pursue the subject. Later maybe, but not now. "If you don't mind, I'd rather not get into that now. I am more interested in knowing what we are going to do now?"

"I suppose you two will have to go back to Manchester," Silas said.

"That's right. I have to work tomorrow." A grimace appeared on Alice's face. If she could she would just fly off with Silas and forget about everything else. But that was not possible. "I am the main servant in the house of the Dickens."

A smile appeared. "I remember the Dickens. Is that good work?"

Alice nodded, but all of a sudden she lost any interest in going back there.

"I have to go back to Cora's father," Silas stated with a serious expression. "He lives right here in Oxford, and tomorrow I have work in London. But can I come and visit you in Manchester? Can I have your address, Alice?"

"You can have more than my address," Alice beamed, "but I suppose a proper exchange of addresses, without the interference of your father and mother, is just about the best place to start."

Silas beamed her a warm smile. "That's indeed a very good start," he said, and they both scribbled their proper addresses on a paper that Baxter handed them. After Silas tucked away the precious address in his pocket, he blushed and said, "Alice… there has not been a day on which I did not think of you. I have missed you so terribly much."

"I did too," Alice whispered back. She saw how Silas reached out to her with his hand. She took it in hers. Warm, tender and comforting… But there was more. Alice felt a longing, a desire, to lay her head on his shoulder or to take his head in between her two hands and kiss his lips. She had never before felt this way, but all of a sudden she understood why people were sometimes doing the bear and what was so nice about it. When she looked up, she saw a flicker in his eyes that only heightened the sensation. Maybe it would be better if she and Baxter would go to the train station.

~

Two months later

Broughton

"Arabella, where are you?" Tyrel Dewar's angry voice echoed throughout the corridors of Broughton. The Master was livid. He stepped with heavy, angry steps through the halls, while clasping a letter. With each step his leather riding boots came down with such force that the wooden floor underneath the carpet groaned and creaked in protest, and all the while he kept yelling at the top of his voice. "Arabella... now! I want you now!"

At last, a door opened, and Arabella's face appeared, her eyes wide with fear. A servant was just busy doing her hair, but had not quite finished yet, and what was supposed to be her feminine glory hung in confusing strings around her drooping shoulders. "W-What is it, Tyrel... did we lose the cotton mill?"

"Of course not," Tyrel yelled back while approaching her. "It's worse than that." As soon as he reached his wife he pushed the letter into her hands. "Read that."

Arabella stared at him with large, desperate eyes and then began to read.

From: Silas

Mother and father, I recently met Alice Matthews again.

Now I know that you both lied. Alice did not hate me as you wanted me to believe, and she wrote me many letters. I can only imagine what you did with them. I know you do not approve of her, but I love her. I now broke off the engagement with Cora Davenport. I know you wanted me to marry her as the cotton mills of the Davenports are rather successful, and a merger would be financially beneficial. But, I do not love Cora. I think that's not a small detail that should be overlooked. I hope you agree. I write this letter to let you know I want to marry Alice Matthews. She has agreed to marry me as well and we will marry, with or without your approval.

Furthermore, I am not bitter about what you both have done. I have been angry, or rather, I have been furious, but I wish you no harm. It's my hope that in time we can see eye to eye again. I will let you know when and where we marry, and if you so wish, you are both welcome to attend the wedding.

Your son

Silas.

Arabella dropped the letter to the floor and her hand flew to her mouth. "He will m-marry Alice Matthews, the street girl? But that is unforgivable."

"Yes, you got that right," Tyrel sneered. "And it's all your fault."

Anger flashed on Arabella's face. "Why is it my fault? I can't help it that our son is so weak that he can't understand the joys we have so carefully placed before him."

"Oh you think so, huh?" Tyrel stepped closer, his nose almost pushing into Arabella's face. "Well, *I* didn't invite Alice Matthews to be Silas' little friend. You told me the boy needed to…," he paused so his words would have more effect, "…*socialize*… isn't that the word you used?" He picked up the letter from the floor and stared at it in disgust. "She didn't help him to socialize… Rather, she poisoned and bewitched him."

"He hates us," Arabella cried in a choked voice, as tears were now brimming her eyes. "Silas hates us and we will never see him again. Oh, Tyrel, we made a mistake."

"Not we, but you," Tyrel grunted. "You caused it all, and now it is too late. Do you have any idea how much money will slip through our fingers now?" He felt his anger rising again. He wanted to kick the walls, break down the doors, scream out in frustration, but when he saw the helpless, fragile figure of Arabella trembling before him, the little bit of good that was still in his heart took over and he calmed down somewhat. All he managed to say was, "You look terrible."

Arabella broke out crying. She walked forward to find shelter in Tyrel's arms, but that was the last thing Tyrel wanted right that moment. He stepped back in dismay and grunted, "Just stay away from me. You've done enough damage."

"Oh, Tyrel," she sniffed. "What are we going to do?"

"It's very simple," Tyrel hissed. "If that boy wants to go down this road, he will also have to bear the consequences. He can't have his cake and eat it too."

"I-I don't understand," Arabella sniffed. "What does cake have to do with it?"

"Nothing, woman," Tyrel cried out in exasperation. "It's a saying. It means you can't have everything just the way you want it. If Silas goes through with this, he is no longer my son. I will write him out of my will."

Arabella's face became ashen, and she let out a gurgle that came from so deep within that it even caused Tyrel to take notice. "A-Are you all right?" he inquired.

"Y-You can't do that, Tyrel," Arabella's voice was bordering the hysterical. "He will be poor. He will have to become a Dog-Whipper or a Chickweed-Seller…* Oh Tyrel… I couldn't stand it."

Tyrel stared for a moment at his wife, just to make sure she wasn't slipping over the edge, but then he said, "My mind is made up. That's what I'll do. I will inform the notary today to rewrite my testament, leaving out his name. It's the only thing that gives me peace."

"C-Can we talk about it?" Arabella asked.

"Just get your hair done," Tyrel answered. "You look terrible. I don't want to see you like that."

"Oh Tyrel…," she cried, "we will get through this. You are always so strong. I am sorry I am not more like you."

At that moment the main servant appeared. He cleared his throat and mumbled, "Excuse me, Master, I hate to disturb you but…

"What is it, man? Can't you see we are busy?" Tyrel felt irritation rising again.

"Yes, sir. Of course, sir. It's just that Master Bud Dewar is here and he wants to see you. He's waiting for you in the visitor's parlour."

Tyrel forced himself to answer in a calm way. "Thank you, James. I'll be right with him."

The servant nodded and judging by how he hastily took his way it was clear he was all too happy to leave the scene.

When he was gone, Arabella looked up at Tyrel, holding her head in both of her hands, as if it would otherwise roll off. "Uncle Buddy?" she cried out, "and I look dreadful. I've been crying. I can't meet him like this… What does he want anyway? He hasn't been around here for months."

"He's my brother," Tyrel spat out. "He's family. He wants family fellowship. That's what he wants. At least, there's somebody I can still trust." Knowing he had to show himself in control so he could keep up appearances for Uncle Buddy, he forced the last remains of his fury away. Just before he turned he gave Arabella one last sneer. "You just get yourself together, woman. You are a Dewar for crying out loud. Never forget it. We are strong. We rule, and nobody will be able to stand in our way. Don't you ever forget that."

* Dog whipper: When foxes were hunted for bounty the tail of the fox was nailed to the church door as proof of capture. The Dog Whipper was employed to deal with the dogs which disrupted the church service, attracted by the tails.

Chickweed seller: A street seller of common weeds, used to feed pet song-birds

∼

Master Bud Dewar was in the best of spirits when he returned to his home that night. Greta Parsley, now his wife, looked up from their faded couch. She was delicately sipping from a glass of port wine. "There you are," she said in a bored voice showing the inside of her mouth as a large yawn distorted her face. "I had expected you earlier."

"I've got news," Bud said with shiny eyes. "Very good news. I've got an idea."

Greta tilted her head, and adjusted her hair with one of her slender hands as if to check whether it was still just as nice as it was supposed to be. Then she asked without giving Bud a second look, "Did you finally find a way for us to go travel the world, see New York and Paris, and places like that? If not, I don't really care to hear about your good ideas." She put her glass down and yawned once more.

"Have a little faith in me, Sugar," Bud said, not wanting Greta's attitude to dampen his enthusiasm.

"Faith in you?" Greta smirked. "You promised me the world, but you never once delivered. Even living as a persecuted Governess in Broughton was better than living in this dump. Look at this place. It's hardly a palace."

"It's a home," Bud replied, gritting his teeth. "I know it's not as fancy as Broughton, but we are not living in the slums either."

"Hear ye him," Greta spoke in a mocking voice. "But with you it's always a lot of smoke with very little substance. Sometimes I wonder if I should have married you at all."

"Thank you, Sugar," Bud replied. "That's really encouraging. But seriously, I think I have found the way to make our dreams come true after all."

Greta fumbled with her wedding ring, staring at it as if she were considering throwing it out the window. But then she straightened herself and asked, "Well, let me hear that *great* news."

"It's young Master Silas."

"What about him?"

"My brother has thrown him out of the will."

Greta looked up and stared at him. "Why?"

Now Bud had Greta's full attention. He smiled and began telling what he had heard that day when visiting his brother. When he was done he said, "Silas, by offending my brother, did for us what the Alvexolol failed to do."

"Sure," Greta replied and studied her nails. "But how does that help us now?"

"Remember," Bud spoke in a whisper as if he were afraid someone would be listening in, "Silas was the main obstacle to getting the inheritance. First we had to get rid of him, and then we would take care of my brother *later… Later* has now arrived." He paused for a moment, hoping to have more impact, and then stated: "What if my brother would have a small accident? Something simple like a little fire in Broughton… "

Greta frowned. "That's stupid. The whole estate could burn down and you'd be burning down your own inheritance."

"It isn't stupid," Bud argued, biting back his frustration at not being understood. "In fact it's very smart." He smacked his lips and continued, "You forget that Tyrel's real money is in the bank, and what's more, the ground on which Broughton stands is worth a lot of money as well. I also believe my brother has some sort of insurance.

But I also would like to remind you that you hated living there."

"I see," Greta replied while carefully thinking it over. Then she shrugged her shoulders and said, "Well, do what you have to do." She picked up the bottle of port wine and served herself another glass. "I will believe it when I actually see the money in your hands. You've disappointed me before."

Bud grunted. "You are a hard woman to please, Greta."

"Oh, you think so," Greta fired back. "Just prove me wrong, Buddy. Make a believer out of me. After all these years of empty promises, I am a little sceptical. I am afraid it will be again much ado about nothing."

Bud Dewar curled his lips in anger and stepped out of the living room, slamming the door behind him. His good mood had soured quickly. Still, this was the opportunity he had been waiting for. Since he knew Broughton inside out, it would not be all that difficult for a small fire to accidentally start in his brother's bedroom…

At last he could take Greta on their trip around the world, and she would look at him with adoring eyes. But she was one ungrateful woman, and that after all he had done for her… he deserved better. Well, if she would not change, he could always divorce her… There would be plenty of women who'd like to live with him… he hoped.

16
THE HOUR OF DARKNESS

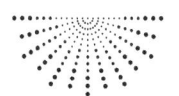

"A dream? You had a bad dream?" Alice looked up from the stove where she was preparing breakfast and glanced at Silas. She was visiting him in London for the weekend as they had planned to finalize the plans for their upcoming wedding. While she kept one eye on the sizzling bacon in the skillet she remembered her own bad dreams she'd had some years ago. "I used to have bad dreams too," she said at last. "All about all my letters to you that never arrived. Turned out my dreams were actually true."

Silas cast her a worried glance. "You actually believe dreams can be true?"

"Sometimes," Alice said and shrugged her shoulders. "But not always. Like my dream from last night for example. It was a happy dream, but it was more likely just the wishful thinking of my unconscious."

Silas cast her a curious look. "What did you dream?"

"I dreamed we were riding horses on the beach," Alice chuckled. "I never ever rode a horse before, so that part was already impossible. Anyway, it was dawn, the sun was just coming up, and the sky was beautiful. There were seagulls soaring by and I could taste the salt in the air." She shook her head. "But then, all of a sudden, we were at Broughton. Baxter was meeting us and it turned out we were living there and you were the Master."

"Where was my father?" Silas asked.

"I don't know. He just wasn't a part of the dream. Anyway, that dream will never happen since your father took you out of his will." She took the skillet off the stove and put the bacon on Silas' plate. "All this to say that not all dreams are true. But…," she arched her brow. "How about you? What did you dream last night?"

Silas sighed. "I was at Broughton too, but there were no horses and Baxter wasn't there either. It was dark. Pitch dark. You know it was the kind of darkness that was just a shade darker than black, if such a thing is possible." He shuddered as he relived the scene again. "Then I heard my mother call out to me in a desperate moan. 'Silas, please help me. Please! She sounded hurt, so I called out, 'Mother where are you?'"

She never answered me, but somehow I knew she was in the kitchen, so I ran through the corridor, but I couldn't find the kitchen anymore. All of a sudden, the hallway was so long... It just never ended, and I kept running. And then...," Silas swallowed hard, "... out of a corner, just out of nowhere there were these wolves with flickering, yellow eyes."

"Wolves? Oh my. How many?"

"I don't know." Silas shrugged his shoulders. "Three, four... I couldn't really see, but the biggest one, a wolf that was blocking my path just jumped at me... That's when I woke up. I was terrified." He cast Alice a helpless glance. "It's not a true dream, right? It's not like your dream about the letters that never got sent."

"Probably not," Alice answered, but she didn't feel much at ease. "I think, it's because you ate too much chicken in that restaurant last night." She broke out in a laugh and hoped it would break the tension that had come over the kitchen table. "I have never see anyone eat that much chicken."

But her cheerful comment on Silas' eating habits did not do much for the young man's mood. He stuck his fork into a slice of bacon and played around with it while thinking. At last he cleared his throat and said, "I need to go back to Broughton."

Alice arched her brows. "Why? Do you think your father

and mother will want to see you? They sounded so mad in their last letter."

Silas sighed. "They are still my parents. They have been so mean to us, but what if something were to happen to them and I haven't seen them for so long? My mother sounded so desperate in the dream."

Alice didn't know what to say. It sure sounded like a noble thought, but she wasn't entirely sure if Master Dewar and his wife could be trusted. She remained still for a long while, but finally Silas broke the silence. "What do you think, Alice? You think I am crazy to want to go down there?" He pressed his lips together. "It's not about the will. I am not hoping to appease him so he'll put me back in… but I want to be able to look them in the face, tell them I am grateful for what they *did* give me, and that I still love them. If they reject me…," his eyes had a sad puppy-look, "… at least, I have cleared my conscience."

"I think you should go," Alice said at last. "As I know Master Tyrel, I do not give you much hope, but you are right, you should give them a chance, so you are free to move on."

Silas took Alice's hands in his. "Thank you, Alice. Then I will go. Do you think we could stay a few days at your Mama's and Baxter's?"

Alice chuckled. "I am sure they have an old straw mattress for you that we can put down in the basement."

"Very funny," Silas said, but his eyes shone with joy and relief.

⁓

A few evenings later a carriage stopped near the gate at Broughton. The side door opened and the bulging body of Master Bud Dewar appeared. He climbed down with some difficulty and once he stood on the pavement he let out a sigh of relief, while leaning heavily on his walking cane. Maybe it was time to do something about his belly... Greta had been on his case about it several times now, and maybe she was even right. But the problems with his overweight were not his concern right now. He would deal with that later. Tonight was the night in which he would get the inheritance. He reached into the carriage and slowly moved a wooden bucket out. It was heavy and it took considerable effort again, but at last he managed to get it out and while his breath came in short gasps he placed it on the stones beside him.

"Looks heavy," the carriage driver said as he had been watching the whole ordeal from his driving seat. His voice was loud and clear in the evening air. Too loud to Uncle Buddy's liking. That man should flap his mouth shut.

"It's not heavy at all," Uncle Buddy grumbled back.

"I can carry it for you to the house," the driver went on, oblivious to Uncle Buddy's concerns. "It's a small thing, Master Dewar. All part of the service." As he said it he moved and was about to climb down.

"No need," Uncle Buddy answered, getting all the more irritated. *That driver knew who he was.* That was something he had not counted on. He licked his lips and said, "It's just marmalade, and I am well able to carry it."

"Marmalade," the driver repeated with a frown.

"Yes, man... marmalade. My brother needs it in the kitchen, and it's *not* heavy."

The driver broke out laughing. "Nanty Narking. I bet your brother is having a marmalade party. My kids would love that."

Keep your big mouth shut. Uncle Buddy was about to get rude. He had no time for such shallow talk and needed to get out of sight as soon as possible, away from this road where other people would pass by. "I warn you man, it's really none of your business." Uncle Buddy said, not trying to hide his frustration any longer. "Remember who you are talking to."

The man straightened up. "Sorry Master Dewar," he apologized. The fear was clearly detectable in his voice. "I did mean no harm. Please do accept my humble apologies."

Uncle Buddy nodded, satisfied that his little correction had the desired effect. People in the despicable class that this man belonged to should know better than to antagonize the direct family of Tyrel Dewar. After all, few people were as wealthy as his brother, and if he, being Tyrel's brother, were to complain about the service he had gotten from this man, it would most certainly mean the end of that man's job.

He walked over to the front of the carriage and asked, "How much for the ride?"

"No charge, sir," the carriage driver stated in a hoarse voice that was dripping with insecurity. "It's on me."

"Well, thank you man," Uncle Buddy nodded in pleased satisfaction and couldn't help but grin. Power was a wonderful thing, and then to think that soon he would have even more of the same. Still, he handed the driver 10 shillings. The driver stared at him with nervously, darting eyes, not sure if he should accept the money.

"Take it," Uncle Buddy said. "But since I am in charge of a surprise marmalade party I just would like it if you will not mention this ride to *anyone*, and I would like it especially if you never talk about the bucket you saw."

"Of course, sir. Absolutely," the driver replied and a greedy smile appeared as he snatched the money out of Uncle Buddy's hand.

"So… we have a deal?" Uncle Buddy asked.

"We have a deal, sir. I have not been to this part of Manchester," the driver stated. "Not tonight, not yesterday, and not last week. Never."

"Very well," Bud Dewar replied. "Then off you go."

The driver yelled a command at the horse and soon the carriage disappeared in the dark.

Uncle Buddy cast a nervous look around to see if anybody else could have spotted him, but there was nobody in sight. It was dark anyway. The moon only occasionally broke through the clouds, and Broughton was not near a busy road. No, there was nothing to worry about. *So far, so good.* He walked back with his walking cane and picked up the bucket.

It *was* heavy.

Having the driver carry it for him would have been a help, but that would be a stupid move. He couldn't risk anything. This was something he had to do by himself. As he pushed the gate to Broughton open and hauled the bucket in, he grinned. *Marmalade?* That was funny. The carriage driver, that nosy idiot, had caught him off guard with his questions. He had not been prepared for questions about the bucket he was carrying. The word marmalade had just rolled out of his mouth, and Uncle Buddy congratulated himself on being so smart. Some folks called it inspiration. Uncle Buddy just called it being wise.

The gate creaked louder than he had wanted, but the main house was too far away for anyone to hear. He would walk up to his brother's bedroom, and just wait until Tyrel and Arabella would go to sleep. Shouldn't take too long, and then, once they were asleep he would open his bucket and go to work.

Coal tar. His bucket was full of coal tar, with its highly inflammable fumes. He would smear it everywhere. On the window, around the window, above and below, and if the window was open he would even drop some inside, and then... party time. The fire would spread so quick and so violent that his brother and the miserable Arabella would be dead before they even knew what had hit them. He had to be still, of course, but since both his brother and his wife were heavy drinkers, it would be unlikely they would wake up. They were usually intoxicated by this time and already in different spheres altogether.

And thus Uncle Buddy stealthily moved forward over the path through the shadows. Not too far away from his brother's bedroom the gardener had planted a strawberry tree. Arabella had wanted it. She said it cheered her when she looked out her window first thing in the morning. Thus Tyrel had ordered the gardener to get it. 'A waste of money,' Uncle Buddy had thought at first. Spending precious money on something so silly as a shrub was utterly ridiculous to him, but tonight he was more than happy to see it. From behind the shrub he had a perfect view of the bedroom while staying out of sight. He put down his bucket of tar and after he had rubbed his sore muscles, he peered through the leaves of the bush. There was a small light in the bedroom. Probably an oil lamp. Who knows, maybe Tyrel and Arabella were already in the bedroom. As soon as the light was put out it meant he could get to work. He would still wait a little while longer, just to make sure both his brother and Arabella were really in dreamland, and then he would strike. It was a perfect plan, Every time he thought about the wealth that would soon be his, an unfamiliar joy bubbled up and made him twitch his nose. *Yes, brother. This is the day of reckoning. Your last hour has come.*

At that instant, a loud angry voice broke through the silence of the night. Uncle Buddy froze as he heard a familiar voice scream, "Never again, do you hear? I never want to see you again. It's over."

Uncle Buddy licked his lips, as they had gotten dry, and nervously peered through the bush in the direction from where he had heard the furious outburst. Had he somehow been spotted?

No, the anger was not directed at him. There on the porch of Broughton stood his brother Tyrel, waving his fist in the air like a madman. Instantly, Uncle Buddy saw who the anger was directed at. There, just stepping off the porch was the distraught figure of... his nephew Silas. What in the world was he doing here?

"I k-know what you are after," Tyrel screamed in an alcoholic slur. "Ho-Hoping to get back in the will, huh? But that's not going to work, you hear me? Y-You are no longer my s-s-son."

Uncle Buddy chuckled. He had hoped his brother would be drinking again. It made his work so much easier. And look at young Silas, all discouraged and unhappy. He was looking so miserable because he wouldn't get a penny. It would all go to him and Greta. "Too late, little nephew." Uncle Buddy uttered a joyful whisper. "You have lost."

The door on the porch slammed closed and Silas approached. Uncle Buddy ducked away behind the bush. Thankfully it was dark. As long as he stayed still and hidden behind the bush he would be perfectly safe.

Silas was close now. No more than 10 feet at the most. Uncle Buddy heard the grinding steps over the path. But then, for some reason, Silas stopped.

Come on, sonny... walk on...

But Silas did not walk on. He peered into the night sky as if something was troubling him.

Was there something in the air?

There was. It was then Uncle Buddy saw it too… Bats. At least three or four bats were soaring low over the path and Silas began to wave his arms around to protect himself as they were zooming over his head, way too close for comfort.

279

Stupid bats. Uncle Buddy let out a soft curse. That was a mistake. A major one but he realized it too late.

Bats have exceptional hearing and can detect even the slightest of sounds, especially an uttered whisper so foul and so low as had just erupted from Uncle Buddy's throat. At that instant, the moon just peered through the clouds and cast silver streaks of light over the ground. One of the bats, a large one, equipped with tiny, yellow pin-point eyes that lit up menacingly heard Uncle's dark mumblings. The beast changed direction and flew right over the bush, almost crashing into Uncle Buddy's shivering head. The man cried out in fear. "Nóóó, get away from me you foul beast." In a desperate attempt to protect himself from the encounter with one of those creatures from the netherworld, he too was now waving his arms around. His cover was blown.

"W-Who is there?" Silas cried out and Uncle Buddy felt his nephew's prying eyes on his bulky frame. "G-Good evening, Silas," he groaned. "What horrible creatures these bats are, wouldn't you agree?"

"Uncle Buddy?" Silas stepped closer. "What in the world are you doing there behind the strawberry tree?"

Uncle Buddy's heart pounded and sweat broke out on his forehead. He had been caught. What was he to do now? Before he could give an answer Silas glanced at the bucket that stood now clearly in sight under the bush, and pointed at it. "What is that?"

"M-Marmalade," Uncle Buddy lied. "Just a surprise for my brother."

Silas' face darkened. "Jam in the garden after dark? A surprise? Let me see that." Instantly he walked over to the bucket, knelt down and without Uncle Buddy's permission, he took off the lid and looked inside.

There was only one thing Uncle Buddy could do. He had no choice, but he had to act fast.

"This is *not* marmalade," Silas stated in a surprised voice. "This is—"

Uncle Buddy let the top of his cane crash down on Silas' head. "Sorry, nephew," he muttered. "You crossed me once, but that will not happen again." The cane broke in two while Silas groaned and fell forward on the grass. Uncle Buddy stared for a moment with satisfied, wicked eyes at the scene before him, but snapped back to reality almost instantly. This had not been part of the plan. Hopefully nobody had heard. He ducked again behind the bush, next to Silas' unconscious body, and stared at the house. *Good. Nobody has heard.*

At that instant, the light in the bedroom went out. The oil lamp had been turned off. Tyrel and Arabella were in bed. Now, he would wait just a bit longer and then finish the job he had begun. He stared for a moment at Silas. What was he to do with his nephew? Then an idea formed and he chuckled. *May as well get rid of Silas in the process even*

281

though he's no longer in the will. After all, I never liked the boy. Good riddance to bad rubbish.

If he had not needed to be quiet and still, he would most certainly have broken out into joyful, pleased laughter. But he would do that later when he was back in Greta's arms. For now he needed to stay calm and collected. Nevertheless, things couldn't be better. Everything was going his way. What a good plan he had cooked up.

17
SEPARATION

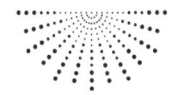

Silas' head hurt bad. Very bad.

He tried to lift his hand so he could feel his head and take away the pain but he could not. He could not move his arms. Somehow, they seemed glued to his body. Why was that, and why was there so much smoke everywhere?

There was smoke In his lungs, in his nostrils, in his head… Ah, what was causing the pain in his head?

There was noise too. Rather, it was pandemonium. A giant roar as of an approaching monster, mixed with the sound of crackling wood and things falling down filled his ears. Silas blinked his eyes and looked around as best as he could. Flames... red, sizzling flames were rolling in. Big ones, small ones, hot ones and even hotter ones. Fire was all around and it was spreading as fast as a hungry swarm of locusts that was stripping a field of all of its verdure in a matter of minutes.

All his dizziness was gone in an instant. There was no time to worry about his hurting head, either. There was only one thing he needed to do, and that was to get out.

Once more he wanted to use his hands, but again, he was held back. As he desperately tried to free his hands he felt how something around his wrists cut into his skin. Tied together... Somebody had tied his hands together. Who had done that and why? How did he even get here?

To his relief he noticed his feet were not tied. He could still get up and run. Instantly, he crawled up and looked around for a way out. Where could he go? Right in front of him was a stove. Several pans stood on the burners, now red hot because of the heat. A stove? Then he knew where he was. He was in the kitchen of Broughton. In spite of hellish flames he recognized the place. On his left was the water pump. Could he use the water to kill the fire? Of course not. The fire was way too big, way too strong. At that instant, the shelf that had once held the jar with the Sugarplums, came crashing down, causing a rain of hot sparks to fly through the kitchen.

. . .

The flames now singed his hair and burned his skin, as if he were face to face with a fire-breathing dragon. A group of small flames, like scouts of an invading army, began to surround him. The door... he needed to get to the door because soon the bigger flames of the fire dragon would completely engulf and destroy him.

Coughing and choking he turned to where the door was to the corridor. But how could he even open the door without the use of his hands? As long as his hands were tied, there was little he could do. But as he uttered the thought, wonder of wonders and unexplainable, the ropes around his wrists loosened and just fell off. How was that possible? Thankfully, whoever had tied him up had done a very sloppy job.

Then he saw the man.

There, right in the middle of all the confusion, the heat, the flames, and the misery, stood a man. Rather, it was a giant. His head almost reached to the ceiling that was already engulfed in flames. There was no panic or fear in his eyes. Rather, he stared at Silas with large eyes that shone with an unearthly light that far surpassed even the brightness of the flames. Silas stood spellbound and somehow knew he was in the presence of a messenger from another world, a sphere of wisdom and rightness. Yet, the expression on the man's face was grim and full of determination. Of course it was... this *was* a desperate, grim situation. But was what he was seeing even real? Maybe he was delusional and the smoke had already affected his brain. Or worse, maybe he was dead already and he was just about to enter the afterlife... A lake of fire, a bottomless pit that offered no hope for those who fell in. Oh God, please... no. But the being before him radiated no anger or fear, and did not in any way resemble the angel of death whose face would have carried a mocking smirk of victory. On the contrary the look was one of deep concern and of utmost urgency. Then the being spoke. In spite of the roar of the fire his voice was clear, and was spoken directly to his mind. Only one sentence, loud and demanding. "Your mother in the guest room needs you."

Mother needs me and she is in the guest room? Instantly Silas saw a picture of his mother, huddled in a corner, weeping and screaming in fear for help. He instantly knew in what room she was too. She was in the room in which Alice had been born. "Do I need to sav—" Silas wanted to ask the being, but there was nobody there. The man had vanished, just like that.

. . .

Nevertheless, the vision had been so clear and so overwhelming. A new sense of urgency filled Silas' thoughts. Mother needed him. And father? Where was he? Both, mother and father had conspired against him and Alice. They had cheated and lied… but right now, that was not important. They were still his parents. The being had urged him that Mother needed him. Silas grabbed a cloth he saw hanging nearby, pushed it with one hand to his mouth and lurched forward to the door. No flames there yet. He swung it open, stormed into the corridor that was fast filling up with smoke, and ran past several chambers. Small flames were already leaking out from under doors and cracks in the wall, and parts of the carpets began to burn. Oh, there was not a second to waste.

At last he reached the room he was looking for. The door was already open and he could see the sea of flames that were destroying the room. He stuck his head through the opening, narrowing his eyes to protect them from the rising smoke, and looked. There she was. Just like in his vision, she sat in a foetal position in a corner, a heap of terrified and confused misery, unable to take any action. She almost seemed oblivious to what was happening around her and Silas figured she was in shock. He had heard that sometimes, people in terrifying conditions, would just turn off an imaginary switch in their brains and thus be unable to move or think rationally. She was just softly moaning and weeping.

. . .

He jumped forward, just as a beam came crushing down behind him, causing another volley of sparks to rain down on him. Was he on fire himself? No time to check. He jerked Mother up by her arm. She looked up into Silas' eyes, her eyes blank and filled with fear, and it did not seem she recognized her son. "It's me, Mother," Silas cried. "I'll get you out of here."

Her response was one of hysterical screaming and weeping. No time to waste or to argue. Silas just grabbed her, lifted her up and threw her over his shoulders. She was surprisingly light.

To the back. To the back. Somehow, and with great clarity, Silas knew where he had to go. Not too far away was a small back door. If they could make it safely there they could escape. Mother did not cooperate at all. She didn't like to be hauled around like a sack of potatoes and screamed almost as loud as the fire. "Put me down. Help! They are kidnapping me."

Silas just tightened his grip on Mother and stumbled forward. He could not stop, he could not reason. He just had to run… faster and faster.

. . .

And there was the back door. It was open. Oh, thank God... In the open door, half obscured by shreds of smoke and sparks stood a woman... Her face was full of wrinkles and when she saw Silas coming she began to wave her arms. "This way... This way."

Silas pressed his teeth together and pressed on. Almost there, almost there. He was now so close to the woman she could almost touch him. But why was his leg hurting so bad? A scorching pain shot up through his spine. But he could not stop. Not now. "Take my mo—" he screamed to the woman who stood there with her arms outstretched, but he could not finish his sentence. The floor under him gave way and he fell forward. The guttural roar that rolled out of his mouth was even louder than Arabella's desperate screams. The next thing Silas knew was that he was on the smouldering carpet. Above him a beam was loose... A burning beam and Silas saw it coming down. Then everything became pitch dark.

∼

The next morning

Alice came running down to the house, throwing the door open, while yelling at the top of her lungs, "Broughton has burned down. Broughton is in ashes."

Mother was just preparing breakfast and looked up. "What, Alice… Slow down. What are you saying?"

"Broughton, Mama." Alice's voice skipped several pitches and was full of panic. "It's gone."

Mother's face paled and she dropped the whisk she was just using to make the pancake batter. "Br-Broughton is gone?"

Baxter, having heard the commotion, came running out of the bedroom and stared with large eyes at Alice, who kept on saying the same sentence over and over. "Broughton burned down to the ground."

"Where is Silas?" Baxter asked the question that had been plaguing Alice from the very first moment the newsboy had shouted out the news.

Alice looked up at him and shrugged her shoulders. "I-I don't know." It was all she could say. She sank down on a chair and began to weep.

The night before, Silas had gone to Broughton. Baxter had suggested he see his parents in the afternoon, but Silas had shaken his head. "The afternoon is business time. No, I need to see them when they are relaxed, and have had their drinks so they will be in a good mood. My best chance is in the evening."

Thus, Silas had arranged for a carriage and had taken off, claiming he would be back on time. But he never returned. In the middle of the night, when he had still not come back, Alice woke Baxter up. "Silas has not returned. I have this awful feeling something is dreadfully wrong."

Baxter rubbed the sleep out of his eyes, but as Alice's words sunk in, he shook his head. "You can't get a carriage at this time, Alice. We will just have to wait and trust. What's more, Silas is no longer the spoiled, irresponsible child he once was. He knows what he is doing."

Alice grunted. Not what she wanted to hear, but she knew Baxter was right. There was little she could do at this hour, and reluctantly she went back to bed. Of course, she had not slept even for a minute. Thus, as soon as the sun was up, she had jumped out of bed, put on her shoes, grabbed a chunk of bread, and ran out the door, intending to go to Broughton. It was then she ran into a newsboy who screamed, "Get the latest… Get the latest. Fire destroys the estate of cotton mill owner Tyrel Dewar."

Alice had literally grabbed the arms of the surprised newsboy and screamed in his face, "Are there any casualties?"

"I think so," the boy said while trying to free himself from Alice's grip, but Alice didn't let go. "Master Dewar, the cotton mill owner is dead," the boy grinned. "Dead as a doornail."

Master Dewar dead? "What about Silas?" Alice literally screamed.

. . .

The newsboy blinked his eyes as he finally managed to shrug off Alice's hands, and cast her a foul glance. "Get lost, lady. Just buy the paper if you want to know the details. I don't know any Silas, and I don't care."

Alice didn't have any coins on her and stared with drooping shoulders at the boy. When the newsboy realized he wasn't going to make a sale, he just turned around and began shouting again, "Get the latest… Get the latest… Fire kills cotton mill owner." All Alice could do was to run back and tearfully share the news with Mama and Baxter.

"We will go down there, right now," Baxter stated in a decisive voice. He slipped on his shoes and ran out the door in search of transport. A short while later, all three of them climbed into a carriage on their way to Broughton.

∼

What a dreadful sight Broughton was.

The smouldering ruins lay before Alice's eyes, and she swallowed hard. It appeared an angry horde of barbarians had stomped through the land, killing and destroying everything in its wake, showing mercy to no man.

The main house was completely destroyed. Only a small part of the servant quarters was still standing. The kitchen, that wonderful place which once had been Mama's domain and where she and Silas had spent countless happy hours, was completely demolished. There really was nothing left of the impressive mansion that had filled her with such awe on that first day when Mama had brought her there. The rubble was still burning and smoking and the air was filled with ashes and small pieces of debris. Alice blinked her eyes as she held Mama's hands, revelling in the security of her presence. While Broughton had brought her pain and confusion, it had also been an important part of her life, and now all of that was gone. The garden was still relatively unscathed. The bench where she and Silas had made their vow was still there, although, like most of the garden, it was covered with dark ashes. All that was really left of Broughton were her memories. The house, the kitchen, the porch…. the cooing doves… it was all gone. The physical house had been crushed to the ground.

Still, none of that really mattered. The only thing that was important was Silas. Where was the man she had come to love so much? As she stared at the smouldering mass before her, tears rolled out of her eyes. No man could have survived such a tragedy… Luckily, there had been no servants, as, since Baxter had been fired, it had been Arabella's policy to not allow any personnel to sleep at the mansion anymore. But what about Silas? Would he have slept there? If the talk with his father and mother had gone surprisingly well and it had gotten late, maybe Arabella had invited him to stay over…

Dear God, let it not be so. It just could not be. It didn't make any sense, none of it did. Even if he *had* been here during the fire, he would have easily been able to climb out of the window and save himself. That thought comforted her somewhat. Maybe Silas was at the hospital right now, helping his injured mother, and he would just show up again, unharmed and well. Then again, the newsboy had claimed people had died. They had found the dead body of Master Dewar... and that was not good. Not good at all.

A rather large crowd of onlookers had formed around the place of disaster. People were standing in small groups together while discussing the cause of the fire. As Alice passed by, she picked up snippets of their conversations. One person claimed the fire was clearly Gods judgment on the wicked rich. Another one, a fat little man with a ridiculous high voice, was certain it was all the cook's fault as she had purposely been burning an apple pie, and yet another woman had it from a trustworthy source it had been suicide. "A strange solution to a marriage gone bad." *Stupid people.* They knew nothing, nothing at all.

And then, Alice froze.

There, not even ten feet away, with his back turned, stood a man Alice would recognize anywhere. *Uncle Buddy.* Alice's hands began to tremble. Upon seeing him an old drawer, tucked away somewhere far off in her memory castle, opened up and a flood of memories that Alice had almost completely forgotten, stormed out. Even from where she was she could smell the familiar scent of his orange flower oil, although that too could have been a trick of her mind, as she was still so many feet away from him. Uncle Buddy… who had tried to kill Silas, who had accused her of being a thief, and who was ultimately responsible for Mama getting fired. Still, would he know something about what had happened to Silas? She let go of Mama's hand and said, "There's Uncle Buddy. Mama, I am going to talk to him. Maybe he knows what happened."

Mama frowned, but Alice was determined to question him. After all, he was Tyrel's brother.

"Master Bud Dewar?" Alice said as she approached him.

Uncle Buddy turned and stared in surprise at the woman who was approaching him. When her recognized Alice his face soured and he gritted his teeth. "Alice Matthews? What are you doing here?"

"I am looking for Silas," she said. "I believe he was here last night. Do you know what happened?"

"Silas was here?" Uncle Buddy answered while wrinkling his nose. "Why was he here? My brother threw him out of the will. He hated my brother, the ungrateful brat."

"Not quite true," Alice replied, trying to sound as polite and respectful as possible. Antagonizing the man would not be helpful. It would ruin her chances of finding out anything important. "In spite of everything that has happened, Silas loved his parents. He came here last night to make things right between them, and I am concerned for him."

"I see...,"Uncle Buddy hissed, and his eyes lit up with wickedness. "Then I know what happened and what caused the fire," he said slowly. "Now I understand... Silas came here last night and unsuccessfully tried to force my brother to change the will. Of course he got angry and retaliated by burning down Broughton, killing his own father in the process." He shook his head and spat on the ground. "What a wicked, evil son Silas was, and...," he moved closer to Alice, "... you and your wretched family of thieves are no better."

"You are crazy," Alice shouted it out, no longer trying to sound nice and polite. "Maybe *you* are behind it all. Maybe *you* did it and used your stupid Alvexolol." Her angry outburst caused several bystanders to look up. They cast a concerned look in their direction.

Uncle Buddy's face darkened as he noticed the onlookers. "Watch your tongue, young lady. I am a Dewar. You don't mess with me you hear me, or..." He did not finish his sentence.

"Or what?" Alice stated defiantly. She was not about to be pushed into a corner by that chubby earwig.

For a moment Uncle Buddy seemed stunned, but then a sly, wicked little smile appeared. "Let me put it this way... I'll let the police know Silas was here last night. I am sure they will be very interested in hearing about his situation."

He shook his head and added, "You know what I think? He is on the run, since he burned down the whole place."

Alice had to fight the temptation to smack the wicked man's face, but forced her fury away and remained calm. "It was a mistake talking to you," she said and turned around. As she walked off, she heard Uncle Buddy call out to a constable who was standing nearby and was trying to keep people from coming to close to the remains of the house. "Constable," he yelled in the demanding, authoritarian voice so common to the Dewars, "there is something I would like to tell you…"

18

PAYBACK TIME

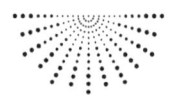

There was no sign of Silas anywhere. Alice stumbled around the burned remains of Broughton for a good part of the day, desperately hoping for a clue as to what may have happened to him. At the same time she was hoping, just as desperately, that she *wouldn't* find a clue at all, for that could mean Silas would possibly still be alive. But nobody knew anything. Nobody had seen a trace of Silas or of his mother. Not here, and apparently, not in town either.

A sympathetic fireman helped Alice to look for some time, but at last he too gave up. "I am sorry, Miss," he said while scratching his head. "There's no sign of either the Mistress or Master Silas. Maybe they are not even here." He shook his head and made an apologetic motion with his hands. "As long as we do not find a body there is hope, but then again... you see the rubble. This was a bad, devastating fire, and their bodies could be buried deep under the rubble."

Alice swallowed back her tears. "Thank you, sir," she told the fireman who gave her a compassionate nod and took off.

That night it was very still in Baxter's house. Nobody spoke a word. Mama had made a special roast, generally Alice's favourite, but Alice wasn't hungry and aimlessly kept sticking her fork in the meat without eating it. Uncle Buddy's terrible words had caused additional fears in Alice's heart. What if Uncle Buddy was right and Silas, in a moment of utter insanity, had gone wild and retaliated by setting the whole mansion on fire and was on the run? It was a ridiculous thought… still, it was there. Silas was kind. He was meek, and not at all prone to violent outbursts like his father. But the thought, like an annoying hornet that insisted on delivering its sting, kept circling around in her mind.

Was he really on the run as Uncle Buddy suggested? If that were true it would be all over. Then, there was no hope of them ever staying together. What was more, if Uncle Buddy pursued his wicked line of thinking, something he was very good at, it was likely the police would show up here at any time. She could hear Uncle Buddy's ugly voice in her mind, "Yes, constable… it's Silas Dewar who did it. He killed his own father in anger. He and his girlfriend conspired to do it. They tried to steal the jewellery of my fiancée before too. They are wicked and rotten to the core. It's them you must arrest."

If that were to happen, what chance would they have? The Dewars were rich and powerful. Even Uncle Buddy, weak and wicked as he was, had considerable influence as a physician. The police would always take his side.

Alice blinked a tear away. She had never known darkness to be so utterly dark and hopeless. And where was God in all this? Why did He not help? She and Silas had *not* been bad. They had *not* walked in the way of the ungodly, they had not stood still with the sinners, and they had not sat down in the seat of the scorner. * Why then all the misery? Why was the outlook so utterly hopeless? It just wasn't fair.

* Psalm 1

"W-Would you like… some eh… tea, Alice?" Mama asked. Her voice sounded strangely hoarse. Alice knew she wanted to encourage her, but it was clear Mama was battling the same cloud of depression and her heart was filled with the same gloomy confusion Alice felt hanging over her mind.

Alice shook her head. "No Moth—"

A knock on the door interrupted them. What was that? *A knock?* Who would be knocking on their door? No one ever visited Baxter's house. Alice cringed and cast Mama a fearful look. "It's the police, Mama," she mumbled. "They will think I planned the fire with Silas."

"Nonsense," Baxter said as he got up. "You did not do anything like that. We have nothing to hide." He got up and walked to the door. Alice admired his faith and courage but when she saw how he stopped in front of the door and hesitated before opening, she knew he wasn't too sure about things either. Then he swung the door open and asked, "Who is there?"

Alice was almost certain it would be the constable pushing Baxter to the side. He would barge in, followed by his underlings. They would step in with their muddy boots, foul up the floor, and make things even more miserable than they already were. She pressed her lips together, waiting for the inevitable.

But it was not the police.

Instead, there was the warm voice of a woman. "Can I come in? I have news." It was a voice that Alice knew well. Instantly, she jumped up. "Miss Thimble." She cried. "What are you doing here?"

Baxter made room and the old woman stepped inside, heavily leaning on her cane. She looked around the room, smiled at Mama, and then placed her hand on Alice's head. It made Alice feel as if she were a small child again, and that was fine with her. Miss Thimble was allowed to do that. Feeling the old woman's hand on her head made her secure, it felt warm and comforting, almost as if an angelic being were touching her.

"Silas is safe," she spoke. "And so is his mother, Arabella."

"W-What did you say?" Alice asked. She had heard the words perfectly well, but hardly dared to believe it. "What?"

Miss Thimble smiled at her ever so sweetly. "Silas, dear… is safe."

Tears now gushed forth from Alice's eyes. "Thank you God," she sniffed and asked barely audible, "W-What happened?"

"It was Bud Dewar," Miss Thimble said. "*He* burned down the estate." She pulled out a chair and sat down next to Alice while grabbing her hands. "Silas caught him with a bucket of tar. Bud Dewar was hiding behind a bush and—"

"I knew it," Alice broke out in an angry yell. "This time he's gone too far. We need to call the police."

"He's a powerful man, Alice, with lots of friends in high places," Miss Thimble stated. "I am sure there is something we can do, but we should proceed very carefully and not do anything rashly."

"Go on, Miss Thimble," Baxter said, "Tell us the rest."

Miss Thimble nodded. "As far as Silas could remember, Bud Dewar knocked him out when he had discovered the tar. He then tied his hands together and dumped him in the kitchen, thinking he would die there in the fire."

"He did *that*? The… the… " Alice could not think of a word that was low enough to properly vent her anger.

"When Silas awoke from the bang on his head, the fire was all around him…" Miss Thimble went on. "And then…" her voice trailed off while her face lit up, "… there was an angel in the kitchen. A huge, large angel that almost reached the ceiling with his head. The angel helped him and then told him to rescue his mother."

"An angel?" Alice repeated what Miss Thimble had said. "W-Where did he come from?"

Miss Thimble laughed. "Where all angels come from, dear. From heaven of course. Angels just appear when they are needed. They just show up."

"And the angel told Silas to rescue Arabella?" What a wonderful story.

"Yes, he did," Miss Thimble replied in a solemn voice. "Silas found her and carried her out. But then, just before they reached me, he stumbled and fell."

"He walked all the way over to your house, and then he fell?" Mama asked while shaking her head.

Miss Thimble smiled weakly. "No, not to my house. I was standing near the back door of Broughton. You see, I had seen the flames from my window. I alerted someone to call the fire brigade and then I made my way over to the estate to see if I could help in any way."

"Bless your heart," Mama said. "Knowing how bad you walk that must have taken a lot out of you."

"It did," Miss Thimble acknowledged, but then there appeared a twinkle in her eye. "But it was worth it all. I am always amazed to see what strength you can get in an emergency. It felt like I was flying."

"But you said, Silas fell just before he reached you? What happened to Silas?"

"There was this burning beam that came down and fell right on top of him," Miss Thimble's voice was very low as she seemed to relive the scene. "I pulled him out, away from the burning corridor."

Alice blinked her eyes and marvelled. "You did all that… you the woman who can't even weed her own marigold garden?"

"I told you, Alice," the old woman chuckled, "God gives you power for the hour. He sure did for me at that moment."

"And Silas? Is he hurt?"

Miss Thimble's gentle smile disappeared. "Yes, Alice. He is. He has burn wounds, but they will heal. But…"

. . .

"But what?" Alice looked up, feeling a new fear entering her heart. "What's wrong with him, Miss Thimble?"

Miss Thimble swallowed hard and her words came out slowly. "He can't see very well, Alice. I don't know whether it is because of the smoke, or because of the beam that fell on his head… Maybe it's just the trauma altogether, but the point is… well, his eyesight is affected."

"Is-Is he blind?" A fresh wave of tears announced its arrival and the joy Alice had felt at the news of Silas being alive drained away. A heavy, sinking feeling took its place.

Miss Thimble did not answer Alice directly. "I am not sure how bad it is. There are herbs and I—"

"Will they help, Miss Thimble? Please make your herbs work."

Miss Thimble gave Alice a sad smile. "I can't heal anybody, Alice. I told you I am no doctor, but I promise you, I will do my best, if *you* do your best too."

"Of course, Miss Thimble. What can I do?"

"Pray, Alice. Besiege the heavens on behalf of Silas."

∽

Uncle Buddy leaned back in his seat and sucked on the large cigar Timothy E. Butters had offered him. The distinguished lawyer with his wavy, silver hair and the small round glasses from the well-respected notary office,

Butters & Butters and sons, gave him a smile. "It's good, isn't it, Bud. It's imported from Cuba."

"Cuban, huh? I can taste that," Uncle Buddy replied. He had a hard time hiding the victorious grin on his face. He had to play the part until the very last moment, but it was clear this was going to be a glorious day. This was what he had been waiting for all those years. His brother had died in an unfortunate fire some weeks earlier. What a tragedy. As he talked to Timothy E. Butters about it he managed to actually look sad and devastated. "My poor brother…." He sniffed. "He died still so young. His best years were still ahead of him. How cruel this world can be at times."

"Very cruel," Timothy E. Butters agreed while adjusting his hair. "But we can't always choose what we get."

That's right, Uncle Buddy thought, *But I can.* He blew out a large puff of smoke and added thoughtfully, "And then to think my brother died after he just disinherited his only son. No, Mister Timothy, it's not always all caviar and champagne in some families. Sometimes the worst of things happen in families that seem so together." It almost appeared he would start crying. "Yes, life can be so cruel at times."

"Still, it seems you think the winds of favour are blowing your way?" Timothy E. Butters enquired while arching his brows.

"What do you mean?" Uncle Buddy asked, barely able to hide the anger he felt rising. "I am heartbroken. How can the winds of favour be blowing my way when my beloved brother just died? And then to think poor Arabella is dead too. Oh, how terrible it all is."

"As you know," Timothy E. Butters continued, apparently unruffled by Uncle Buddy's lamentations. "Arabella Dewar wasn't a big part of the will."

Uncle Buddy nodded. "I know. My brother told me. She is…," he paused to find the right words, "… well, how should I put it…?" He lifted his eyes and looked at the ceiling to find inspiration. "Well, to be frank, Mister Timothy," he said at last, "my brother confided to me that she was always complaining… wearing him down, you know." He leaned forward and said, "You know what I really think, Mister Timothy?"

The man shook his head. "No, Bud, *what* do you really think?"

"She was just riding on my brother's coattails. She was just in it for the money and had wormed her way selfishly into his life." His face dropped and his sad face appeared once more. "But nobody deserves to die like that. Dying in a terrible fire … Even your enemies deserve better. Apparently his son died too, that little brat Silas. So sad."

"Well, they never found their bodies, Bud," Timothy E. Butters remarked. "For all you know they will show up one day when you least expect it."

"Nah," Uncle Buddy shook his head. "I've seen the ruins. That fire must have been hellish. No man could have made it out of there alive." He narrowed his eyes and spoke in a whisper, "I'll be frank with you, Mister Timothy. I really thought for a time that young Master Silas had lit the fire in revenge for having been thrown out of the will and that he was on the run. But I now understand the police believe there was no indication of foul play. It must just have been a most unfortunate accident."

Uncle Buddy leaned back, congratulating himself and trying to hide the satisfied smirk he felt coming. *I did a good job making it look like an accident. Greta should be proud of me.*

"Most unfortunate, indeed," Timothy E. Butters agreed and while both men sucked on their cigars an uncomfortable silence erupted. At last, Uncle Buddy tapped his fingers on the desk, smacked his lips loudly and asked, "Well… eh… shall we begin. I don't have all day. Please, can you read the will?"

"We are still waiting for someone. I am sorry," Timothy E. Butters said as he knocked the ashes off his cigar. "We can start soon, I am sure."

"Someone else?" Uncle Buddy's face turned red. "There's no someone else. My brother died, his wife is not in the will, Silas is out of the will, and there's nobody else. Come on, Mister Timothy, let's get on with our business."

At that moment the door opened and the youthful face of Isabel, the notaries' secretary appeared. "They are here, sir. Shall I let them in?"

"Of course, Isabel. Let them in."

Uncle Buddy gritted his teeth. *They? That secretary said 'they'?*

Seconds later the door opened again. Uncle Buddy craned his neck to see who was coming in. He cursed. Not hidden, but out loud. First Arabella appeared, and she was followed by… Silas Dewar. The young Master had risen from the dead. But this could not be possible? He had been left for dead in the kitchen… there was no way Silas could have ever made it out of there alive. He had even tied his hands… *You forgot his feet, you fool. That's what did it.* A dark voice from deep within Uncle Buddy's villainous heart rebuked him. This was not good news. Silas had seen the tar. Surely, even a child could put two and two together.

"Hello, Uncle Buddy," Silas said in cheerful tones. "What a surprise to see you again."

"Yes… eh… g-good to see you too," Uncle Buddy managed to say. "Arabella… What a surprise." He felt sweat forming on his forehead. That needed to go off right away. That would look suspicious. He pulled out a handkerchief and forced a grin on his face. "Hot here, isn't it?"

"It's not hot at all," Silas remarked. He studied Uncle Buddy's face and said, "You don't look too well, Uncle. Maybe you have a fever and should go to bed."

"You have something in your eyes," Uncle Buddy growled. "You don't see too well."

Silas let out a chuckle. "Well, that would be almost true. For a while I could not see, because of the fire I was in, but it's getting better every day, due to prayer and Miss Thimble's herbs. No, Uncle, I see very well, and I can see you don't look too good."

"I am not sick," Uncle Buddy fired back, almost losing it. "I am here to collect… eh… to hear the will of my dear brother."

"That's right," Timothy E. Butters agreed. "Let's turn to the will." He opened a drawer and pulled out a stately paper. Uncle Buddy could see the logo of *Butters & Butters and sons* and felt his mouth getting dry. Something was weird. Something didn't make sense… No, it was worse, something was wrong.

Timothy E. Butters licked his lips, cleared his throat and stared for a long while through his glasses at Uncle Buddy.

"Bud," he began, "I don't know how to say this, but I have no other option but to be perfectly honest with you."

What's that shrimp talking about? Uncle Buddy bit his lip in anger. He tasted blood.

"I am certain you are familiar with The Wills Act that our parliament accepted in 1837?"

"Of course," Uncle Buddy fired back, no longer willing to hide his anger and frustration. "That is the act that confirms the power of every adult to dispose of their real and personal property by will on their death. That's why I am here."

"Right," Timothy E. Butters confirmed. "I will skip all the technical words and so forth, but the point is that in the Wills Act it states that a will has to be signed by two independent parties for it to be valid…"

"So…? What are you hinting at?"

Timothy E. Butters grimaced and then moved the testament before him to the others. "Look."

"Look at what?" Uncle Buddy groaned, but began to nervously scan the legal document before him. There it was, in black and white … *Bud Gregorius Alfred Dewar* (that was his full name) *would inherit all of Tyrel Dewar's money and assets.*

It said so right there… All of it.

He heaved a sigh of relief and cast Timothy E. Butters a pleased smile.

"But what's that at the bottom of the page?" the solicitor asked.

Uncle Buddy frowned. "At the bottom?" He tilted his head and looked again. There was nothing there. "I see nothing," he stated, not comprehending what Timothy E. Butters was hinting at. "Nothing at all."

"Exactly," Timothy E. Butters stated with a solemn voice. "Nothing. Nobody signed. Not your brother and not any of the witnesses."

It was as if a cannonball hit Uncle Buddy right in the stomach. Everything around him began to twist and whirl and a strong nausea welled up from deep within. "W-What does that mean?" he managed to stutter.

"It means," Timothy E. Butters stated flatly, "that this testament is not worth a dime. It's not valid." He picked up his cigar, sucked long and thoughtfully, and then, while his face momentarily disappeared in the smoke, he said, "Your brother was about to sign the document. He had found two reliable witnesses and he was to meet with me here in the office. Alas… one day before our appointment he died in that *unfortunate* fire."

Uncle Buddy sank back in his chair, resembling a sailor who could no longer stand on his feet by means of one too many whiskeys. "I-I… get nothing?"

"Yes you do," Timothy E. Butters continued and he pulled out another document. "This here is the original testament. Since the other testament is not valid I have no alternative but to switch to the only valid testament there is. Would you like me to read it?"

"Please do," Silas said and Arabella nodded her agreement.

"Well then," Timothy E. Butters said while he readjusted his spectacles. "Let me read it to you."

Uncle Buddy heard nothing. His ears could not even comprehend the simple English five-year-olds spoke, let alone the technical language of a testament, but when he heard his name and he realized Timothy E. Butters had finally come to the good part, he perked up.

"And to my beloved brother, Bud Gregorius Alfred James…," the solicitor spoke in a soft, but business-like voice, "…I leave the physical estate of Broughton..."He paused and looked over his glasses to Uncle Buddy. "That is the building that is no more." Without waiting for Uncle Buddy's response he went on. "The grounds upon which the estate is built will go to my wife Arabella Conchita Dewar. For the rest, all my assets, my money and my other investments, of which there will be a list below, will go to my dear son Silas Stephanus Dewar."

There was more, but Uncle Buddy no longer heard the droning voice of Timothy E. Butters. All he had heard was that he would get… nothing, Nothing at all. Everything had been in vain and everything was going to Silas. When Timothy E. Butters was finished reading, Uncle Buddy, as

313

white as a goose, stammered, "…and-and you knew all this?"

The man nodded. "I did, Bud. Sorry."

Silas cleared his throat. "When my eyes were better, I went to the police. I told them I had seen the tar in the bucket. They confirmed to me the fire had been lit. We searched for more clues… we found a carriage driver who told the police you gave him 10 shillings for keeping his mouth shut. He saw you entering the estate with a bucket, the same bucket I spotted that was full of tar. The police kept it all quiet for the sake of the investigation, but they are at the door."

"All lies. All lies," Uncle Buddy screamed at the top of his lungs. "It's a conspiracy… You are all full of the devil." He waved his finger hysterically into Silas' face. "*You* brought the tar. *You* burned down the estate. I had nothing to do with it." All at once fury overtook him. Uncle Buddy felt a rage he had never before felt. Overpowering and all-encompassing rage. Everything around him became black except for the face of Silas who cast him that stupid grin. "You were supposed to be dead, you lousy kid. I left you in the kitchen to die. How come you are not dead?" He jumped up, pushing the fancy chair of *Butters & Butters and sons* with such unbridled force against the iron wood stove, that it crashed in twain. Timothy E. Butters jumped up too, causing his spectacles to fly off his nose. The floor had now turned into a battleground as Uncle Buddy had thrown himself upon Silas and tried to beat him to a pulp.

"H-Help," Arabella screamed. "Help!"

Instantly the door to the office swung open and the police stormed in. Two armed officers grabbed Uncle Buddy by his arms, pulled him away from Silas and held him in an iron grip.

"Calm down," one of the policemen yelled in his ears. "You are under arrest."

Under arrest. Me? Oh, why is this happening? The whole world is turning against me. Uncle Buddy stared at the scene before him and saw how Silas clambered back up on his feet, still wearing that pleased grin. How dare he? Uncle Buddy wanted to attack again, strike that smirk off that frog's face, but he could not. The police held him firmly.

"I suppose everyone here heard from Bud Dewar's own mouth that he tried to kill me." Silas looked at the constable who had entered the room as well. "I think, we are done here." He nodded at Timothy E. Butters. "Thank you, sir. It's been a great pleasure doing business with you." He turned to Arabella. "Come Mother, I think we need to go."

But before Uncle Buddy saw them leave, Timothy E. Butters cleared his throat and said, "Just a minute, Silas. Let's not make the same mistake twice. If you want the inheritance, you still have to sign." He turned the paper to Silas and Arabella. "Thank you, Mr. Butters," Silas said. "I will most gladly sign."

EPILOGUE

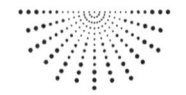

And so this story comes to an end.

Silas and Alice married shortly after, although at first there was some confusion as to when they would do so. Silas wanted to tie the knot immediately, but Alice wanted to wait a bit longer, and start the rebuilding of Broughton first. "Marrying around the bench where we made our vow to be friends forever and ever, and even a bit longer, would be my dream."

"The rebuilding of Broughton may take years," Silas objected, but at last they found a compromise. The garden would be brought back to its original state, the rubble of the fire removed, and a small, temporary wooden cabin would be built where Alice and Silas could stay while the main rebuilding of the mansion took place. And then, when the mansion was rebuilt, they would officially move in, together with Mama and Baxter, who were given the best room in the house.

Silas offered Arabella a room too, but she refused. "It's kind of you, Silas," she said. "But I feel the need to go in a different direction. I have lived under a cloud for years. I have always loved you, but I am afraid I've made many wrong turns in my life. I feel I must leave England and have a fresh start elsewhere."

At first, Silas did not agree. "Alice and I have wholeheartedly forgiven you, Mother," Silas explained. "There's no need to run. We all have made our mistakes, and we all need forgiveness. You are welcome to stay at the new Broughton."

But Arabella shook her head. "The strangest thing has happened, Silas. Last week, I woke up in the middle of the night…"

"And?"

"A man stood by my bed."

"A man?" Concern filled Silas' eyes. "A burglar?"

"No burglar. On the contrary, it was an angel. He was *so* tall his head almost reached the ceiling. Then the angel spoke. Firm, and full of conviction. He said, "The boat, Arabella… travel by boat so you may find your destination. Then he was gone… just like that."

"He said that?" Silas narrowed his eyes, but he had seen too much to doubt or question what his mother said. Thus Silas bought the ground of Broughton that Arabella had inherited so she would have enough money on her travels, and she took off with the promise that if things did not work out, Silas and Alice would take care of her. Her travels didn't lead her to Paris or New York as Greta Parsley had always wanted, but the last Silas heard was that she had joined a convent and had turned her back on the world.

Eventually, Alice got three happy, healthy children. Daughters they were, and they became the pride and joy of Hazel, who let no moment pass by in which she could spend time with them. "Spoiling them," as Silas put it, but if you would have seen those happy, cheerful faces of their offspring, you would have to agree it did not harm them in the least.

Uncle Buddy was sentenced to hang, but Silas, hoping the man would have a change of heart, fought successfully on his behalf and got his sentence reduced to a life time in prison. Eventually, years later in 1878, he was put on a ship to Australia together with a whole slew of other ruffians, where he was forced to serve out his days in a labour camp.

And Nana? Did anything happen to Nana? With Alice's help, she managed to stop drinking, but she did not live long to enjoy her new life. The drinking had so damaged her liver that only a year after Silas and Alice had gotten married, she died in her bed, holding on to the tiny hand of Alice's first baby.

And so, as said earlier, this is where the story ends, right at the favourite spot in Alice and Silas' garden at Broughton.

That was their stone bench, their *vow-bench* as they now called it and one balmy evening they were looking back over all that had happened in their lives.

"It's been a good life, Alice," Silas said as he was sipping a glass of cold lemonade. "Remember, when I was young and I told you I wasn't sure if there was a plan, a reason, and a purpose to it all?"

"I sure do," Alice answered him with a chuckle. "I am so glad you changed your mind about all that."

"Me too," Silas answered with a tender smile. "How could I not; after all the wonders that have happened? Small wonders, greater wonders, and even the greatest wonder of all, which is that love conquered all. God always knows best, and I am so glad I learned to trust Him." He took Alice in his arms and kissed her long and affectionately.

THANK YOU FOR CHOOSING A PUREREAD BOOK!

We hope you enjoyed the story, and as a way to thank you

for choosing PureRead we'd like to send you this free book, and other fun reader rewards…

Click here for your free copy of Whitechapel Waif
PureRead.com/victorian

Thanks again for reading.
See you soon!

IF YOU LOVED THE MANCHESTER MAID

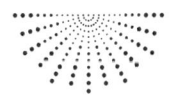

Continue reading with another PureRead tale of romance and resilience.

For your enjoyment here is the first chapter of The Slum Mother's Sacrifice by Dolly Price.

"Let me help you with them clothes, Katie."

Katherine Foley peered around the flapping white bedsheet, although she didn't need to see who was speaking to know that Gerry Murphy was on the other side.

Gerry smiled, his warm brown eyes crinkling at the corners when his gaze met hers. Katherine smiled in return, then wished she had not done so, because Gerry's response was to smile more broadly, his visage telling her he knew that she'd mourned her dead husband a year. It was, his smile said, time to move past the dead and toward the living.

"Thank you, Gerry," she said primly, "but I'm sure you've plenty of work to do yourself and 'tis not for me to keep you from it." She batted smuts of soot from the freshly washed sheet. Too soon, it would be getting on for the cooler weather with autumn arriving. Folks who'd enjoyed the summer for its heat and the money saved in fuel would soon be burning coal and firewood. The chimneys of thousands of people in Birmingham, England, warmed the insides of tenements and palaces alike, while expelling the dust and dirt into the air.

Washing clothes for a living was hard enough for an Irish widow with two young children to raise, but it would be especially hard come winter. She'd have to hang the clothes inside the cramped two-room flat where the family lived so that the garments would dry. The rooms were crowded enough as it was: stringing a line from the front room where the cooking, eating, and washing up were done, to the tiny bedroom where she and the children slept, would make the Foleys feel even more squeezed within the walls. But it was no more than any of her neighbours, desperate Irish workers in flight from the Great Hunger who'd come to Birmingham for the sake of their families, had to deal with and in fact, the Foleys were less crowded, with only three in the dwelling.

Gerry shrugged. If he sensed a rebuff in her words, he gave no indication of it. He continued to move along the clothesline, to pluck the washed and dried linens and garments from it and put them into the waiting basket. "Where are Rose and Seamus?" he asked.

"Over at Bridey McKenna's, playing with her brood. I'll be calling them in for supper soon." Katherine folded the shirt as neatly as she could, so that ironing it would be easier.

"Supper," Gerry said as he removed another sheet from the clothesline. "I'm still dreaming of that grand stew you made not a month ago."

He smiled when he said it to take the edge off his bald effort to invite himself to the family meal. Gerry was a charming man, and good looking, with the brown beard and moustache that he found time to keep neat and trim despite his long hours at the textile mill. He was hard-working and kind, patient and attentive with children, traits no doubt earned as the eldest of a raucous brood of siblings. He didn't drink more than the average and didn't

323

spend his wages in the taverns. He laughed easily and went to mass on Sundays. If she were looking for a husband to replace Jimmy, Gerry would have been the obvious choice.

He certainly thought so. But Katherine wasn't looking. Jimmy Foley, big and brawny, with a laugh as vivid and loud as his carrot-red hair, had gone to his death on the public works back home in Ballygowl.

"Speaking of that fine stew," Gerry said, lowering his voice, "I'm thinking it's time for another. What d'you say?"

Katherine maintained a noncommittal expression as she took down another garment from the line. Inside, however, her heart started racing with the combination of eagerness and fear that always greeted an announcement that Gerry was ready to go poaching again.

It would mean a night of no rest in order to leave the teeming noise and eyes of Birmingham to walk to the farthest outskirts of the city, far enough that the dense, dark woods replaced the sleepless, watchful eyes of the slums. It meant being vigilant and awake through the night to quickly snare a pair of rabbits or partridges that could be surreptitiously killed and hidden in a satchel to be brought back home for skinning and gutting. And cooking, for poaching meant meat for her children, a welcome reprieve from the gruel, potato parings, and rotting vegetables that made up their daily fare. Another stew, strengthened by meat and perhaps a few fresh vegetables if she could spare the money for them, would do wonders for Rose and Seamus, especially now with Rose so prone to coughs. Katherine could use the bones to make broth, which would add flavour to a soup, even if the vegetables she'd be able to afford would be past their best days.

Katherine hid her face from view as she lowered her head to fold the man's shirt she'd taken off the line and put it into the basket. If her mother were alive now, she'd be mortified to think that her daughter had turned to poaching to feed her family. But Ma had died before the Famine, and Pa had died before her. They'd known hunger, but not starvation.

"Aye," she said, not meeting Gerry's intent gaze as she brushed a loose lock of damp auburn hair that had come loose from the pins. "When?"

"I'm thinking night after next," Gerry said. "Should be a clear night, Ma says her bones tell her it's not going to rain." He grinned, accepting his mother's rheumatism as sufficient proof of the weather forecast. "A clear night, a three-quarter moon..."

"Do you not think we ought to wait," Katherine said anxiously, "for an overcast night when we're less likely to be seen?"

"And risk the rain?" Gerry scoffed. "We'd get naught but mud and chills for our efforts."

Katherine knew he was right. Gerry had been working and living in Birmingham for two years, providing for his family with the wages he earned from the textile mill and from a spot of poaching now and again. He had four sisters and a brother whose ages ranged from eleven to sixteen, and a mother who took care of their lodgings and did the cooking and cleaning. Mary Murphy seemed to have no qualms about her son's illegal means of procuring food for the family, but then, Mary was a fierce Irish patriot who regarded the poaching of English game as one way of striking back at the loathed tyrants. Katherine's mother although not fond of the English, had been even less fond of lawbreaking.

Seeing her hesitate, Gerry said, coaxingly, "Ah, c'mon now, lass, 'tis food for your children and the forest has plenty more. 'Tisn't as though we're trespassing on some great lord's property now."

Katherine knew that Gerry was trying to make her feel better by smoothing the rough edges of laws which, in his view, were designed to keep the poor downtrodden.

Although Gerry didn't discuss politics with her, Katherine knew that he and his mother, indeed, the entire Murphy family, were passionate Fenians, dedicated, at least in their speech, to ridding Ireland of the cursed invaders who had robbed the Irish of their liberty long before a potato was ever planted in an Irish field. For the Murphys and their forebears, and many of the other Irish who lived in the Birmingham slums, worked in Birmingham factories, and starved on Birmingham wages, the resentments against the English had not abated since Henry the Second and his Normans invaded the island in the twelfth century.

Jimmy had always stayed out of politics. It was his dream that someday the Irish would be led by canny politicians who would guide the nation to independence, but he didn't favour violence as a means. *O Jimmy*, Katherine thought as she weighed the limited options before her, *I do miss your good sense.*

But Jimmy wouldn't want his children to go hungry.

Katherine nodded, saying nothing. There was no need to voice her assent. Poaching was serious business, with a severe punishment. She could be transported from England to the wilds of Australia, and then what would happen to her children?

"Aye, then," Gerry commented, reading her acquiescence. "Saturday, then. I'll send Althne over to your crib to mind Rose and Seamus. She'll keep her wits about her."

Althne was the eldest of the sisters, a quiet, responsible girl who could be trusted to see to the children. She would, of course, know where her brother and Katherine were going but she'd never let on to the children or to anyone.

"Thank you," Katherine said. She might have been thanking Gerry for picking up the basket of folded laundry and carrying it into her lodgings, but they both knew that there was a greater reason for her appreciation. By including her in his forays to the forest to poach, Gerry was helping her to provide for her family. Katherine knew that he was a good-hearted young man, genuinely fond of the children and willing to help a widow if he could. She also knew that the day would come when Gerry would naturally assume that his kindly gestures would be accepted as wooing, and that, when she thought herself ready, he would be the man she'd choose to be a father to Rose and Seamus. She could not think of such a development now, so she thanked him again.

He paused at the door, his brown eyes resting upon her face as if he found it pleasant to do so. "If you need aught," he said, "you know where to find me."

"Two streets down, first door in," she repeated. It was how Gerry had introduced himself when she'd first moved into her two-room lodging, in Birmingham. She'd sold nearly everything they had owned to pay for the journey to Birmingham and the flat, with its uneven floor, smoke-stained ceiling, and windows papered over to keep out the draft where the glass had cracked, was all she could afford. She could have cried when the children looked around in mute disbelief.

It had been Gerry who'd found furniture for her to use: a table, wobbly to be sure, but it worked for them; a bench to sit on made of a rough-hewn plank with no shortage of splinters; a straw tick mattress big enough for the three of them to sleep on; an odd mismatch of plates and cups;

threadbare blankets that kept them covered if not entirely warm in chilly weather; and various items that she was grateful to receive.

He'd found her customers so that she could earn wages doing laundry and he'd brought her a big metal tub and a washboard, crowing with triumph because he'd bargained successfully for it. He'd refused to take so much as a shilling for anything, claiming that the Irish had to stick together or the accursed English would rob them blind. Then he'd apologized, with a cheery smile, for bringing the English into what was meant to be a civil conversation.

Gerry grinned. "Never forget it," he said. "Now, lock the door after me. There's ruffians about."

He always cautioned her against being lax in keeping her home secure. She knew the streets were not safe, for even though there were many fellow Irish living as her neighbours, there were just as many thieves, drunkards, and ne-er-do-wells. Not a night went by, after she and the children had said their prayers and Rose and Seamus were sleeping soundly, one on each side of her, that Katherine didn't lie awake and long for the familiarity of the green fields of home, where she had never locked her door nor had reason to.

"Saturday night, then," he said softly as he stood outside the door to leave.

"Saturday night," she whispered, closing the door.

As Katherine added water to stretch the precious cooking oil in the frying pan, she stood over the fire, stirring in the potato peels and the cabbage she'd gotten from the street vendor that morning, and tried to stave off the rising momentum of fears. How much longer could she live like this? The children were growing out of their clothing—how would she afford the thread, the cloth, everything she'd need to sew them something new? When cold came, how would she afford the extra wood she'd need to keep the fire going so that the laundry would dry inside the kitchen? What if Rose suffered another cough like the one she'd had last winter? What would Katherine do for medicine?

The walls of the rooms in which she and the children lived felt as if they were pressing closer, as if they intended to trap her inside this dismal place so that she would never again wake up to the sun on her face in the morning and the lush, verdant countryside all around her. If she did not find some way of protecting her children from the poverty and despair which engulfed Birmingham as much as the thick shroud of smoke from the coal fires that kept the factories running, she would never be able to make Jimmy's dreams for his son and daughter come true…

∽

Continue Reading The Slum Mother's Sacrifice on Amazon

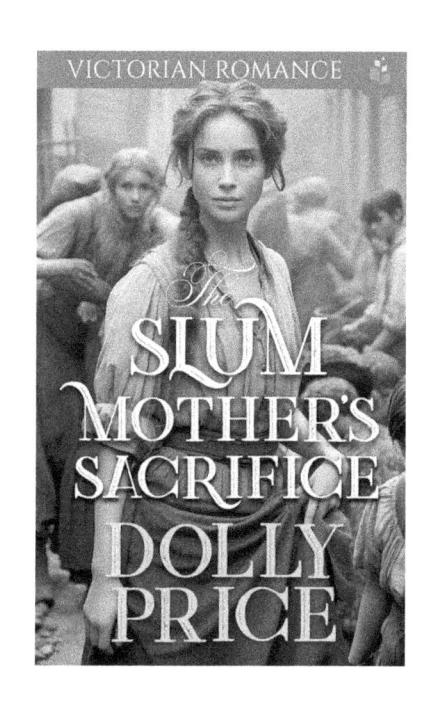

VICTORIAN ROMANCE

THE SLUM MOTHER'S SACRIFICE

DOLLY PRICE

LOVE VICTORIAN ROMANCE?

If you enjoyed this story why not continue straight away with other books in our PureRead Victorian Romance library?

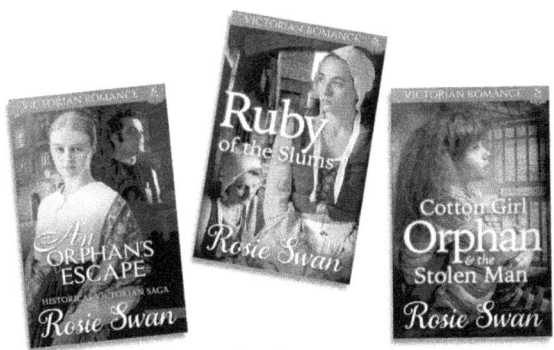

Read them all...

Orphan Christmas Miracle

An Orphan's Escape

The Lowly Maiden's Loyalty

Ruby of the Slums

The Dancing Orphan's Second Chance

Cotton Girl Orphan & The Stolen Man

Victorian Slum Girl's Dream

The Lost Orphan of Cheapside

Dora's Workhouse Child

Saltwick River Orphan

Workhouse Girl and The Veiled Lady

OUR GIFT TO YOU

AS A WAY TO SAY THANK YOU WE WOULD LOVE TO SEND YOU THIS BEAUTIFUL STORY FREE OF CHARGE.

Our Reader List is 100% FREE

Click here for your free copy of Whitechapel Waif

PureRead.com/victorian

At PureRead we publish books you can trust. Great tales without smut or swearing, but with all of the mystery and romance you expect from a great story.

Be the first to know when we release new books, take part in our fun competitions, and get surprise free books in your inbox by signing up to our Reader list.

As a thank you you'll receive an exclusive copy of Whitechapel Waif - a beautiful book available only to our subscribers...

Click here for your free copy of Whitechapel Waif

PureRead.com/victorian